AMBER

DAUGHTERS OF THE DAGGER SERIES - BOOK 3

ELIZABETH ROSE

ROSESCRIBE MEDIA INC.

Copyright © 2013 by Elizabeth Rose Krejcik

This is a work of fiction. All characters, names, places and incidents are either a product of the author's imagination or used fictitiously. Any similarity to actual organizations or persons living or deceased is entirely coincidental. All rights reserved. No part of this book may be used, reproduced or transmitted in any form whatsoever without the author's written permission.

Cover created by: Elizabeth Rose Krejcik

Edited baby Scott Moreland

ISBN-13: 978-1500821159

CHAPTER 1

BOWERWOOD ABBEY AND MONASTERY, ENGLAND, 1357

*V*espers had just finished, and Amber de Burgh of Blackpool, novice of the Sisters of St. Ermengild, blessed herself as the doors to the church slammed open, and in entered the devil himself.

All heads of the congregation of praying nuns and monks turned toward the door. Father Armand who was conducting the service looked up sharply in surprise.

"Lucifer!" he cried out, startling everyone inside the church. "Bid the devil."

Commotion broke out and the occupants of the church parted like the Red Sea. The nuns huddled together in a hurry, quickly blessing themselves and praying aloud. The monks gathered together at the other side of the church conversing in hushed whispers.

Amber raised her chin, looking over the heads of the nuns, surprised to see a man standing in the doorway instead of the horned and hoofed demon she expected to find. A bedraggled man with a chain around his neck and chains on his wrists stood in the entranceway. His legs were spread, and his hands raised to stop the doors of the church as they hit the wall and swung back toward him. Lightning illuminated him from behind and thunder boomed from outside. Rain pelted down like a barrage of arrows from the sky, crashing against the stone steps of the church directly behind him.

"Father," the man said in a low voice through clenched teeth, and Amber realized he was speaking to Father Armand. "I will see you in Hell before I do your bidding again, you bloody bastard!"

Cries of shock went up from the group around Amber. One of the nuns swooned, ending up prone on the floor in a tangle of her black robes and long veil. Several of the sisters rushed over to assist her. The monks at the other end of the church continued talking to each other behind their hands. Amber curiously made her way from the wooden bench at the front of the church closer to the door to gaze upon this spawn of the devil.

"You are naught but the devil," shouted the priest. "Lord Jesus Christ, we beg your forgiveness for this possessed man who has entered into your house of worship." The priest made his way down the steps of the dais, raising his book of prayer to the sky as he walked a straight line toward the angry man.

"God's eyes, look what you've done to me," spat the devil man in the doorway. That's when Amber noticed the gashing wound in his side and the trail of blood behind him as he took a step forward.

"You will not use blasphemy in the house of the Lord," reprimanded Father Armand. "And you will remove yourself from these premises immediately."

"I will not!" shouted the man the priest had called Lucifer, stumbling forward. Catching himself on the edge of a bench, he bent over. "I seek refuge and ministrations and, dammit, I will get what I came for and not be sent away again." His words were filled with anger and venom. Amber felt the fear in the room as the nuns cowered together watching with wide eyes and the monks huddled together in the shadows. The priest grabbed hold of a tall, freestanding iron candleholder, slowly making his way toward the wounded man.

Lucifer had shoulder-length dark blond hair now soaked from the rain. The water ran in rivulets down his dirtied face and neck. His coarse, brown tunic was ripped down the front exposing his naked broad chest that was scratched and scarred. His face was covered by a mustache and full beard that made him seem as though he'd been on the road for quite some time. The man had a traveler's bag made of canvas with a long strap slung across his chest that hung down across one side of him. On his waist, he donned a sword and also a dagger. Bent over, he held his hand on his side and slowly stood up, holding his palm outward for all to see it covered with blood.

Shrieks went up from the nuns. Sister Dulcina, the abbess, gathered the women closer.

"Get away from him quickly," she instructed, moving her large frame in front of them in a protective manner with her arms outstretched as she herded the women together at the front of the church.

Amber had been a novice of the Sisters of St. Ermengild at Bowerwood Abbey and Monastery in Kent for three months now. Her petition to become a nun and live by the ways of God had been granted easily. She supposed 'twas because of the sizeable wealthy dowry that had accompanied her. It was eagerly accepted by Father Armand who oversaw the double monastery that housed both nuns and monks. Still, it didn't matter to her. She'd made her decision to atone for the sins of her family, and she would do whatever it took to ensure an easy path to Heaven for those she loved.

She'd passed her trial month of being a postulant and was

now in training that would last a full year before she took her final vows. There were only nine months left until she would become a full-fledged nun.

Amber came from a noble and wealthy family, being one of the four daughters of the Earl of Blackpool. While her older two sisters, Ruby and Sapphire, were married, her twin sister, Amethyst, still resided with her father back home at Blackpool Castle.

Amber had decided she would never be married to anyone but God. She would pay for the greed and deceit of her deceased mother who had tried to steal, and also the sins of killing a man and adultery committed by her older sisters. Aye, she would devote her life to prayer and helping the less fortunate. She hoped to bring about the grace and forgiveness for her family that was required in order to assure a successful place in God's domain once they passed on.

"He's hurt," said Amber, hurrying across the room toward the man, her instinctive nature to help and serve winning over her fear. But she never made it to the man. Father Armand's arm reached out to block her, his prayer book dropping to the ground at her feet.

"He's dangerous. Stay away from him," the priest warned her.

"Sister Amber, come join us quickly," begged the abbess from the other side of the church.

"But 'tis our duty to help the sick and wounded, and to take in travelers on their journey as they pass through." She bent down to pick up the priest's prayer book. From her position she could see the stranger's face clearly.

Lucifer's chin lifted slightly, though his body was still bent over. His hand pushed upon his wound to try to stop the flow of blood. The man's eyes were angry yet captivating at the same time, as they were birdlike, and the lightest blue she'd ever seen. They were also the most dangerous. His face held the look of a man gone mad, and his gaze was locked directly on her.

Too frightened to move, and in the same moment too intrigued to look away, she stared into the eyes of the devil. Oddly, she found herself mesmerized by this man though she didn't understand why.

He tried to stand upright, and when he did, Father Armand swung the iron post with the lit candle upon it, right toward him.

"Nay!" Amber shouted, gaining the stranger's attention just in time for him to raise his hand and clamp it around the iron rod, keeping it from hitting him. The hot wax from the candle splattered on his chest making him flinch as the stub of the candle fell to the floor and extinguished itself. His face came closer to the face of the priest as he leaned toward him, both of them still holding on to the rod. And though the man spoke in a low voice and she was sure the nuns and also the monks at the opposite sides of the church could not hear him with the raging storm, she could still make out every word he said.

"Drop it, Father," Lucifer warned the priest.

"Leave here now, or I'll be forced to take action."

"Haven't you already taken enough action?" She saw him swallow deeply. His nostrils flared as he inhaled sharply, making her realize he was wincing from pain.

"You were sent on a pilgrimage to atone for your sins," the priest answered.

The man moved his hand away from his wound, the chains around his wrists rattling as he did so. That's when Amber saw the lead badges from each shrine he'd visited upon his pilgrimage, attached to his torn tunic. There were many and she wondered how far he'd traveled or how long he'd been on the road.

"I believe you sent me to atone for *your* sins, you lying bastard. You will rot in Hell for what you've done," he spat.

Amber got to her feet, shocked by the foul words spewing from the man's mouth in such a holy place. He spoke of Hell, so perhaps he was the devil after all. She hurriedly made the sign of the cross, hoping to ward away any evilness he could possibly bring forth.

"I am a man of the cloth and live by the rules of the church and the word of God. I have no sins." The priest smiled sardonically when he spoke. Amber thought it an odd action for such a pious man.

"Well, now, I believe I'm living proof that you are lying once again. The guise is up," Lucifer snarled. "Your secret is no longer safe, and I refuse to do your dirty work any longer of –"

The priest took his hand and punched it into the man's wounded side.

Lucifer let out a gasp and wailed a loud moan of pain. Releasing his hand from the iron rod, he used two hands now to cover the bleeding of his side. His wail echoed through the church, reverberating off the stone walls. Thunder boomed again outside the open door and a gust of wind blew in, extinguishing all the candles and leaving the church in the dark.

Several of the nuns whimpered in the background. Sister Dulcina tried to be brave and comforted them, but Amber could hear the tremor in her voice.

Then a flash of lightning lit up the inside of the church. In that instant, she saw Lucifer reach out his hand toward her, and she heard him call to her as well.

"Help me," he said in a whisper. Amber felt startled, not sure what to do. He looked right at her, reaching for her, and then it was dark once again. She could not see him, but his image was burned into her mind. A shiver wracked her body and she bit her lower lip, but did not move.

"You fool," said the priest in a low voice, malice dripping from his words. Then, as lightning lit up the room again, she gasped as she saw Father Armand raise the iron rod and, in a split second, bring it down right on the head of the wounded man.

The room was dark again, but she heard the crack of the iron rod against the man's skull and the rattle of the chains around him and then a thud as he fell to the ground.

One more rumble of thunder followed by another flash of lightning, and when she looked back to where the man had stood – he was gone.

A scraping sound was heard and then the flicker of fire was seen as the priest lit a candle. He replaced it in the iron rod holder as if nothing had happened. Amber's eyes dropped to the wounded man on the ground, lying in a puddle of blood.

"He doesn't deserve to die," she found herself saying aloud. Her eyes widened and her mouth dropped open as she shook her head. Then when she looked up at the priest, his eyes bored into her, making her feel more frightened than she'd been of Lucifer – the man that the priest had referred to as the devil.

"What is the matter, Lady Amber?" asked the priest. "Or perhaps I should say Sister Amber, since you will soon be one of the Order."

"Is he . . . is he dead?" she asked meekly, her eyes traveling back to the man on the floor.

"He fell and hit his head on the bench," said the priest nonchalantly.

"Nay," she objected. "I saw you –"

"You saw me what?" asked the priest calmly. It was calculated, as if he'd not just been in the middle of this harrowing incident.

"You . . . you had the candleholder in your hand."

"I was protecting you from the devil, my dear. Just as God would want me to do."

"You killed him."

"Nay, I never touched him. He just fell and hit his head."

"But I saw . . ."

"Whatever you thought you saw, you are mistaken."

"Nay, I'm not. You hit him! I saw you do it."

"What has happened?" asked Sister Dulcina, hurrying over to Amber's side.

"This novice has lied and accused a man of the cloth of purposely trying to hurt or even kill another," said the priest. "She will need to be reprimanded for this, as well as to come to me for confession. I will have to assign her the penance I feel appropriate for such an action."

"Of course, Father Armand," said the abbess, taking Amber by the arm to lead her away.

Confused, Amber knew what she had seen, yet the priest denied it. The image of the man named Lucifer reaching out to her and asking for her help was embedded in her brain. She looked at him lying on the floor in a puddle of blood face down and not moving. She was sure he was dead and that the priest had killed him.

"What about him?" asked Sister Dulcina, nodding her head toward Lucifer. "Shall we take him to the infirmary and tend to his wounds or is he dead?"

"I'll handle him," said the priest, flicking dust from his robe.

As Amber turned to go, she heard the voice of Lucifer, soft but distinct, from behind her.

"Amber ... will tend to me ... not you ... you sack of dung."

Amber froze in her tracks, glad to hear the man's voice and happy that he had not died. But at the same time, she was shocked to hear her name springing from his lips as if he knew her. The devil requested her presence at his side, and just the thought of it made her feel ill. A wave of fear ran through her. Her body stiffened at the idea of serving and applying ministrations to a man who could very well be the devil. She didn't want to be around him nor around Father Armand. All she wanted was to go back to her chamber and lock herself within and drop to her knees and pray.

Tonight, she had witnessed something she didn't understand, and now she was to be punished. And perhaps because of it, she might never have the chance of taking her final vows.

She turned slowly to look at the man, and when his piercing

eyes lifted to meet hers, she felt a fire within her that she'd never felt before. 'Twas as if a spark had been ignited that hadn't been there earlier. It made her feel strangely alive inside.

'Twas the fires of Hell, she realized. What else could it be? And now the devil himself would be taking control of her actions. The priest's prayer book slipped from her grip and landed with a thud at her feet. She raised her hand slowly and blessed herself as the man's gaze burned into her, making her feel as if he'd just violated her thoughts as well as her very soul.

"Aye," she said, nodding her head hypnotically. "I will tend to your wounds . . . Lucifer." And as she agreed, she felt as if she were surely making a deal with the devil.

CHAPTER 2

*L*ucifer's eyes slowly opened as he felt the gentle touch upon his skin. There before him in the light of one nighttime candle next to the bed was the girl with the big, green eyes and full lips that were ripe and ready to be kissed. He'd been dreaming about this beauty all night. In his dreams, he'd made love with her and she'd screamed out in passion.

Pleased to see the girl of his dreams was a reality after all, he grew hard just from his thoughts. She didn't notice he was awake at first, and reached over him, dabbing a wet rag against his far arm. That left her face very close to his. As she worked, her breasts rubbed up against him and he felt the want inside of him grow.

Then, as if she felt his eyes upon her, she stilled and turned her face toward him. Such soft-looking skin, such clear, innocent eyes. His body ached for her since he hadn't had a woman in some time. Lucifer, or Lucas as he preferred to be called, was still in a half-daze from the pain or he might have realized just what he was doing and stopped himself. Too late. He raised his hand around the back of the girl's head and pulled her closer, his lips locking on to hers firmly. His tongue shot out and pressed between those full, luscious lips, and he sampled the sweetest essence of a woman he'd ever tasted in his life.

Her eyes opened wide in horror and she dropped the rag and pushed away, holding her hands to her chest. Then before he knew what was happening, she reached out and slapped him hard across the face. The sound of skin against skin and the feel of the sting on his cheek led him to believe he'd not only been washed and had his wounds wrapped, but someone had also shaved him.

"How dare you!" Her hand went to her lips, those gorgeous lips, and he saw her tongue shoot out to lick away his essence. The action about drove him mad. "I am a nun," she retorted. "And you, sir, are surely the devil as Father Armand has called you."

"A nun?" It took a moment for him to realize just where he'd seen this green-eyed beauty in the first place. Then his memories of his encounter at the church came creeping back into his brain. He let out a deep sigh. It had been over four months since he'd been back to Bowerwood, and he'd almost forgotten how much he hated the place.

'Twas at the church he first saw her, he remembered now. While everyone turned away from him in fear, she'd bravely moved forward, wanting to help. He surveyed her long, black gown with sleeves down to her knuckles, and wondered how he could have forgotten this part. It surely wasn't in his dream.

She wore a scapular over her work robe that covered her shoulders. The long, white woolen strip of cloth with a hole in the middle for her head, hung down the back of her as well as the front. A rectangular piece of cloth was belted around it to keep it in place. On her head was a white wimple that covered her hair and sides of her face. Over the wimple was a short, white veil instead of the nuns' normal black one. That told him she was a novice – or a nun in training to take her vows.

"I'm sorry," he said. "I should have realized that you were dressed in the clothes of a frigid woman."

"I'm not frigid. I'm celibate," she corrected him, keeping her distance and pushing a stray strand of hair back under her headpiece.

"Same thing," he muttered. "And what a waste. With those beautiful, big, green eyes and such luscious lips, sweetie, you really shouldn't be a nun."

"I would appreciate it if you kept your inappropriate comments to yourself. And stop referring to my sex." She fussed with straightening her habit.

"I said nothing of sex, but now that you mentioned it, the subject has been on my mind lately. I'm sorry, but I enjoyed the kiss and I'd venture to say you did, too."

"I did not," she said, looking away rather than meeting his gaze, assuring him he was correct in his assumption. "Such conversation is not tolerated, so I'd appreciate you refraining from talking while you are in my care."

"I knew from the moment I first laid eyes on you in the church tonight –"

"Yesterday," she corrected him.

"What?"

"You have been asleep for a full day now. I was starting to wonder if you'd ever wake up."

"Yesterday?" he asked, moving slightly, causing his side to ache. His hand went to it. "So, I've been having those dreams for longer than I thought. No wonder I'm so hard – I mean – having a hard time remembering," he corrected himself when he saw the scowl on her face. His hand slipped under his bandage and he realized his wound had been sewn up. "Do I have you to thank for sewing me back together?"

"I did what I could," she said, "but I don't know how much of a scar it'll leave. I've only done embroidery and sewn clothes before, never human flesh."

"Well, one more scar won't mean a thing to me, so I thank you."

She just looked at him coolly and nodded. Then she reached out her hands and held them over his wound. "In the name of the Father, Son and Holy Mary," she said. "The wound was red, the cut deep. The flesh will be sore, but there will be no more blood or pain until the Blessed Virgin bears a child again."

"Now, that, I'd appreciate if you kept to yourself," he told her.

"I have cleansed your wound with wine and I've rubbed egg whites on it for a soothing balm."

"You did what?" he ground out. "It sounds to me as if you're praying over a meal. A simple stitching without wasting the wine or eggs would have worked just as well."

"I am doing as I've been instructed."

"I'm sure you are, since I don't think anyone would be able to make that up on their own." His hand went to his jaw, his fingers running over the smooth skin of his chin and under his nose as well. "I see you are skilled with a sharp edge, too."

"That wasn't me. That was Sister Dulcina, our abbess. She insisted on shaving your face, as she said your appearance within the abbey's walls would not be tolerated. But you have me to thank that she didn't give you a tonsure as well."

His hands flew to his head next, feeling the length of his hair still down to his shoulders. Then he patted his scalp to make sure he wasn't shaved bald atop his skull like a monk. The chains dangling from his arms rattled in the process. The old abbess had given him a tonsure once before and she hadn't been merciful. He never wanted her touching his head again.

"Well, thank you for that, my pure, little dove. Now what can you do about getting these chains off my wrists and neck?"

"Why are they there?" she asked curiously.

"Because Father Armand believes me to be flawed and full of sin. He made me wear these as punishment while on my pilgrimage."

"Only nobles are punished with chains on a pilgrimage to

point them out to others. So, you are a knight perhaps? From a foreign land?"

She was right about the first part. Lucas never did understand why the priest had put the chains upon him since he wasn't a noble. But the priest had convinced him that he'd been living a life of sin ever since he left the monastery and he needed to repent. Lucas hesitated before he answered her question. "Nay, I am not a knight."

"Well, you seem to travel, so mayhap you are a knight errant? Out looking for an adventure?"

"Nay," he answered again. "And my idea of seeking an adventure is not being clad in chains for four months and wandering the lands on a pilgrimage."

"A mercenary then?" Her head tilted to one side and her eyes narrowed. She was too curious for her own good and also very smart. He was a mercenary, but didn't want to tell her.

"What difference does it make?" he asked. "Does a title truly make a man? Is it by title only that one is judged? Shouldn't a woman or man devoted to God and the church accept everyone as they are, without expecting them to live up to one's expectations?"

"You sound as if you have something to hide," she surveyed. "And an axe to grind as well. So, tell me, does your situation have to do with Father Armand? Your words in the church were heated and filled with venom."

"I am sorry you had to hear that, but it doesn't concern you. So please stop asking questions." Lucas liked the girl and wanted to impress her. But by telling her of his hard and twisted life, it was sure to repel her instead. After all, she was almost a nun and would not accept him for who he was or what he'd done. Nay, he'd just keep his past to himself.

"You sound as if you know Father Armand, so I'd guess you are perhaps from around these parts." She busied herself with her healing ointments, not looking at him when she spoke.

"You could say that. But then again, it really shouldn't concern you."

"I saw a man on the road not long ago who resembled you. Perhaps I've met one of your family since I've been in Bowerwood?"

"Quit playing games. Don't you think I know that you probably haven't set foot outside the monastery since you got here? It doesn't do you good to lie. After all, that is not a quality of a nun. Now you will have to confess your lie and receive penance for it. If you have something to say, then be direct."

"All right, I will." She wiped her hands and put the rag on the table and then put her hands on her hips. "First of all, I don't lie. And I leave the abbey, or monastery as most people seem to call it, once a week to give alms to the poor in the village. I did see a man who reminded me of you, but he was a knight. Therefore, I am sure he could not have been related to you after all. You are obviously naught but a mercenary who hires out his sword to the highest bidder with no regard to chivalry or honor. I sincerely doubt that you have any morals at all."

"Well, Sister, you are more perceptive than I've given you credit for. And just to satisfy your burning curiosity, you are correct in everything you've said. Now, does that repel you? I can offer that I am sure it does."

"You are not very perceptive if you believe that. After all, if I must remind you, I was the only one who took measures to help you in the church when everyone else was cowering in the corner. If it weren't for me, you might be dead from the blow on the head Father Armand gave you."

Lucas rubbed the top of his head, noticing the welt from the candleholder still stung, but the swelling had eased. She was right. If she hadn't accepted him, she never would have tried to help him.

"I am sorry, as I am the one who has judged you prematurely. But you must realize that I am not used to anyone wanting to help me or purposely be near me. Actually, I relish the conversation. This is the longest I've conversed with anyone for in as long as I can remember."

At one time, Lucas had been friends with everyone in the double monastery. But that was when he was in training to become a monk. When he left to become a mercenary, everyone seemed to shun him. He had a feeling Father Armand was behind their actions.

"So, your parents were mean to you then?" she asked. "Or did they send you away to be fostered and that's where you've experienced this inner pain?"

The girl touched a part inside of him, and he realized she was right. He held a lot of inner pain and that was the cause of all his misery. No one in the monastery had ever seemed to care enough to ask him questions about himself. He enjoyed the conversation. Mayhap he'd tell her just a little about his life after all.

"I never knew my parents," he told her, not wanting to relay the fact that he was an orphan abandoned as a baby on the steps of the church.

"Oh, so they died when you were young then. I'm sorry," she said. "I was just curious. I didn't mean to bring up harsh memories."

If she only knew how harsh his memories really were. Nightmares of his past haunted him still. Growing up without the love of a single parent. The turmoil of his present life, and the trials he'd been enduring lately, too. He no longer looked forward to the future as there was nothing there for him. He was an empty shell living a life of a lie every day, never knowing who he was or where he'd came from. Unwanted and abandoned since the day he'd been born, he pushed everyone away from him. He couldn't take the chance of being hurt anymore.

"The only thing you need to worry about is helping me heal so I can get away from here," he said, no longer wanting to talk about his pathetic life.

She turned back to fuss with items on the table, shaking her head, obviously not approving of his language. He wanted to tell her the truth of his past, but since he'd returned from pilgrimage, he wasn't sure of anything anymore.

He no longer knew what was truth and what was a lie. He'd heard a story from an old woman while on his pilgrimage overseas that she was once passing through the parish of St. Ermengild years ago. 'Twas a stormy night and she'd hid under a tree until the rain let up. That's when she spied a wagon pull up to the church. A noblewoman got out and laid a bundle atop the church stairs. She'd thought it to be food for the poor until she'd heard the crying of a baby. Then a priest ran out and picked up the baby, and she saw the woman hand him a large pouch that she could tell was filled with coins.

The pilgrim woman had said she went to the church the next morning and found Father Armand with the baby. He'd told her the child was abandoned on the church steps. When she'd asked the baby's name, he thought for a moment and then replied that the baby's name was Lucifer. It was the devil's name and that is why, to this day, the pilgrim woman had not forgotten it. She also said the baby had the same pale blue, piercing eyes as Lucas.

It was too much of a coincidence, in his opinion. Could this noblewoman she spoke of possibly be his birth mother? It was too similar to have been someone else. Did Father Armand know who his mother was all these years and keep it from him? If so, he would kill the priest, he swore. He would find out the truth from that deceptive cur that called himself a priest if it was the last thing he ever did.

Amber reached out and gently applied the wet rag dipped in a poultice of healing herbal water to his scratched arm. He reveled in the soft touch of her fingers as they accidentally skimmed across his skin. He closed his eyes, trying not to look at her, and trying not to think about his dreams last night.

"Oh, I'm sorry. Am I causing you pain?" she asked.

"More than you'll ever know," he said, hoping she didn't notice the tent under the sheet at his waist.

"What happened to you anyway? Were you perhaps in a battle?"

"Attacked by a band of ruffians while on pilgrimage," he said in a low voice.

"What were they after? Did you have a lot of money or valuables on you perhaps? I am surprised they didn't take your weapons, or that you didn't use them."

"I used them," he said. "If not, the bandits wouldn't be dead right now."

"Oh!" she said, holding her hand to her mouth. "So, you killed them."

"It was either them or me. And as you can see, I almost joined them."

"I suppose it was self-defense then," she said, making it seem as if it didn't bother her that he'd killed several men, but he could see in her eyes that it did.

"If it'll make you feel any better, I also protected and saved the lives of several women and children and an old man."

"Well, I suppose it was for a purpose then."

"Where is my traveling bag?" he asked, hoping he hadn't lost everything after he'd almost died to save its contents.

"'Tis on the table next to the bed," she said with a nod of her head. "And the metal badges you wore from each of the shrines are next to it as well. I had to burn your tunic since it was torn beyond repair. Your sword and dagger are being held by Father Armand. He said you were dangerous and he didn't want you striking out with them."

"Aye, I am dangerous," he agreed, thinking of how he'd wanted to use the weapons on the priest right there in the church. But even as angry as he'd been, his upbringing made him hesitate to pull a weapon in a house of worship.

"What is in that bag anyway?" she asked, curiously eyeing his possession. "It is full and very heavy for having been on pilgrimage. After all, pilgrims usually only have the clothes on their backs and a traveling staff and naught else."

"You ask too many questions," he told her, assuring himself the bag was still there and then closing his eyes with a sigh. "Don't worry yourself with things that don't concern you."

"Is your name really Lucifer?" she continued, not letting up for a moment with the questions she fired at him.

His eyes popped open at that, as his name had always been a sore spot with him throughout his whole life. He hated the fact Father Armand did this to him. After all, why would a priest name an innocent child after the devil in the first place?

"It is," he admitted sadly. Her hand stopped its movement and her eyes grew wide as she surveyed him.

"I've never known anyone to be named after the devil," she said, sounding shocked.

"I'm not the devil, even if I do have the devil's name," he pointed out. "So, don't you worry your pretty little head that I'll take you to my lair of fire and brimstone. And I prefer to be called Lucas, so please refer to me by that name from now on."

"I see."

"I SEE?" he asked mockingly. "You sound as if you don't agree with the name I've chosen to be called."

"Your birth name is obviously of importance to someone if they chose to call you such an oddity in the first place. Why did your mother do that?"

"Is your name really Amber?" He didn't want to answer her question, so he turned the conversation toward her. This wench was much too curious for her own good. He'd never seen anything like it.

Her head snapped up, and he could see the anxiety on her face by his question.

"How do you know that? I've never met you before, nor have I told you my name, but I heard you say my name in the church. Do you have some sort of magical powers to know such a thing?"

Well, the distraction worked and he almost laughed aloud. This girl was too easy to control.

"If I had magical powers, I'd use them to get you to kiss me again."

Her face reddened and she looked away. "*You* kissed *me*, not the other way around. And I beg you to never do it again."

He reached out and grabbed her wrist, not enabling her to leave his side. Her eyes fell upon his hand and, slowly, she raised her gaze up his arm and to his face. He could feel her body trembling under his touch.

"Relax. I'm not the devil nor a sorcerer, just very observant. I know your name because I heard Father Armand say it in the church, even if I was half-dead on the floor at the time. I always know everything going on around me. And I promise you – some day you will be begging me to kiss you again, not turning me away – mark my words."

"I am a nun," she retorted, pulling her arm out of his grip. "And you are surely the devil to be trying to tempt me like that."

"I did naught to tempt you, but only made the suggestion. The devil only exists in one's mind, as he is not real."

She blessed herself and started praying when he said that. He was sure she'd never heard anyone deny the existence of the devil before.

"And as for being a nun," he continued, "I see no ring of God on your finger nor the black veil of a woman who has taken her final vows. To me, you are no different right now than any other woman."

"Your words are daring by denying the existence of the devil," she said. "You must be careful with what you say or God will punish you. Or don't you believe in Him either?"

"Don't worry yourself to death about it. My soul is so blackened that even if I did believe in Hell, I'd probably not even be wanted down there."

"I'm not sure what you've done in your past, but God is forgiving. With penance and prayer, even someone like you could possibly enter the Kingdom of God."

"How long have you been a novice?" he asked. "You already sound like a full-fledged nun. Are you close to finishing your year of training yet?" He decided to fire questions at her the way she'd done to him. "Have you made it to Matins to pray at two in the morning every day or have you been a bad girl and overslept and had to be disciplined? After all, I can see you obey the vow of poverty by the simple way you dress, and there's no doubt you obey the vow of chastity by the way you kiss. But what about your vow of obedience? With the way you've been firing questions at me, I'm willing to bet they gave you a job at the monastery that keeps you out of everyone's hair."

"I asked you not to mention the kiss again," she said, looking over her shoulder, obviously hoping no one else entered and heard their conversation. "You seem to know much of an initiate of the church. That surprises me that a man like you would know anything that goes on inside the walls of God."

"You'd be very surprised if you knew how much about the church I really know. So, tell me, which it is? Do they have you reading from the Book of Hours aloud at the meals since you can't seem to refrain from speaking, or are they hiding you away doing some weaving in order to give their ears a rest? You do realize there are some branches of the Order that don't even speak at all."

"If you are trying to be amusing, I'd like to point out that I am not laughing. And for your information, I work in the scriptorium."

"Really? Impressive. So, you obviously know how to read and write. Considering it is all in Latin, I'd say you are from a wealthy family to have learned that. Perhaps the daughter of a baron or an earl."

"I am an illuminator in the scriptorium and, yes, I know how to read and write in several languages. I am Lady Amber, daughter of the Earl of Blackpool."

"Ah, so I figured. And I'll bet you have several older sisters and that's why your father put you in a nunnery, rather than having to dish out a hefty dowry to marry you off."

"I chose to come here!" she retorted. "And although I have two older sisters named Ruby and Sapphire who are already married, it makes no difference. I also have a twin sister back in Blackpool, and my father would give a dowry for each of us. As a matter of fact, he did give a wealthy dowry to the church when I arrived, so you are wrong in your assumption."

"All named after gems," he said. "Interesting. You say you have a twin? Another one like you?" he stroked his chin in thought. If this one wasn't available, perhaps he'd look into meeting her sister. "Does she have big, green eyes and voluptuous lips like you? And please tell me she isn't a nun, too."

"My sister, Amethyst is my twin but our looks are not identical," she retorted. "And you can calm down, because I can tell you right now she wouldn't like a man like you."

"A man like me?" he asked. "How can you say that when you don't know anything about me at all?"

"I know you are a ruffian with a blackened soul who likes to tempt women sexually and you're named after the devil. What more is there to know?"

He laughed and scratched his chin. This girl was not only beautiful and chatty, but she was also very entertaining. He laughed again and, this time, he felt the sting of the pull of his stitches and stopped suddenly, holding his side.

"You see what happens if you laugh at others?" she said. "God is punishing you."

"You have no idea of my life, so don't pretend you do."

"Then why don't you tell me?" she said, crossing her arms in front of her in challenge. But before Lucas had the time to say anything, the door to the infirmary burst open and in walked both Father Armand as well as the abbess, Sister Dulcina.

The priest was tall, with short, gray hair and dark eyes, and a very fair complexion. He was in his early fifties. The abbess, on the other hand, was short and stout, and about forty years of age. She wore a large cross on a chain around her neck, marking her as the abbess. None of the other nuns were allowed to wear jewelry or crosses of any kind. And on her face was that stern look he'd grown up seeing that always made him want to run and hide.

Lucas had been raised inside the holy walls after his mother had abandoned him three and twenty years ago. He'd been reared by the unforgiving hand of Father Armand. He'd also been disciplined by the strict Sister Dulcina who was obviously under the priest's control though she had earned the title and position of running the double monastery by herself. And if Lucas hadn't stopped his training by rebelling and leaving the monastery, he would have been a monk by now. Ever since he'd returned, the priest had been doing all he could to make Lucas' life miserable.

"How is he?" asked the abbess, walking forward with a threatening stare to peruse Lucas.

"Sister Dulcina, I have done my best," Amber told her. "His stitches have remained clean, and the rest of his wounds are healing nicely, including the bump on his head."

Lucas put a hand to his head when she said that, remembering now why he felt as if his skull were splitting open. Because the man who'd raised him had also tried to kill him.

"Has he taken to a fever?" Sister Dulcina slapped her beefy hand on Lucas' forehead, then roughly tore off the sheet, inspecting his chest. She was reaching for his wounded side when he stopped her.

"I am fine, no need to check." He held up one hand and

covered his wound with the other. "Sister Amber has seen to all my ministrations with a gentle hand and the finest of care. I have no fever." He looked over to Amber whose eyebrow raised and so did the corner of her mouth as she almost smiled. This led Lucas to believe that she approved of his compliments. He felt his body reacting to her beauty as he remembered the kiss. Yanking at the sheet to cover his lower half, he was thankful he was still clad in his braies. "No fever, that is, that can be remedied by herbs or ointments, anyway," he added, thinking how hot and bothered he was right now. Damn, what was this girl doing to him with just a look?

Amber's eyebrow dropped and her slight smile turned into a frown. She once again did not approve of him relaying his thoughts aloud.

"Sisters, you can leave now," instructed Father Armand. "Sister Amber, now that Lucifer is awake and healing, you no longer need to stay at his side. You can resume your normal routine. I expect you to meet me in the church for confession first thing in the morning. I will decide then what your penance will be for the way you addressed me in the church last night."

"Of course," she told him, keeping her eyes focused downward as she headed toward the door right behind Sister Dulcina.

Lucas could tell Armand was trying to get rid of them, and he knew the conversation between them was going to be far from pleasant.

"Well, hello, Father," said Lucas sarcastically. "I didn't expect such a smashing reception or I would have worn a helm." He rubbed his head as he spoke. "After all, I almost died trying to save those worthless relics and the money they brought us."

The priest's eyes burned with fire and his head snapped around toward the door. The abbess had already quit the room but Amber stopped and turned her head slightly upon hearing his words. Father Armand turned back to Lucas and shook his head as he spoke to Amber without turning around.

"Is there something you need, Sister Amber?" the priest ground out. "If not, be on your way and close the door behind you."

Amber didn't even acknowledge him, and Lucas was secretly glad. The priest didn't turn around or continue talking until he heard the click of the door as it closed. Then he quickly glanced over his shoulder checking that she'd left, and turned back with his dark eyes focused on Lucas.

"What are you doing, talking like that with the women in the room?"

"Well?" asked Lucas. "You seemed to have no problem trying to kill me in front of them at the church so what does it matter?"

"I was only trying to shut you up," said the man. "You can't be barging into the church spouting blasphemy. I'll have to punish you for that or the abbess will question my actions."

"It seems to me you're finding reasons to make me suffer every time I return to the monastery."

"You were supposed to be a monk, not a mercenary wandering the land."

"You are just angry that I didn't end up as a man of the cloth who abides by the rules and doesn't sin at all. Just like you, Father, right?"

"I did all I could to raise you right and in the eyes of God since the day I found you on the church steps."

"Speaking of that," said Lucas, sitting up straighter. "I met a very interesting woman on pilgrimage who told me she'd witnessed a noblewoman dropping off a baby at the church steps three and twenty years ago."

"That happens all the time, so why should this news seem to surprise you?" The priest paced back and forth, his usual nervous self.

"Mayhap because this noblewoman gave the baby to you along with a bag of coins."

"Sometimes coin is left along with the babies to ensure I can tend to their upbringing until I find a family to take them in."

"But they are not all named Lucifer and have the piercing light blue eyes of a bird, now do they?"

The priest stopped his pacing, and grabbed hold of the back of the chair. Stepping around it, he slid down onto it slowly. "I have no idea what you heard, but I assure you it is naught but idle gossip. I advise you to ignore it."

"This is one time I am glad for wagging tongues. Because now, I realize that you have known the identity of my birthmother all these years but yet you've kept it from me."

"That is utter nonsense."

Lucas swung his feet over the side of the bed and sat up. He felt his fury rising. "So, are you going to sit there and lie through your teeth like you've done for the last three and twenty years every time I asked you about my parents?"

"Keep your voice down," he said, nervously glancing toward the door.

"I will not, until you give me an answer."

"All right, calm down. So, I had seen your mother before in the village, but I tell you I never knew her name."

"Was she a noblewoman like the pilgrim told me?"

"I . . . suppose so. She paid dearly for me to take you off her hands."

"Why didn't you find a family to take me in? I find it odd you kept me at the monastery and raised me yourself."

His eyes opened wide and then they turned to squints. His mouth was pursed as he seemed to be thinking of what to say.

"She made me promise to keep you here until she could one day return for you again."

"And did she?" Somehow, he had a feeling the woman had come back and there was more to this than the priest was telling him.

"She did," he admitted. "Not more than a year later. But she told me she couldn't keep you since her reputation would be tarnished. It seems she had you out of wedlock."

"So, she *was* a noblewoman, or she wouldn't have cared about her reputation."

"Aye, I suppose so."

Lucas' side started aching and, at those words, he sank back down onto the pillows.

"What did she look like?" he asked, staring across the room at nothing in particular. "Was she pretty?"

"I guess, but I don't notice those things. Lucifer, I am not concerned with them."

It was a lie, as Lucas had seen Father Armand eyeing many pretty women over the years as he'd spoken to them after mass.

"You told me you named me. Is that true or was it my mother?"

"That is true," he told him. "You were a newborn and had no name. She didn't even know what I'd named you until she returned a year later."

"Why did you name me Lucifer? What would possess you to do such a thing?"

The priest looked to the ground and just shook his head. It took him a moment to answer. "It doesn't matter. Now, give me the bag of coins you brought back from selling the relics."

"It matters to me," said Lucas. But he knew he'd find out nothing more from the man at this time. His wound was hurting him as well as his head, and he was tired. He had no more strength to argue with the priest right now. "Fine," he said, "but this conversation is far from over."

Lucas reached for the bag on the table, surprised the priest hadn't just taken the coins when he was unconscious. He realized he had probably waited because he didn't want Amber to see him doing it. His hand stopped in midair. He turned back to the priest.

"Take off the chains first," he said, holding his hands out to him. "And I want my weapons returned at once."

"Give me the bag," he countered. "You are too weak and wounded to use a sword right now, nor is it appropriate to have it within the monastery walls. I'll hold on to your weapons until I feel you are ready to have them returned."

"These chains are reserved for nobles on pilgrimage," he pointed out. "You knew I was the son of a noblewoman and that's why you put them on me in the first place, wasn't it? But no one else knows that, so you needn't have wasted them on me."

"It was necessary to make sure people respected you enough to buy the relics from you without questioning the authenticity of the pieces. Besides, you punched me before you left on pilgrimage in one of your angry fits. You had to do penance for that, or have you forgotten?"

"I haven't forgotten. I hit you because I was angry at the way you treat me as well as others. And they are fake relics," he reminded him. "You disgust me to be taking advantage of poor innocent people who are trying to buy their way to Heaven."

"Now, now, Lucifer. If they were innocent they would most likely never be on a pilgrimage to begin with or be trying to collect all the relics they could to ensure the saving of their souls. And the money goes to the double monastery. Bowerwood is large and takes much coin to run it. So those sinners were only helping out the church, and for that they will be smiled upon by God. Besides, I let you keep your weapons to protect those people, so they were in no real danger."

"You are no priest, but the devil in disguise," ground out Lucas. "You will burn in Hell for your greed and deceit."

Father Armand reached out and grabbed the chain around Lucas' neck and pulled, causing the metal to chafe his skin. Though his hands were not bound together, they were encircled with metal rings and chains hung from them as well. It was a form of punishment and embarrassment that he could have done without.

"Well then," said the priest, his face getting very close when he spoke, "I guess I'll have company in Hell as you'll be right there alongside me as my accomplice."

Lucas tightened the muscles in his neck, surprised at how strong the man was when angered. He didn't want to fight a priest, but neither did he want to be subservient to the man any longer either.

"I almost died trying to carry out your scheme. And if I'd had anywhere else to go at the time, I would have left you and your deceptive ways in a minute."

"You're in too deep, Lucifer, and you know it. You owe your life as well as your soul to me for raising you and keeping you from a life of poverty."

"You promised me my own castle after this pilgrimage, and I want it!"

"Nay, you never finished the pilgrimage, so you get nothing until you deliver." The priest dropped the chain and it hit Lucas in the chest.

The man's lies once again had him trapped as well as angered. He'd been living on borrowed promises, doing his penance for leaving the church, thinking he was saving his blackened soul as well as ensuring a wealthy lifestyle for himself. That's the only reason he agreed to sell the fake relics for the priest to begin with.

It seemed an easy way to make money quickly. The reward he was to be given when he finished was more than he could ever attain from being a mercenary.

Being a hired sword was a cold, cruel job. Wandering the lands was unfulfilling. He knew damned well he'd never have a pot to piss in if he kept up that lifestyle. No mercenary who wasn't a noble would ever have his own castle. The church had more wealth than most the nobles and, by God, he wanted some of it. He'd seen Father Armand's lifestyle and it was impressive, indeed. If a church were to give him a castle, he'd be accepted, be he a noble or not.

Lucas had nothing in life. No wealth, no lands, and no one to love or care for him. He'd been promised a castle after he did the priest's bidding, and now he was being denied it. Father Armand controlled the strings of the coin pouch for the double monastery though that position should have been controlled by the abbess alone. And as the priest was his surrogate father, Lucas felt he deserved to share the wealth as well.

"You bastard," he spat, raising a hand to hit him, but Father Armand stood up and moved away quickly. The priest stumbled backward and steadied himself by grabbing on to the table.

"What's the matter?" Lucas growled. "Been nipping too much wine from the chalice again?"

"You'd better watch your words. I'll not allow you to hit a holy man and get away with it again. I'll have you excommunicated."

"I was well in my cups when I punched you the first time, but I am more than sober now. If you need to excommunicate me from the church, then do so. There is nothing here for me anymore, so it doesn't matter."

"I sent you away before, and I'll do it again," said the priest, standing up and smoothing down his robe. "As soon as you're able to leave the bed, you'll finish your pilgrimage as was our deal. I need you to go to Canterbury where one of our biggest shrines to the saint, Thomas Becket, is just crying out for someone to sell relics. Besides, Canterbury Cathedral has a relic I want and you are going to retrieve it for me as well. Actually, it's not a relic, but one of the treasures of Canterbury."

"Retrieve?" he repeated the word. "What you really mean is that you want me to steal from a church, don't you? You've gone mad."

"I want the parish of St. Ermengild to have the best relics in the land. Real ones, that is, and also the best treasures. The archbishop of Winchester will be visiting soon and I need to make a good impression in his eyes. If he likes what he sees, I am hoping he will put in a good word to the Pope about me. With any luck, I'll be a bishop soon and have my own diocese instead of just a parish. Besides, this won't be the first time a relic or treasure is stolen from a rivaling church. This has been going on amongst the churches for years. It is not anything new, I assure you."

"Perhaps not, but you are asking me to do it. I almost died from a band of ruffians with very large blades on your little mission already. It was only by my own training with a sword that I was able to protect the other pilgrims and kill the bandits. And I assure you it didn't help that I had these to slow me down." Lucas held up the chains to show him. "Had they not used the chains to hold me down I never would have been wounded. 'Twas only because I had my feet free that I was able to get out of their holds."

"I suppose that could be a problem. But I knew you could take care of yourself, Lucifer, so I wasn't worried."

"I admire your vote of confidence. But the fact doesn't change that we made a deal and I'll not let you renege on it."

"Of course not. Just finish the pilgrimage and get me my relic from the cathedral of Canterbury and I'll make good on all I've promised."

"Fine. But since this mission sounds even more dangerous than the last, I want more than just a castle when this is finished. I want lands and a wife, too. And more wealth than an earl."

The priest thought for a moment, and then nodded. "All right," he said. Canterbury Castle will belong to the church soon, as I've heard the lady of the castle's husband has died without an heir and he has left it as well as his land to the church. I want you to go there after your pilgrimage and court the woman. In the meantime, I'll make the arrangements needed. In order not to lose her lands, she'll have to marry you. Then you'll have not only your castle, but your lands and wife, too."

"Why would she marry me? I'm not a noble. I have nothing to offer."

"She doesn't need to know that. I'll pay someone to write up the appropriate parchments so it'll look like you're a baron or an earl."

"Nay. I'll never be able to convince anyone of that. I'll go to the castle, but as a knight errant only. I've taught myself to fight, but I'll live by the rules of chivalry that are expected. I will earn my title of knight and lord, though the castle will be your gift to me for what you've put me through. As for a wife, – I will take Lady Canterbury but only if she so pleases me. I'll not have a wife who is old or ugly. I've spent my life in a monastery of drab nuns. I want a wife who is alluring and very lively and who will see to my lusty needs. Well then, now that our agreement is settled, I will not have these chains on me another minute. I demand that you release me."

"So be it," said Father Armand. "But I warn you if you breathe a word of this to anyone, I will not carry out my end of the deal, do you understand?"

"This is the last time I'll do your bidding. And believe me, I have no intention of telling anyone anything that could keep me from the lifestyle I truly deserve."

"Hrmph," sniffed the priest, getting a reaction out of Lucas.

"You never did tell me anything about my mother. Nor if you know who my father was. For all I know, I could have been sired by the king."

"There's no chance of that, Lucifer, take my word on it." With that, Father Armand pulled a key out from the folds of his robe. "Give me your hands."

Lucas held his hands forward and as the priest unlocked them, the chains fell to the ground with a loud clang.

"I'm surprised you didn't hack them off yourself," said the priest unlocking the neck collar as well.

"I thought about it, but since you were the one to put them on me, I wanted the pleasure of seeing you regretfully take them off. Besides, we had a deal and I was upholding my end."

"There," said the priest, dropping the collar to the ground and then placing the key on the bedside table. "Now hand over the coins, and be sure to restock the relics before you go."

Lucas grabbed the canvas bag with fake relics, dumping them atop the bed. "Pig bones, horse hair, old teeth from the beggars at the gates . . . why do people believe these are body parts from saints? 'Tis garbage and not worth a rat's ass."

"Because they want to believe, Lucifer. It doesn't take much to convince someone of anything if they are crying out in their mind, wanting to believe in something."

Lucas knew how that felt. He'd been crying out silently for years to believe in something. He'd thought at first it was the church. But when he'd seen how corrupt Father Armand was and yet he still wore the holy robes, he knew his faith had been misplaced. If there was a God, then why hadn't He helped him by now instead of making his life so miserable?

"Now the coins," said Armand, his long fingers jutting out toward Lucas, the greed showing in his eyes. "It looks like that pouch is full."

"It is. And don't forget I almost died to keep it." He picked up the heavy pouch filled with coins collected from the sales of the fake relics for the past four months. He was about to hand it over, then decided against it and clutched it to his chest instead. "I think I'll keep this for now to make sure you'll deliver your end of the deal."

"You can't do that. That money belongs to the church. Now, hand it over."

"You mean it belongs to you, don't you? I have no doubt in the least that neither the church nor the monastery ever sees a penny of this. I'll hold on to half of it. After all, I'll have traveling expenses. Though I'll be on pilgrimage, this time, I'll be stopping at inns to eat and sleep along the way instead of begging for food and sleeping on the damp earth. I think I might even buy a horse, as I tire of walking."

"Lucas, that wasn't the deal, now hand it over."

"It wasn't part of the deal that I almost got killed either, so I'll take my share as I feel is fair." He dumped most of the coins on the bed and shook the pouch, looking inside to inspect what was left. "There you go." He pulled the strings closed and tossed it to Father Armand. "Your thirty pieces of silver, Judas."

"Don't call me that!" snapped the priest, shoving the coin pouch under his robe.

"Why not? After all, you have betrayed God. Besides, being called Judas is admirable compared to being called Lucifer, don't you think?"

CHAPTER 3

Daughters of the Dagger

*A*mber rushed to her room and closed the door, then threw herself down at the side of her pallet. On her knees, with her hands folded in prayer, she blessed herself and tried to calm her breathing.

"Forgive me, God," she prayed. "I never meant to kiss the man. I am devoted and would never do this of my own accord. It was he who saw to kiss me. I despised every minute of it."

She went into a mantra of Hail Marys, but stopped when she thought once again about the kiss. Lucas' piercing blue eyes were dangerous and perusing. He'd tasted like power and strength as he'd thrust his tongue into her mouth.

Her heart beat even faster just thinking about it, and she realized she was lying to God when she said she despised it. She'd felt a flutter in her chest and a tingle against her skin when he'd touched her. She could still remember the softness of his lips and the way she'd almost melted under his slight embrace.

"Nay!" she cried out and squeezed her eyes shut. It was wrong to be feeling this way about a man. Especially such a dangerous one that everyone referred to as the devil. But a part of her came alive today that she'd never known existed. She enjoyed the kiss just like he'd said. But she would never beg him to kiss her again as he predicted. She would make certain of that.

She never wanted to see him again. He was just like that fallen angel Lucifer to try to coerce her into sexual pleasures. He was a vile man to even touch a nun, even if she was only a novice. Amber still deserved the same respect as any of the other Sisters of St. Ermengild. She needed to focus. Her training was in midstream and, before long, she would take her final vows and become married to God for life. This was something she didn't need right now, as it was going to spoil everything.

There was a purpose for her being here. It was up to her to save her family's souls. Her mother had been dishonest and dishonorable, and her older sisters both had committed mortal sins. How could anyone who killed a man or committed adultery ever make their way to Heaven? It was up to her now, and she needed to concentrate on her goal. The last thing she needed was doubt creeping into her thoughts about becoming a nun. She was doing the right thing, she told herself. She would just keep far away from Lucas and she would have nothing to worry about.

Locked inside the abbey with all the nuns and monks, Amber would have no trouble keeping her mind on prayer. But she had kissed a man now, and she'd have to confess it. Her only hope was that when she went to confession in the morning, Father Armand would be forgiving. He was already upset with the way she spoke to him at the church, so there was no doubt her penance was going to be hefty. But no matter what, she would accept her penance with grace, and repent for her sins. To keep her soul from being

blackened, she needed to stay far away from the King of Temptation himself – Lucifer.

* * *

IT WAS JUST AFTER LAUDS, the five o'clock in the morning prayer session, and Amber was leaving the church when she saw Lucas standing under a tree watching her from across the cloistered walkway. She was surprised to see him there, and even more surprised that he was even standing after seeing the severity of his wound. But he had been healing nicely, and she had a feeling he was a man who would only stay in bed for one reason. And to heal himself was not the reason.

She slowed down and glanced over, but when their eyes interlocked and she felt that odd fluttering sensation in her stomach, she quickly looked away. She sped up to join the line of nuns making their way across the cloistered walkways, returning to their rooms or going about their duties of the day. Looking back over her shoulder, thankfully, he seemed to be gone.

The abbey was housed with both nuns and monks, actually being called a double monastery. It was one of the few in all England that housed both, and was headed by the abbess. Of course, Father Armand made his presence there prominent, and though they needed a priest to serve communion, hear confessions and say the masses, the abbess was skilled in all other matters and in charge of how the monastery was run.

The main building of the church of Bowerwood Abbey and Monastery was cruciform, or shaped like a cross. It was the largest of all the buildings. Just outside it, was a small cemetery. Leading from it, and all around the monastery, were cloistered, or covered, walkways. And in the center, was the garth – the gardens meant for serenity and contemplation to be used by the nuns and monks.

Along the cloistered walkways were long buildings made of wood and stone, such as the refectory, or eating hall. The kitchen was in a separate building to guard from fires. The monastery also had a cellarium – or underground storehouse for roots and crops to be used during the winter. There was the tithes barn that housed whatever was collected from the villeins for taxes, or one-tenth of their income. It was often collected in livestock or crops. There was a granary and also a brewery, as the monks were skilled in brewing ale.

Opposite these on the other side of the gardens were the infirmary for the sick or wounded, the guesthouse for travelers passing through or for nobles to stay on their journeys, and also the chapter house where the nuns and monks met with Father Armand and the abbess for daily meetings. It was right next to the library. Next to that was the scriptorium where she and others copied books and illuminated script.

Across the back of the cloistered walkways were the stables and the garderobe. A warming house was the only place besides the infirmary or kitchen where a fire was allowed. And just beyond the stables were the fields of crops and the orchards, as well as a small pond for water and to catch fish.

Most the dorters, or dormitories, were on the second stories above the main buildings. They had a nighttime staircase and passageway leading directly into the church to enable them to get there quickly and safely in the dark for early morning prayers.

On one side were the small, simple rooms of the nuns, and on the other were those of the monks. There were two larger, more luxurious rooms that had more than just the simple straw pallet, chair, table, and hooks on the walls. Those belonged to the abbess and the priest.

Amber's room was tiny compared to the large chamber she'd had at her father's castle. But it didn't matter anymore because she had hardly any possessions. Other than the clothes she wore, with one extra robe to be worn on washdays, she had a crucifix on the wall, and her bible. Everything else, including her favorite gown, was confiscated upon her arrival and given to those in need.

Even her dowry that included an amber ring and necklace – her only remembrance of her deceased mother – was gone now. Her mother was dead, and though she was only three when it happened, she missed her dearly. She also missed her father and sisters, and had no idea becoming a nun would be so challenging or so lonely.

Quickly making her way up the stairs to her room, Amber clutched her prayer book to her chest. Opening the door, she hurried inside, then closed it and placed her head against it with a deep sigh. Her heart still raced from seeing Lucas. She had to wipe him from her mind completely before she started thinking about that kiss again. It could only lead to devious thoughts and trouble.

She turned to the bed meaning to read from her Bible until it was time for Prime, the second prayer session that started in less than a half-hour. But she stopped suddenly in her tracks when she saw the devil lounging upon her straw pallet.

"Good morning, my little dove," he said, lounging back on her pallet with his arms behind his head. His tunic had ridden up, showing the bindings around his side covering his wound. He still wore his boots.

"Lucifer!" she gasped.

"Now, now, sweetheart, I thought I told you I like to be called Lucas."

"What are you doing here?" she asked. "How did you get here? You shouldn't be in my room." She backed up until she touched the wood of the door behind her. Her body trembled and she didn't know if it was from fear or just excitement. "These rooms are off limits to any male."

"I took the short cut – the nighttime staircase," he told her. "You know, it really is quite fast. And I have good reason to be here. My wound is aching and I need you to take a look at it."

"Then you'll go to the infirmary as is proper. Sister Dulcina should be there right now and she'll tend to you."

"Nay, I don't think so. She is too rough with me. Actually, I fear the abbess as she is usually grouchy and doesn't like me much. I rather liked the gentle touch of your hands and would like only you to tend to my wounds."

"Quit calling me . . . sweetheart and . . . dove." She could barely repeat the endearments aloud. She'd never been called that by anyone before, and it appalled her. Well, actually, she rather liked it. "I have a name and I prefer that you use it."

"All right, Amber, I will. And remember, I'm Lucas to you, not Lucifer."

"It's *Sister* . . . Amber," she told him, watching his eyes devouring her from the bed. She wet her lips as her throat became suddenly parched.

"All right then . . . *Sister*, are you going to tend to my wound or not? I hope it's not infected."

"Infected?" She straightened her stance. "Do you have a fever?"

"I can't tell," he said, slapping himself in several spots on his forehead.

"You're not doing it properly," she scolded. Without thinking what she was doing, she rushed to his side. Hurriedly placing her prayer book on the simple wooden table, she leaned over him and laid the back of her hand against his forehead. "Nay, you seem cool."

"I'm not," he rallied. "I am burning up inside."

"You don't feel hot." She felt under his chin and then at the base of his neck.

"I am quite hot, I assure you. You're just not feeling in the right spot. It is my loins that are on fire." He turned his head and placed a small kiss on her arm. She tried to pull away but he grabbed her wrist in his hand. "My fever is not from the wound but from just seeing you. You make a man fill with desire, forgetting the fact that you are almost a nun."

"Let go of me," she spat, but he didn't listen.

"Please, check my wound," he told her with a smile. She found herself worried about his health, and couldn't deny him.

"All right, but you need to promise not to touch me."

"That's like asking me not to breathe, but I will do my best." He released her arm from his hold.

"Thank you." Amber gingerly lifted his tunic a little higher, careful not to touch his skin. She'd cleansed all his wounds while he'd been unconscious and knew every scar and scratch on his body. The only part she hadn't seen, and wouldn't go near, was what lay beneath his braies. She was only too glad now that he hadn't been awake at the time, or he might have pulled her down on the bed . . . and she might have let him.

Easing back the binding, Amber took a look. And when he let out a small moan she dropped it quickly and pulled his tunic down to cover him once again.

"Your wound is fine," she said. "'Tis healing incredibly fast. Now please get off my bed and leave at once."

"Now, now, is that any way for you to talk to a man who only wants to be healed?"

There was a knock at the door and then the muffled voice of one of the nuns was heard.

"Sister Amber, it is time for Prime, are you coming with us?"

Her eyes opened wide and she looked first at the door and then back to Lucas.

"Don't say anything," she whispered. Then she called out, "Go without me, Sister Ursula. I'll be along in a minute."

Any moment, the door could open and anyone could walk in. If she were seen with a man in her room, there would be no explaining. She would be finished as a novice and sent on her way back to her father's castle.

"I'm going to prayer service and then I am going to the refectory to eat," she announced to Lucas. "After that, I will attend confession and then retire for the rest of the morning to the scriptorium to work."

"Well, thank you for telling me where I'll be able to find you every minute of the day."

"Nay! I am telling you so you can be sure not to be anywhere near me again. I am sorry, Lucas, but I need to focus on my prayers and you are too distracting."

"I am distracting? In a good way, I hope." His mouth turned up in a lopsided grin and his eyes were starting to mesmerize her again with their clarity. She felt her face flush. She had to get away from him fast.

"Please," she told him. "I already have enough horrid sins to confess, and I don't need more to add to the list."

"You?" he chuckled lowly. "I sincerely doubt you have any sins to confess at all. Now, what could you have done that was so horrid?"

"It's none of your concern. Now, as soon as I leave, I want you gone, do you understand? And don't let anyone see you leaving my room."

She left then, making sure not to open the door wide, not wanting anyone in the cloisters to see him. Then she hurried down the steps and across the courtyard toward the church, realizing she'd forgotten her prayer book but not daring to go back to get it. If she did, she might find herself under Lucas' spell again, and then she'd only have more to confess.

CHAPTER 4

Daughters of the Dagger

Lucas paced the floor of the church waiting for Amber. She would be showing up for her confession and he really wanted to try to talk to her again. Besides, he knew Father Armand was coming here, too, and he needed to discuss the plans of when he would be leaving on pilgrimage.

He wanted to try to talk him out of this mission of having to steal the treasured item at Canterbury Cathedral. He didn't even know what this treasured piece was, since the priest had been very vague. Lucas also needed to try to talk him into divulging the secret of his mother's identity. The man claimed he didn't know her name, but Lucas could tell he was lying. He'd wanted to beat the information out of him, but he thought it to his advantage to just bide his time and not anger the priest more.

The sun shone in through the stained-glass windows high overhead in the tip of the vaulted ceiling on both sides of the transepts, cross sections of the church. A round window was displayed over the altar. The scenes depicted the life of Christ, but they didn't display his whole life since there were only a few windows.

These were donated years ago by a wealthy nobleman.

Though the windows of red, yellow, and blue hues were beautiful, Father Armand had always complained that he wanted as many as were in Canterbury Cathedral. This was a rare and expensive item to behold, and St. Ermengild, being one of the poorer parishes, was lucky to even have them.

Lucas' wound was healing nicely thanks to Amber, but he still felt as if he wouldn't be up to traveling for at least another few days.

He'd eaten his meal of bread and fruit in the refectory hall alongside the nuns and the monks. They were pious and humble and didn't eat much. They only ate meat on special occasions, though they did have an occasional duck, goose, or perhaps fish.

He was still starved when he'd finished, as it did naught to fill his empty stomach. He'd noticed Father Armand had quite a spread of assorted cheeses and meats to accompany his meal, and though Lucas could probably have had some if he just asked, he didn't. He was too distracted watching Amber from across the room. His stomach was in a knot thinking how, in a few months from now, she would be a nun.

Lucas felt guilty for toying with her earlier, but he couldn't help it. 'Twas in his nature to be that way. He was tired of living the life of a pauper or a monk as Father Armand had expected him to be. Lucas wanted to start living the way the nobles lived. And although Father Armand had raised him and was like a father to him since he had no other family, Lucas still had to be true to himself.

He had respected the priest up until recently, and always did everything the man asked. Lucas felt he owed it to Father Armand for taking him into his care. But lately, he felt otherwise. Ever since he left Bowerwood Abbey and Monastery in a rage five years ago, he started seeing what it was like outside the monastery walls. That's when he knew that he was never meant to live the secluded life away from the rest of the world that Father Armand expected of him.

Lucas had wandered the land, teaching himself to fight, and acquired weapons along the way. He'd hired himself out as a mercenary, fighting for whoever paid the most, never thinking twice about taking a life. He'd consumed ale and wine, and played dice and cards. He'd even frequented the whorehouses of Bankside along the River Thames, and tried the temptations of the Winchester Geese, as the legalized whores of the Archbishop of Winchester's diocese were called.

He'd found out that nothing is as it seems. Even the priests of the church with so much power and wealth could be corrupted though they were holy men. The Archbishop of Winchester saw to it that prostitution was allowed in his diocese, yet right across the river in London it was illegal. He collected the taxes from the working girls for the church and, from them, became rich. Then he'd turned his back on the Geese, by not allowing the whores that died to be buried on consecrated land. Oh, what a twisted world it really was out there.

That's why he'd returned to Father Armand and Bowerwood. Because he realized you can't run from greed and deception and certainly not from yourself. But to his surprise, his surrogate father was no better than the Archbishop of Winchester. He'd said Lucas needed to atone for his sins and in order to do that, he had to go on a pilgrimage. And while there, he had to sell fake relics to make money for the church. It was to pay for the years of his absence when he should have been helping out.

Lucas had gone as instructed and done Father Armand's bidding. But he'd realized years ago that the man was never satisfied and always wanted more. Lucas wanted more, too, and would do whatever it took to find out who his mother might be. He needed to find out who he was and stop hiding from himself whether it be inside the walls of the monastery or out on the road. He needed to find out his past and face his future no matter what happened, and just try to always make it better.

He wondered if Amber had joined the Order inside the holy

walls just to hide from herself. He felt as if he needed to find out more about her. And he also felt as if he needed to remind her of what she'd be missing once she took her final vows.

Still, he struggled with himself, thinking mayhap he should just leave her alone. The girl seemed determined and focused on her prayers and studies, and he was only tempting her. But it was easy for him to see that a girl like her should never be a nun to begin with.

Nunhood should be reserved for the old and widowed, or at least for those who were undesirable and ugly. Amber was none of these. She was in the prime of her life, probably not any older than two decades at most. And she was thin and beautiful with eyes that could lure any man to her bedchamber with just a glance.

She didn't really want to be a nun, and he knew it. He saw it in her eyes every time he looked at her. He'd also felt it in her kiss. Lucas was once in this position, and he knew what she must be going through. Or so he thought. He just really needed to find out.

The front doors to the church opened, and he spotted Amber coming across the nave, the main section of the church. He suddenly changed his mind, realizing that being here wasn't such a good idea after all. She had pointed out that she didn't want to see him, and it would only upset her. If he was going to try to get her to accept him, the first thing he had to do was stop riling her.

He slipped behind a curtain quickly, peeking out to see her headed right toward him. Then, he realized his mistake. He'd hidden in the confessional and that was exactly where she was headed, coming to tell Father Armand her sins.

She entered the confessional next to him and disappeared behind the curtain. He was about to leave when he heard her speaking to him from the other side.

"Bless me, Father, for I have sinned and I have come to ask for your forgiveness."

Lucas jerked backward in surprise, knocking into the chair in the small partition, making quite a loud noise.

"Father?" she asked from the other side of the curtain.

He planned to remain silent or just slip away, until he heard her next words.

"I have kissed a man, and I am horrified to say that I liked it."

"Really?" he spoke aloud, and slowly settled himself on the chair, very interested in her confession since it was about him. He had to stay now. If he stayed, he could find out what she really thought about him. If he knew she was having illicit thoughts about him the same as he'd been having about her, then that would surely mean she was not meant to be a nun. His suspicions would be confirmed.

"You sound different, Father. Are you ailing?"

Lucas cleared his throat and tried to speak in a raspy whisper. "Yes, my dear, my throat is feeling scratchy."

"I am sorry to hear that. Perhaps I can give you something to soothe it later if you come to the infirmary."

"Aye." He cleared his throat again and spoke in a slight whisper. "So, tell me about this kiss. Who was it you shared it with and tell me how you felt afterwards."

"It was with the devil," she replied.

"What?" he said much louder than he'd intended to speak. He didn't like her referring to him in such a manner.

"'Twas with Lucifer, Father."

"Oh, you must mean Lucas, my dear."

"Aye . . . but I've never heard you refer to him by that name before."

He realized she might see through this guise if he wasn't careful. If so, he would never know for sure how she felt about him. So he bit the inside of his cheek and went along with the name he hated.

"So . . . why did you kiss . . . Lucifer," he asked. "Does the man interest you?"

"Oh, no, not at all," she said quickly, making Lucas feel as if someone had kicked him in the side. The stitches pulled at his skin and he covered the wound with his hand letting out a small moan.

"Father? Are you feeling ill?" she asked again.

"I guess you could say that," he answered, feeling so disappointed that she had just said he didn't interest her at all.

"He was the one to kiss me, actually," she told him.

"And you said you liked it?" he asked curiously, hoping he'd heard her right the first time.

She hesitated. "I did," she admitted slowly and with a deep sigh. "I deserve to be punished severely. I will take any penance you give me without complaining."

"Why should you be punished for enjoying something that most men and women enjoy together all the time?"

"Pardon me?" she asked.

"You are a woman, darling, and need to be true to your wants and needs."

"But I am soon to be a nun!" she gasped. "I surely should not be having flutters in my stomach nor tingles upon my skin every time I am near the man."

"You do?" His mouth turned up in a grin and he thought mayhap he wasn't so wrong about her after all. "So, this man does interest you as well as excite you, doesn't he?"

Another pause. "Aye, Father. And now I must confess that I've lied to you when I told you that he didn't."

Lucas felt a newfound surge of energy wash through him. He had to do something to help Amber get in touch with her true self before she was cloistered away from the world and also herself and it was too late.

"Are you sure that the calling of a nun is for you?" he asked.

"Oh, yes. Mostly definitely."

"Be honest."

"Well . . . I think so. But lately, since I've met Lucifer, I have been having doubts. I don't understand it, Father. I was so certain that I wanted the life of a nun until I was tempted by that devil!"

Devil? She was back to calling him that again, was she? He didn't like it. Especially since she'd just admitted she was attracted to him.

"Now there is no reason to call the man names. After all, you should be thanking him for helping you realize that, mayhap, you have made a mistake in coming to the abbey in the first place."

"Father? What are you saying? That I don't really know who I am?"

"Well, it sounds to me as if you need some time to figure it out before you waste your life."

"Waste my life?" she asked, shocked.

"I meant waste your time . . . in prayers that is, when you should be taking action."

"I don't understand, Father. I have taken the vows of chastity, obedience and poverty. Prayer is what is expected of me, but you're telling me that this isn't so?"

"Nay!" he said a little too loudly, knowing he was not handling this well at all and he was already regretting his ploy. "I just meant that you should get to know Lucas – Lucifer first, and explore your feelings for him before you take your final vows."

"Oh, I see. Yes, perhaps you are right. But I am not sure how I'd do that here in the abbey."

This was true. She would never drop her guard within the holy walls. If she were going to be true to her own feelings and be able to relax, she'd have to be somewhere other than here.

"Well, what is my penance for these horrible sins?" she asked.

She sounded as if she truly believed what she was feeling was bad. He needed to do something to remedy that at once.

"Your penance is . . ." He didn't feel right giving her a penance, but if he said nothing, then she would know he really wasn't the priest. He couldn't let her find out – not yet. Not before he knew for sure how she truly felt about him. "I think your penance will be to spend time with Lucifer."

"What?" she asked. "That is not a penance. Father, this doesn't sound like you at all."

"Hell," he said under his breath, knowing the guise was over. She'd hate him forever now.

"What did you say, Father? I couldn't quite hear you."

"Pell – pilgrimage," he said, trying to cover his mistake. Then he realized that this was a wonderful idea after all. "Aye, you will accompany Lucifer on a pilgrimage to Canterbury in a few days' time."

"A p-pilgrimage?" She sounded frightened. "But that is dangerous, is it not?"

"Lucifer is skilled with a sword and will be there to protect you so you needn't worry." He smiled and nodded, knowing this would impress her.

"Aye, I've seen how skilled he is with a weapon. That wound in his side that almost killed him proves it."

"He was trying to fight off a band of robbers with chains on his wrists," he spat. "If he hadn't been hampered by them he could have taken down all the marauders before they'd injured him."

"Hrmph," she said, and it sounded like disbelief. "So, my penance is to go on a pilgrimage. Anything else?"

"Well, you should allow yourself to be tempted while on it."

"Tempted? Whatever for?"

"To see if you can resist temptation. If so, you will know your choice of being a nun is correct. But if you cannot, and give in to the passion between you, then you will know what you'll be missing by taking your vows."

"Missing? What do you mean?"

"I mean . . . you'll know you were missing your true calling and that it is not right to take your final vows at the abbey after all."

"Yes, Father, I understand. What about my penance for speaking brashly to you in the church the night Lucifer arrived?"

"Oh, that." In order to sound like the priest, he would need to tell her something. After all, the priest had seemed upset and determined to punish her for what she'd done. "One Hail Mary and one Our Father will be sufficient."

"One? Only one of each?" she asked. "Do you mean one rosary for each bead on it that represents both of the prayers?"

Lucas knew the rosary well, as he had said it often in his days of training as a monk. There were six Our Fathers and fifty-three Hail Marys on it. That would mean she'd have to say fifty-nine rosaries which would take forever. He didn't want her spending any more time in prayer since she was already going to the services eight times a day and also praying in her room. Mayhap it was selfish of him, but he wanted her to spend any free time she had with him instead.

"Nay, just one of each, not a rosary for each."

"But . . . but I've never heard of such an easy penance."

"All right, then two. But that is enough. Now go."

"Aren't you going to bless me and give me grace, Father, to absolve me from my sins?"

Lucas froze. To pretend he was a priest and listen to her confession was one thing. But to absolve sins – he just couldn't do it. If he were caught absolving sins, the punishment was to be burned at the stake. He feared that more than he did his soul burning in Hell.

"You need no absolution for your sins, as you really haven't sinned, my dear. You are just feeling human, that's all, and there is naught to forgive you for."

"But I lied to you, Father. Surely I need to be forgiven for that!"

"You didn't know at the time it was a lie, I am sure. You are confused and just trying to decipher your decisions. Now I bless you, so go quickly. And don't forget – you'll be leaving on pilgrimage with Lucifer in just a few days, if not sooner."

"Thank you, Father." He heard her bless herself and then the rustle of the curtain as she left. He sat back in the chair and folded his arms over his chest and smiled. Good thing he didn't believe in Hell. Because if he did, that's exactly where he'd end up for this outrageous stunt. Still, it felt good. Now he was going to get to spend time with Amber after all, and outside the holy walls. She wouldn't fight him since she thought it was her penance. And what a fun penance he planned on making it be.

Lucas heard the door of the church close as Amber left. He sat there for a minute, still smiling to himself. Anything could happen, and he was looking forward to finding out what.

When he heard footsteps again, he ventured to peek out, seeing it was Father Armand coming from the sacristy – the small room where the extra vestments were stored. Lucas had his hand on the curtain and was about to step out and speak to him when someone else came in, causing him to stop in his tracks.

There in the doorway to the church was a monk he recognized as Brother Gervase. He collected the tithes from the villeins each week. The peasants were expected to give to the church one-tenth of what they earned. If they couldn't give it in money, they had to give up crop, seeds or livestock instead.

"Brother Gervase, have you finished collecting the tithes and put them into the tithes barn as ordered?" asked the priest.

"I have collected the twenty percent of their earnings, although most of it is in livestock and grain since the villeins do not have the coin to pay."

Twenty percent? Lucas wondered how long this had been going on. Ten percent of their earnings was already asking too much. The people of the parish of St. Ermengild were poor with little or nothing to begin with. With Father Armand taking their food sources away now, they were going to starve as well as have no seed to plant come spring. It was nearly autumn, and they should be stocking their larders as well as their granary, but they were stocking the coffers of the monastery instead. Especially lining Father Armand's pockets, he was sure.

"Where is the coin you collected?" asked the priest eagerly.

"I've put it in your room, Father, where I always put the coin."

"Good. Now remember, not a word to the abbess about how much we're collecting and that you put the coins in my personal chamber. I'll give her pittance to suffice her and not rouse suspicion, just as I always do."

"Of course," he said and held out his palm.

Father Armand grumbled and pulled a coin from his pocket and handed it to the monk. "Don't waste it at the alehouse in town next time you collect. I have plenty of wine hidden away in the cellarium. You can have a tankard or two with every delivery of tithes you bring me."

"Aye, Father. Thank you." The man shoved the coin into the fold of his robes and started away.

"Oh, and Brother Gervase," called out the priest.

The man stopped and turned around.

"Does anyone in the village seem to be close to dying?"

"Not that I know of, why?"

"Just keep a watch. I'll be needing more teeth, hair, and bones, soon. I'm sending Lucas out on another pilgrimage and he's going to Canterbury. With the popularity of Becket's shrine there and the number of pilgrims flocking there every day, we'll need more relics to sell. Send someone out to see if the cordwainer has any old shoes. And see if you can get one of our cooks to give you some blood next time they slaughter an animal for a meal. Those types of relics seem to sell better than the rest. People believe they've been healed and cured from relics and we're going to give them hope. I'm thinking we'll bring in enough to possibly get another stained-glass window for the church soon."

"That much?" asked the man. "Just from relics?"

"Fake relics," he reminded him. "But soon, we'll have a rare treasure at Bowerwood. That is, the Regale ruby. It was given as a present from King Louis VII from France, two centuries ago and it resides at St. Thomas Becket's shrine."

"That is in Canterbury Cathedral. We'll never secure it," protested the monk.

"Just think. If we had the ruby at Bowerwood, then the pilgrims would flock here, too, just to see it. We'd be rich in no time."

"How do you plan on securing the ruby? I hear it is well guarded."

"I have my ways. Just keep it to yourself. Now go."

Lucas waited until the monk left. Then, as Armand turned around, Lucas stepped out of the confessional.

"Lucifer!" The priest's eyes opened wide. "How long have you been in there?"

"Long enough to hear your scathing plans and how you're wringing everything out of the villeins. Why don't you just squeeze blood from them instead of the livestock? After all, they have nothing left to give."

"You heard everything, didn't you?"

"I did. And I am not surprised by your greed, as I'm used to it. But I am appalled that you'd take everything from the peasants as well as steal the ruby for your own personal gain."

"It's not that way at all," he explained, trying to put his arm around Lucas. Lucas shook him off and just glared. "Walk with me," Father Armand said, leading him out of the church.

"Where are we going?" he asked.

"I want you to see the tithes barn and what's in it."

Neither of them said another word until they arrived at the barn. Two monks that Lucas knew were less than honorable were guarding the door. Father Armand nodded and they let them pass. Once inside, Lucas' jaw dropped at what he saw. He had no idea that through the years the priest had collected so much from the villeins and stored it in here.

Grain was piled high along the walls. Fruit, nuts and wool were stacked in barrels. There was also furniture and personal objects that were taken from the serfs. A far door was open at the other end and Lucas could see the barnyard with pigs, cows, geese, many chickens, and even a horse all pushed together in the pens.

There were many different types of seeds in open troughs along the walls that the peasants would need desperately for planting their winter crops.

"This is outrageous," said Lucas. "This is gluttony, as these things will spoil or be infested with bugs or eaten by mice before they can be consumed. You claim to have taken the vow of poverty yet these are the coffers of a king."

"Not a king, but perhaps a bishop," he told him. "Did you know the Archbishop of Winchester even owns a few stews which bring in more money for the church than everything else put together?"

"So now you're going to buy a stew?" he asked. "Somehow that doesn't surprise me."

"Nay, I'm not. I'm just pointing out how wealthy one can be if they know how to go about it."

"You are so greedy and deceitful that I can't believe you call yourself dedicated to God. Now I've seen and heard enough! Return my sword and dagger as I plan on leaving for pilgrimage as soon as possible. And once I have my castle, I'll have naught to do with you again."

"Now who is the greedy and deceitful one?" the priest asked.

"I don't think of it as greed, but rather as back payment. After all, you've been collecting your little treasures for some time now, and I've never seen any of it."

"And, why should you?"

"Doesn't a father usually bestow his wealth on his son?"

Father Armand's head jerked up and he narrowed his eyes. "What do you mean by that?"

"Well, you are the only family I've ever known, so I guess that makes you the closest thing to a father that I'll ever know, though it pains me to say it."

The priest didn't say anything. He led the way to his chamber and opened the door which was locked. Ironic, since this was a place of honesty and trust and no other door in the place was ever locked.

"There are your weapons by the trunk at the foot of the bed. Now get them and get out."

Lucas made a beeline to the bed, trying not to even look at the wealth and riches that lined the walls and floor of the priest's personal chamber. While Amber had a small room with naught but a thin straw pallet and only a chair and table, this room looked like it belonged to a king.

Statues of saints that were gilded in gold with embedded jewels lined shelves on the walls, and oversized crucifixes looked down upon the warm woven rugs that lined the floor. There was a padded chair used by the nobles, and Father Armand's bed was lifted off the floor on a pedestal and surrounded by thick, velvet drapes.

There were pieces of furniture and trunks lining the walls, each one of them overflowing with fine clothes as well as jewelry and golden chalices and plates. And in the corner hung some of the finest swords he'd ever seen.

"No wonder you lock the door," Lucas said under his breath, knowing that it would do the man no good for anyone to know what was behind it. He picked up his weapons. As he was fastening them on, he spied a trunk with a noblewoman's gown of burgundy and gold made from some of the finest velvet, taffeta, and silk. Next to it, on the top of another trunk, was displayed a gold necklace with amber stones in it and a matching ring as well. He picked up the ring and studied it, thinking what a beautiful piece it was.

"Nice, isn't it?" the priest asked.

"Where did you get all this?" asked Lucas. "I know it wasn't from the peasants."

"I often – I mean *the church* often receives gifts from the nobles trying to buy their way to Heaven. For a promised prayer, they'll give you just about anything if they think it'll help pave the way to redemption after they die. Most people fear the devil and Hell and rightly so."

"So, I see," he said, picking up the necklace next.

"Those trunks with the things you're looking at came with our new novice, Sister Amber, as part of her dowry from her father, the Earl of Blackpool."

"I thought you were supposed to give away to the poor the things you took from the nuns and monks when they entered the order."

"Why?" he asked. "The peasants, by law, cannot wear the clothes of a noble, nor would they have a need for fine things. The goods are better off just staying here with me for the time being."

The priest was standing in the open doorway trying to keep it partially closed when all of a sudden it was pushed out of his hand and swung open. And there, before them, stood Amber.

"Father Armand, I am glad I caught you," she said. "I wanted to thank you for that light penance you gave me and tell you how generous it was of you to –"

She stopped in midsentence when she spied Lucas. Her gaze fell to the jewelry in his hand.

"That's my mother's jewelry," she said, pushing past Father Armand even though he was reaching out to stop her. She walked up to Lucas and looked down at the trunk. "This was my favorite gown." She picked it up and ran her hand over the soft surface. "What are these things doing here?"

"Sister Amber, you are not allowed in my chamber. Now remove yourself at once," the priest shouted.

"Aye, this is your dowry," explained Lucas. "The good Father

Armand was just telling me that he did not give away your things because he wanted to make sure you'd made the right decision by entering the Order. If you decide to change your mind, he plans on returning everything in your dowry to you before you return to Blackpool."

"You do?" Amber looked at the priest with wide eyes. "That is so thoughtful of you, Father. Thank you. These things mean a lot to me. I must admit I've been thinking about my mother's jewelry lately, but only because it was my last remembrance of her and I miss her dearly."

Lucas didn't miss the evil glare coming from Father Armand's eyes. He hoped Amber hadn't noticed.

She suddenly took a good look at her surroundings. "Why are all these things in here?" she asked. "I thought priests took the vow of poverty as well."

There was silence for a second and then the priest cleverly changed the subject. "What did you mean you wanted to thank me for your light penance, my dear?" he asked, feigning a smile that didn't reach his eyes.

"Oh," she said, focusing her attention on him. "I just never heard of any priest assigning one Hail Mary and one Our Father for penance and that's it."

"Two," Lucas corrected her. When her head snapped around to look at him, he knew he'd made a grave mistake.

"Yes, that's right," she admitted. "How did you know?"

"I . . . I . . . Father Armand told me," stuttered Lucas.

"What?" Her head snapped back around to look at the priest. "You told him my penance? I thought what was discussed in a confessional was private."

"I don't know what you're talking about," said the priest, making Lucas realize he had to intervene.

"Sister Amber," explained Lucas. "Father Armand had to tell me that you and I would be going on pilgrimage together so, you see, he couldn't keep your penance a secret."

"She's not going on pilgrimage with you," snapped the priest.

"I'm not?" asked Amber.

"Of course, you are," Lucas interrupted. "Father Armand thought that some time away from the abbey might be beneficial to your state of mind." Lucas motioned with his eyes to the wealth around the room so only the priest could see him. "Didn't you, Father?"

"Oh . . . yes, that is correct," said the priest. "You'll leave tomorrow."

Lucas shook his head, trying to tell the man tomorrow was too soon, but he didn't pay him any attention.

A bell rang from the church tower, echoing across the courtyard and thankfully interrupting their conversation. Amber dropped the gown back into the trunk. "'Tis time for Compline, and I still need to get my prayer book from my room." She rushed to the door and was about to leave, but turned back to the men. "Father, although you told me my confession was not a sin, I would still like your absolution."

"Of course, you are absolved from your sins." He made the sign of the cross in the air. "Now go, Sister Amber. Sister Dulcina will not be as gracious as I've been when you show up late for the last prayer session of the day."

"Thank you, Father," she said with a smile. Then her eyes interlocked with Lucas' for a mere second before she dropped her head and hurried out the door.

Father Armand slammed the door behind her. Then he turned toward Lucas with fire in his eyes and his arms crossed over his chest, though he maintained a cool composure. "So . . . how gracious was I?" he asked. "And what sins did she confess that I thought to tell her were not sins at all? After all, that's what you were doing in the confessional wasn't it? Pretending to be me?"

"She has no sins," answered Lucas, scratching the side of his neck. He didn't want to tell the man that he'd kissed Amber. It wouldn't play well for her and he didn't want her punished.

"You know that if you gave her absolution you'll be burned at the stake for such an act," the priest reminded him.

"I didn't. You heard her just now ask for it, didn't you?"

"Well, it's good to know you learned something with all that training I gave you and that it wasn't just a waste of my time."

"I was just trying to get her out of the monastery since I know how much she upset you the night I arrived. But we can't leave tomorrow, as I could use a few more days to heal."

"Nay," he said, his hand going to his chin. "The sooner you leave the better. Now that she's seen what's in my room, she'll be dangerous to me. Plus, she heard you talking about the relics the other day. She knows too much. I can't have her in the monastery anymore."

"That's why I'm taking her with me."

"That's not what I mean. I'm not talking about just for a sennight or two. I'm speaking about forever."

"You don't think she'll make a good nun?"

"I don't think she'll keep her mouth shut about what she saw and heard. It's too risky, with the archbishop's visit so close and all. You'll have to do something about it."

"Me?" he asked. "What do you want me to do? Keep her away longer by taking her on an extended pilgrimage? I hope not. Because I'll tell you right now I have no desire to do it. I'm going to Canterbury and then I'm never setting out on another pilgrimage as long as I live."

"She can't be allowed to become a nun, no matter what. If so, my fate is doomed," protested the priest. "If she stays out of the monastery, it might not be so bad. Even if she does talk, no one will believe her."

"So, what are you suggesting I do? Kill her?" asked Lucas. His hands clenched into fists at his side.

The priest's eyebrows arched in question. "Would you even consider it?"

"God's teeth, don't tell me to harm her because I would never do it," growled Lucas. "And I cannot believe you would even order such a thing."

"I'm not. Calm down." The priest paced back and forth with his hand to his chin. "There must be another way of keeping her from becoming a nun. Such as . . . if she didn't obey the vows. If that were the case and she came to me to confess it," he looked up, "which she would, because she is ever so obedient when it comes to rules . . . then I would not forgive her but tell her she had to leave the Order for good instead."

"But she is determined and very structured. There is no way she would ever break her vows of chastity, poverty and obedience willingly."

"That's where you come in, Lucifer. You've got to help her do it."

"What are you suggesting?"

"Take her on the pilgrimage and . . . bring this along to tempt her." He picked up the gown and jewels and shoved them into Lucas' hands. "These seemed to mean a great deal to her. Get her to try them on for you." The priest nodded in satisfaction. "That should do it."

"Just because she tries on a nice gown and jewels doesn't mean she'll keep wearing them," Lucas pointed out.

"Then do something to make sure she doesn't take them off. Also do something to get her to break her other vow."

Lucas knew what *other vow* he was speaking of, and he couldn't say it hadn't entered his mind. "Then you . . . want me to . . . defile a nun?"

"Nay, you're not going to defile her." The priest swiped his hand through the air. "Besides, she's not a nun, she's only a novice. Just do what it takes to make her come to you of her own free will, and she will bed you!"

The thought excited Lucas beyond measure. But the fact that the idea came from a deceitful priest with greed in his heart and that he was ordered to do it, made Lucas want to retch. The rebellious part of him now made him want to keep his hands off of her, and that made him more confused than ever.

"Get out of my way," hissed Lucas, shoving the gown under his arm and grasping on to the amber jewelry as he pushed past the priest. "Because if I stay here a moment longer, I swear I am going to punch you."

CHAPTER 5

Daughters of the Dagger

*A*mber sat still and focused in the small room of the scriptorium, trying to concentrate on illuminating the capital letter A on the script in front of her. Sister Ursula sat behind her on a stool inspecting finished works. Two monks she just met recently named Brothers Walter and Victor kept bent over their pages as they copied script faster than anyone she knew.

She learned much about working in the scriptorium since she'd arrived, from the way the animal skins were turned into parchment and soaked in lime, to the way they were stretched to dry. The pages for the books were cut to the right shape and size, then smoothed down with a pumice stone before her work even started. She had to rule the lines on the pages by first pricking the pages to indicate the spacing for the lines.

There were horns of colored ink on her workbench as well as gold leaf for gilding. She'd used glair, or the sticky substance from the bottom of a bowl of whipped egg whites, for her binding element. She trailed it out with her quill made of a sharpened goose feather to make the curly intricate designs. Then she'd added a dove to the artwork. It had dried enough now, and she leaned forward to blow her breath on it to make it tacky again and ready for gilding.

Picking up her gilder's tip, she carefully balanced the very thin sheet of gold leaf and dropped it over the parchment where it almost seemed to jump into place. Then she used her thumb to press it down with a clean piece of silk, and picked up her burnishing tool which was naught more than a dog's tooth mounted on a handle. Amber burnished the edges and top of the gold to make it shine. Next, she picked up her soft ermine-haired brush and swept away the excess gold to reveal her work of art.

She was trying her hardest to concentrate, but found it difficult after what she saw earlier today. It wasn't right for a priest to have such wealth in his chamber. And although Lucas had told her that Father Armand was going to give her dowry back if she decided not to finish her training, she didn't believe it for a moment.

Something odd was going on here and she didn't know what to do about it. She wanted to ask questions to some of the nuns and monks, or mayhap tell Abbess Dulcina, but she knew how angry Father Armand would become if she were to say anything. She was thrilled he'd given her a light penance earlier, even if he seemed not to remember it. However, she was already being punished by having to go on a pilgrimage with a man who was most likely to distract her in more ways than one. Nay, she didn't need another penance like this one.

The two monks put away their works, extinguished their candles, and silently left the scriptorium. It was almost time for Sext – the prayer service that started at noon and was followed immediately by dinner in the refectory.

"Are you coming, Sister Amber?" Sister Ursula stood next to her with a smile on her face. She was a young nun probably a few years older than Amber's age of eight and ten years. Ursula had entered into the Order, just having taken her final vows several months ago. She was a noblewoman also, so Amber felt comfortable around her.

"I'd just like to finish this first," said Amber, burnishing vigorously with her tool.

"All right," said Sister Ursula, turning to go.

"Wait."

The nun turned back to face her. "What is it, Sister Amber?"

"Tell me," said Amber. "While you were in training did you ever have thoughts that perhaps you didn't really want to be a nun after all?"

"Why, of course not. Are you having those thoughts?" she asked.

"Nay," she said quickly, then put down her tool and looked up. "Aye. I mean . . . I'm not sure."

"You sound as if you are perhaps smitten with a man and don't want to admit it."

"Me?" Amber's heart raced just thinking of it. "Why would you say that?"

"I was in love once before I came to the abbey," she told her. "And I see the way you look at Lucifer while we're eating in the refectory though you don't think anyone notices."

"I'm not in love," she blurted out, feeling the color rising to her cheeks. "Not with anyone, and especially not Lucas."

"Your voice trembles when you say his name. And though the rest of the monastery has always called him Lucifer you are basically the only one to call him Lucas. That alone tells me that you have feelings for him."

"I don't," she blurted out, embarrassed by even bringing up the subject. But not wanting to lie to another nun whom she considered her friend, she decided to tell her the truth. "Oh, Sister Ursula, can you keep a secret?"

The girl's eyes lit up and she grabbed on to Amber's arm. "Yes. Tell me, please. I have been so bored with the conversation since

I've been here that if this has anything to do with Lucifer, I'd love to hear it."

"He . . . kissed me," she said, biting her lip, not sure what reaction she would get from Ursula.

"Really?" she asked with wide eyes.

"It was in the infirmary when I was tending his wound. He said I had beautiful eyes and . . . luscious lips. And that I should never be a nun."

"Oh, Amber, that is so wonderful!" Ursula's smile was wide. This was the most life Amber had seen in the girl's eyes since she'd arrived here.

"It is?" she asked.

"Yes, it is," said Ursula excitedly. "You may have a chance to find the kind of love I once knew before I lost my husband to the plague."

"Oh, I am sorry, I didn't know."

"Thank you," she said. "But tell me more. Did you like it?"

"I did," she admitted and smiled. "And he did something odd – he entered my –"

"He did?" the girl gasped.

"My mouth with his tongue. During the kiss," Amber explained. "Just thinking about being so intimate with a man has my body tingling." Amber hid her face in her hands. "Oh, I am a horrible person for enjoying it. I must pray more and ask for forgiveness for my thoughts alone."

"'Twill probably not happen again, since he knows now you are a novice. So, do not give it another thought." Ursula tried to assure her, but Amber wasn't so sure.

"But it might happen again," she said. "For my penance, I am to go on a pilgrimage with the man."

"Oh, I see."

"I am frightened, yet at the same time mesmerized and excited by him. I don't know what to think."

"Well, he does have a temper," stated Ursula in thought. "After all, I've never seen anyone hit a priest before."

"What?" asked Amber, taking her hands from her face. "When did he hit a priest? I was in the church when he arrived and he did nothing of the kind."

"Nay, not then," her friend explained. "I first met Lucas about four months ago, right here at the abbey. With my own eyes, I saw him punch Father Armand in the face. That's why Father sent him away on a pilgrimage with his hands and neck in chains. He said he was dangerous and needed to repent."

"Why was he here at the abbey in the first place?" Amber asked curiously.

"I'm not sure, but you might want to ask Abbess Dulcina. After all, she is the oldest one here and has been a nun for as long as anyone can remember. She knows everyone and everything that goes on around here. All I know is that everyone in the double monastery, except for the new novices, all seem to know Lucifer very well."

"That is odd. He didn't tell me that. I wonder why that is."

"Why don't you ask him?" said Ursula. "Here he comes now." She smiled and nodded with her head to the door of the scriptorium. To Amber's surprise, she saw Lucas standing in the doorway, looking even more handsome than he had yesterday. And twice as dangerous.

He was dressed all in black, his long-sleeved gypon hanging down just past his hips, allowing her to see his long legs filling out his hose beautifully. He wore black hose as well as black leather boots that reached up to his calves. His hair was clean and golden, illuminated from the sun at his back. It hung down to his shoulders. His face looked so regal with the angles of his cheekbones. It only enhanced his clear, light blue eyes that now stared right at her. He reminded her of a nobleman, and she had to remind herself that he was not. She felt that fluttering sensation in her stomach again, and had to look away.

"Don't leave me here alone with him," whispered Amber, thinking how dangerous it was to be alone with this man in a darkened room.

Sister Ursula smiled and whispered back. "No kissing in the scriptorium, Sister."

"Thanks a lot," said Amber already regretting that she hadn't finished her work sooner. If so, she would have left the scriptorium by now and not be facing Lucas alone.

Lucas held the door for Ursula as she exited, surprising Amber by his small act of chivalry.

"Good seeing you again, Sister Ursula," he called her by name, proving to Amber that mayhap he did know everyone here after all.

He closed the door and with it went the sunlight, leaving them alone together in the dark only lit by the one candle that Amber had yet to extinguish.

"You are not allowed in here," Amber told him frantically as he came closer.

"Why not?" he asked. "Besides, Father Armand sent me to gather up the script you copied for a man who is waiting in the courtyard. Something about the knight's Code of Conduct."

"Oh, of course," she said, getting up quickly to get it. She was so nervous that she knocked into the horn of ink atop her worktable and spilled it. Lucas' hand shot out quickly and he pulled away the book she'd been illuminating. The ink spilled on the flat wooden worktable where the book had been just seconds ago. "Oh, my! In my haste, I almost spoiled all my hard work. Thank you for saving it. I have never seen anyone move so fast before."

"Aye, I have a reputation for my fast moves." He reached for the rag on the table to wipe up the spill at the same time as she did, and their hands touched. She pulled back quickly as if burned. He smiled. In the firelight, she could see his straight, white teeth, making him seem even more handsome though she didn't think it was possible. She felt her body heating up, as she hadn't missed the intention of the double meaning of his words.

"I know I put that knight's Code of Conduct here somewhere," she said, leaving him to wipe up the spill, trying to move far away from him. She picked up one scroll after another, unrolling them quickly to find the right one.

"You do beautiful work," he commented, putting down the rag and looking at the book in his hand. He cocked his head and scrutinized her artwork. "Most illuminators just do simple designs but I see you've added a dove, for the pure, little dove that you are."

"Thank you for the compliment, but please – I asked you not to call me a dove."

"The colors you used around the gold leaf are vibrant and clear. It looks like . . . vermillion, vine black, saffron, and possibly the most expensive pigment, ultramarine."

"Yes, you're right," she said, finding the scroll and looking upward curiously. "How do you know that?"

"I know not only that, but also the fact that some of these pigments were made from insects, plants, minerals, grapevines, and others from boiling iron nails in vinegar. The ultramarine is made from the lapis lazuli stone."

"Thank you. I'm impressed with your knowledge, but I know these things already. It is my craft."

"But did you know that there are a few things in these pigments that are a secret that you'll never hear anyone say out loud?"

"Like what?" she asked curious to know.

"Like urine and earwax," he told her with a straight face.

"You are jesting," she said, laughing, and he smiled, too.

"I wish I were," he said with a grin. "I know first-hand it's true, because I more than once had to make these fine paints. And before you ask, I did not make up the recipe for the vile potion, so I take no blame for that."

"You made the paints?" she asked. "How could that be?"

Just then, the church bell atop the tower rang out, calling all to the prayer service.

"Oh, I must go," she said, taking the original scroll and rolling it together with the copy she'd made. She handed it to him, taking the book back in the process. She laid it down flat on a clean part of the worktable to finish later. "I mustn't be late for Sext," she said.

"Aye, I agree, it's not a good thing to be late for sex."

"What did you say?" She stopped in her tracks and looked at him, knowing exactly what he said and the meaning behind it, but she wanted him to admit it.

"I said – don't be late for Sext, darling. That's all." He reached over and blew out the candle.

He followed her out into the cloistered walkway and all the way to the church.

"So, I see you decided to join us in prayer today," she remarked snidely, knowing he had no intention of doing that.

"Nay. Just following you. I like to watch you walk."

She stopped in her tracks and he barreled into her. Dropping the scroll, he wrapped his arms around her to keep her from falling from the impact.

Amber got that feeling again and it was getting stronger. That is, that tingling sensation flitting across her skin from his protective touch, and that uneasiness in her stomach.

She turned to reprimand him. Their faces were so close that if he just leaned forward they'd share another kiss. He did naught to remove his arms from around her and, for one second of her life, she felt as if they were a couple. He was looking at her mouth and she couldn't help but look at his, too. Then she realized they were out in the open. She was a nun in the arms of a very persuasive, handsome man. Quickly pushing away from him, she busied herself straightening her wimple.

"What's the matter?" he asked. "Afraid I might bite you?"

"Afraid you'll kiss me again," she retorted.

"I wouldn't object, if you wouldn't."

"Stop it. This is very inappropriate. And if we are going to be traveling together, you need to promise me right now that you won't touch me again."

Lucas didn't want to lie, as he planned on touching her a lot on their little journey. But he also couldn't alert her to it or she might try to come up with a reason not to go on the pilgrimage with him after all.

"Lucifer," came Father Armand's voice from behind him. Though Lucas hated that name, he was glad at the moment for the distraction. "Lucifer, do you have the scroll that Sir Romney has asked us to copy for him?"

Lucas bent over and picked it up quickly, dusting it off and handing it to the priest. "Here are the Codes of Conduct of a knight, copied in the beautiful hand script of the very talented Sister Amber." He flashed a smile at her when he said it, but she scowled and rolled her eyes in return.

Father Armand stood there with Sir Romney, as well as with a lusty tart.

"Take a look, Sir Romney," said the priest handing the man the scroll. "See if it is to your liking."

Amber poked Lucas in the back and he turned to her. She leaned over and whispered behind her hand.

"I told you I saw a man who reminded me of you, and that he was a knight. This is that man."

"What?" He turned back to look at the knight, surveying his dark hair and deep eyes. Lucas was blond. He didn't see a resemblance at all. Though the man was the same height and build as him, he looked to be a few years younger. "I see no resemblance at all," he told her. "Other than we are both knights."

"You are not a knight," she said. "You told me so yourself."

"That's right," said Father Armand, overhearing the conversation. "Lucifer is a knight errant. He will be knighted as soon as he finishes his pilgrimage to Canterbury."

"Canterbury? That's where we're going," said the whore, looking up at Sir Romney and smiling. Lucas had seen this girl before at the Cardinal's Hat, one of the whorehouses in Southwark. As a matter of fact, if he wasn't mistaken he'd even had her once. Aye, he was sure of it.

"That's right," said Sir Romney, rolling up the scroll and placing it under his arm. "When are you going? Mayhap we can travel along with you."

"That would be wonderful," piped in Amber. "I would love to have someone to talk to on the road."

Lucas knew she was only saying that so she wouldn't have to be alone with him on the journey. Well, he couldn't allow that. He had work to do with her and a third and fourth party along would only make it harder for him when he tried to woo her.

"Nay, we won't be leaving at the same time," said Lucas quickly.

"Oh, that's a shame," said the whore, eyeing up Lucas. "I really want you to come." When she licked her lips, he suddenly remembered exactly who she was. Mirabelle. And she was very good with her mouth. He also remembered having had no money at the time she'd serviced him, and so he'd left without paying her. He only hoped she didn't recognize him as well.

"I bet you do," he said under his breath.

"We are leaving in the morning," said the knight. "In case you change your mind and want the company."

"That's when we're leaving," said Amber, making Lucas wish she'd shut up already.

"You are going to be late for prayers, Sister Amber," he reminded her through gritted teeth.

"Oh, that's right," she said. "But first, my name is Sister Amber," she told their guests. "Just as you've heard Lucas call me.

I know your name, Sir Romney, since I've heard Father Armand mention it. However, I don't know the lady's name."

"Her name is Mirabelle, and she is not a lady. Now get going," growled Lucas as he gave her a slight push in the right direction. She took a step forward and then turned around and was back again.

"How did you know that?" she asked.

"I . . . just know."

"Mirabelle?" she asked the girl. "Really! That was my mother's name. Oh, I do wish you would come with us on the morrow. I would like that so much."

"Nay, you wouldn't," mumbled Lucas.

"Yes, I would," she told him.

"Sister Amber, I don't think it would be appropriate to be going on a pilgrimage with one of the Winchester Geese," Lucas said.

"Don't call her a goose," Amber said in a low voice from the side of her mouth. "'Tis not kind to compare her to a fowl."

"You don't understand," protested Lucas.

"I understand that you are being rude, Lucas."

"But she's not like you, sweetheart," Lucas continued.

"That's fine," she answered. "As long as she is nothing like you."

"God's eyes, don't you understand that the girl is nothing but a . . . she is . . . not a lady." Lucas was trying to be subtle, as he didn't really want to call the girl a whore in front of a priest and a novice. Besides, he didn't know how Sir Romney would accept his words either. He didn't need a fight when his side was still sore.

There was a gasp, but not from any of them. It was Abbess Dulcina, coming to join them. She blessed herself and collected Amber into her arms. "Come, my dear, you are late for Sext and you cannot miss or be late for another prayer service again."

"Late for sex?" Mirabelle laughed and so did the knight.

"Father Armand, what is this woman doing inside our holy walls?" asked the abbess, obviously appalled by the whore's presence.

"Sister Dulcina, we have provided a service to Sir Romney, and he is about to pay me for the copy of his document." The priest's hand shot out with palm upward.

"Oh, of course," said Sir Romney. "A shilling, was it?" He reached into his pouch and pulled out the coin and laid it in the priest's hand.

"It was two." Father Armand still stood with his hand open and ready to collect more.

"Nay, I remember exactly. It was one," protested the knight.

"Well, since your memory is poor, Sir Romney, perhaps you'll consider the other coin a tithe to the church," suggested Father Armand. "And if you make it a full crown I'll let you and the girl stay in the guest house tonight and give you a meal as well."

"The knight can stay, but *she* is not welcome here," spat Sister Dulcina, glaring at the whore. She then pulled Amber into such a protective hold that Lucas thought she'd choke her. "And that woman will not be accompanying one of the novices of the Sisters of St. Ermengild anywhere."

"Now, now, Abbess," the priest said in a controlled but firm tone. "Everyone is welcome in the house of God. If you don't believe me, I am sure you could ask the Archbishop of Winchester, since he accepts women of her kind."

Aye, he accepts them for the money their profession brings in, thought Lucas, but he dared not say it aloud.

Sister Dulcina just sniffed and turned up her nose and whisked Amber away with her.

"Pay him, Romney," the whore whined. "I want a real bed tonight."

"Oh, all right." Sir Romney placed a full crown in Father Armand's hand and was about to take back the shilling when the priest snapped his fist shut and pulled back his hand.

"May God bless you both and absolve you of your sins," said the priest, waving the sign of the cross in the air.

"Did you hear that?" asked Mirabelle with a giggle. "I'm absolved of my sins."

"That won't last long," Lucas said under his breath and the whore shot him a daggered look.

"At least some people pay for services rendered," she replied, obviously a subtle reminder that she remembered him after all.

"And some people charge for services that are normally free." Lucas looked toward Father Armand when he said it, as travelers were usually welcome into the abbey with no charge. If they so choose to make a donation, that was their choice.

"Lucifer, I think it would be a grand idea if these two accompanied you and Sister Amber tomorrow on your journey," said the priest.

"What are you saying? It would be a bad idea, I assure you," Lucas answered.

"Feel free to make your way to the refectory for a bite to eat," the priest told their guests with a smile. "The meal will start at the end of the prayer service. And you'll both stay tonight in the guest house as well."

"Well, thank you, Father Armand," said the knight with a slight bow. Mirabelle grabbed on to his arm. "And I'll have to be sure to tell Sister Amber personally of the superb job she did on my parchment." They headed away, and when they were out of earshot, the priest leaned over and spoke softly to Lucas.

"This is perfect," he said.

"Nay, 'tis a horrid idea. I need to be alone with Amber and this is going to wreck the plans."

"On the contrary, Lucifer, I believe having a *woman of profession* along might just help to change Amber's mind about becoming a nun. With any luck, she'll have a full turn around and never want to return to the abbey."

"Or it may appall her and do just the opposite," Lucas pointed out. "I still don't like the idea."

"Since you're posing as a knight errant, you might want to learn as much as you can from Sir Romney," the priest told him. "Take a good look at that knight's Code of Conduct while you are at it. You'll need to learn all you can by the time you reach Canterbury if you plan on becoming lord of the castle and being dubbed a knight."

"I'm really being dubbed a knight?" he asked in shock, but very pleased. "How could that be?"

"Don't worry about it. I will take care of the details. All you'll need to concentrate on is reversing Amber's decision and securing that ruby. I'll show up in Canterbury a day or two after you to collect the ruby. At that time, we'll seal our deal. In the meantime, find a way to stay at Canterbury Castle and just wait for me."

"And how am I going to do that?"

"Well, while talking with Sir Romney, I discovered that his sister is the widow of the late Lord of Canterbury. Actually, he is on a journey to console her. Do what you have to, but get invited to stay. I'll take care of the rest. And while you're at it, try to sell some of our fake relics to Sir Romney. I saw the amount of coins in his pouch and he can afford it."

Lucas didn't like the idea of traveling with the two. Especially since Mirabelle remembered him. He didn't want Amber to know the girl had, at one time, serviced him. The only good thing that could come of all this is if Mirabelle taught Amber how to use those luscious lips of hers in more ways than one.

CHAPTER 6

Daughters of the Dagger

'Twas just after Lauds, the five a.m. prayer service, and Amber walked next to Ursula as they made their way toward her room.

"Oh, Sister Ursula, I must admit I am excited to be going on a pilgrimage with Lucas today. I already have my bag packed as I was told we were going to get an early start."

She didn't have much in her bag, just a change of her long, black gown, her rosary, and a traveling cape in case the nights got chilly. She would add the prayer book she clutched in her hand to the pack as soon as she got to her room. She owned nothing else, since it wasn't allowed.

Still, she couldn't stop thinking of her favorite russet gown and her mother's jewels sitting in Father Armand's chamber. That only brought to mind the jeweled amber dagger she'd had as a child. She wished she had it now, because the journey would be long and dangerous. But then she reassured herself that no one would harm her if she were donned in her habit. Besides, Lucas would be there to protect her, too.

"Aren't you afraid to be alone with him?" asked the nun.

"I was. That is why I made sure we would have other people

along on the trip. We will be traveling with Sir Romney and his lady friend named Mirabelle."

Sister Ursula giggled. "Lady friend?" she asked. "You mean the Winchester Goose."

"Why is everyone referring to her as a goose?" Amber asked curiously. "I don't understand."

"Oh, Amber, you are so naïve. The Winchester Geese are whores!"

Amber's mouth dropped open and Ursula covered her own mouth quickly and then blessed herself. The abbess was across the courtyard moving toward them and Sister Ursula gave Amber a quick hug.

"I'll see you when you return," she said. "*If* you return." Then she winked.

"I will," Amber said with conviction. "However, now that I know Mirabelle is a whore, I'm not even sure I want to go."

"Don't be that way," said Ursula. "It would be nice to have another woman along to talk to. In case you need advice with Lucas, that is."

"Nay! She is the last person I'd ask for advice."

"You'd better keep his interest, Amber. Because if you don't, she just might."

With that, Ursula hurried away just as Sister Dulcina joined her. The woman had her rosary in her hand, and a worried look painted her face. Amber was afraid she'd grab on to her again like yesterday and she'd find it hard to breathe. So, she hurried toward her room instead of standing still.

"Sister Amber, I need to talk to you," said the abbess, hurrying behind Amber as she climbed the stairs leading to her room.

"I'm in a hurry, Sister Dulcina. I am about to leave on my journey."

The nun blessed herself and shook her head. "That's what I want to warn you about. I don't think you should go."

"Don't worry, Abbess. I will not judge the woman even if she is a whore."

Amber opened the door to her room and entered.

"Don't say that word in the abbey," warned the nun, her thick finger lashing out in a scolding wave in front of Amber's face. "And that's not who I was warning you about. I meant Lucifer."

"He prefers to be called Lucas," she said, picking up her traveling bag and shoving her prayer book into it quickly.

"Whatever name he goes by, he is still the devil."

"He is not," she proclaimed. "He is a man, that's all."

"You cannot trust him," the nun warned her.

"Oh, I think you have him all wrong." She laughed, stepping around the abbess, meaning to exit the room.

"You don't know him the way I do."

"Well, mayhap it is time I get to know him." She opened the door wider and the abbess stopped it with her hand.

"Nay," she said. "I have known him since he was a child and I tell you he has a wild and defiant streak and a temper that can be ignited for no reason at all."

"You knew him as a child?" she asked, her hand sliding down the door. "How can that be?"

"He was raised in the double monastery by Father Armand," she told Amber. "I thought everyone knew that."

"He was raised here? I didn't know that. He told me he never knew his parents."

"That's right. He was abandoned by his mother on the steps of the church, and if Father Armand hadn't taken him in, he would have starved and frozen to death as well."

"He is an orphan?" Suddenly, all the ill thoughts she had of Lucas dissolved. Her heart went out to him. She knew how hard it was to grow up with only one parent. But not having either parent must have been so sad and lonely. "Oh, Sister Dulcina, I feel so sorry for him."

"Don't." Her arms crossed over her ample bosom. "Father

Armand spent the best years of his life raising Lucifer to be a monk. And then just before taking his vows, the boy left the monastery to wander the world as nothing more than a murderer."

"Do you mean a mercenary? He told me that. But are you saying he was supposed to be a . . . a monk?" Somehow, she couldn't picture Lucas with his head shaved in a tonsure or attending prayer services eight times a day either. "What happened?" she asked. "Why did he leave?"

"I don't know, but he was gone for years. Then he returned about four months ago and punched Father Armand in the face. That's why he was sent away in chains to repent for his sins."

"Oh, my," was all that Amber could say. She had wondered about Lucas' past, and he seemed to avoid answering her. Now she understood why he knew so much of a novice's training and also why he knew how to make the paints for the scriptorium. He obviously wasn't jesting with her like she'd thought. "Well, thank you for telling me," she said in a half-daze, heading out the door.

"You can't trust him," the abbess said. "Father Armand has given everything to him and lived a hard life just to teach him to read and write and be trained as a monk. And then he did this to the man who raised him. Father Armand has suffered greatly and this is the thanks he gets in return."

Amber thought of all the wealth she'd seen in the priest's chamber. He was the one who couldn't be trusted. Although she wanted the abbess to know, she felt it wasn't her position to intervene.

"Perhaps Lucas is not the one we need to be concerned with," she said. "After all, even the holiest of people can be deceiving at times."

"What are you trying to say, Sister Amber?"

"Nothing," she answered. "Just that I am going on a pilgrimage because it was my penance from Father Armand."

"Nay," she said, shaking her head. "I am sure he never would have given you that as a penance."

"But he did," she explained. "Along with one Hail Mary and one Our Father."

"One?" she asked shaking her head in disbelief. "You must be mistaken."

"Oh, you are right," she said with a smile. "It was two. And one last word of advice, Sister Dulcina, before I go . . . if you are missing anything, you might want to check behind doors that are off limits."

With that, she hurried across the courtyard and away from the abbess. She stopped just outside the chapter house, seeing Brother Walter coming from within.

"Good morning, Brother Walter. Have you seen Lucas by any chance this morning?"

"I saw him a while ago heading for the stables," he told her.

"Thank you," she said and hurried off. She all but ran across the courtyard and to the stables, not wanting to be stopped by Sister Dulcina again in case she should decide to follow. All she wanted was to be away from the abbey where she could think about everything the abbess had just told her. Why hadn't Lucas told her he was once training to be a monk? Mayhap because she probably wouldn't have believed it anyway.

She walked into the stables, but saw no one, as it was still early. Then she heard a slight thumping noise and thought one of the horses was getting frisky. She headed toward the noise, now able to hear what sounded like the heavy breathing of someone as well as the voice of a woman.

"Ohhh, give it to me, please," she heard. "Harder, faster." Then the woman squealed out in delight. "Oh, yes, yes, more, more, more."

She rounded the corner to see Mirabelle bent over a pile of hay with her skirts thrown up over her head and Sir Romney's naked backside. The knight pumped into her over and over again until he growled so loud she thought he'd scare the horses.

"Oh!" she cried, holding her hand up to her eyes and turning her head. She realized she had just walked into the midst of the act of coupling.

"Amber?" Lucas shot out from inside one of the stalls, and she saw that he'd been busy saddling a horse. "Bid the devil you two, stop that!" he shouted to the couple. "You are inside the walls of a monastery not in a brothel." He put his arms around Amber and pulled her to his chest, cradling her head in his hand, not letting her turn to see as the couple finished up.

"I . . . I didn't know," she said, feeling her body trembling in his arms.

"Shhhh," he said, running his hand over her wimple. "There is nothing to be frightened about, so you needn't tremble. I am just sorry you had to see that." She felt him kiss her lightly atop her head.

She wasn't trembling because she was frightened, but it was only because she found herself curious and slightly aroused. Being pulled tight in his embrace only made her want to know what it felt like to be with a man. She had never coupled with a man, but she'd heard from both her married sisters how wonderful it was. Her sister, Sapphire, had even been mistaken for a whore and taken to an upstairs room in a tavern by her husband before they were married. She'd let him touch her and couple with her then though she was married to someone else – a very evil man. She'd had a weak moment, but didn't regret it at all.

This was one of the reasons Amber had decided to be a nun. To pray for Sapphire's soul as well as her sister Ruby's. Killing a man was a mortal sin as well, even if Ruby had done it in self-defense.

Well, now that she'd seen what her sisters were talking about. It made her curious to know this feeling before she took her vows and never had the chance to experience it in her life. What was the matter with her? Why was she thinking this way? She felt ashamed of herself and also shocked by her less than moral thoughts. She had always been the virtuous one of the four siblings. Now, she was starting to seem no better than the rest of them. Now she needed to pray for her soul as well, because thinking of coupling was almost as bad as doing the act itself.

She pushed out of Lucas' embrace and blessed herself, dropping to her knees right in the soiled straw on the floor and reciting one prayer after another.

"Get up, Amber," he growled pulling her to her feet. "This is no place for that."

"And neither is this the place for that," she said, turning around to see Sir Romney tying his hose and the whore nonchalantly brushing the straw off her gown.

"All right, I'm ready, let's go," Mirabelle said as if she'd done naught more than her morning business in the garderobe or perhaps a menial chore.

"Yes, I am ready as well," said the knight, strapping on his sword and heading over.

Amber stood there with her eyes fastened on them and her mouth opened wide, not knowing what to say or think.

"What is the matter with you two?" Lucas ground out. "You just did that in front of a nun!"

"Sorry about that," said Mirabelle with a giggle.

"Let's get out of here," said Lucas, bringing forth the horse he saddled. She could see the travel bags were already full and tied to the horse's saddle.

"I'll get my horse and we'll be on our way," said Sir Romney. He headed off and Mirabelle ran after him.

"We're taking horses and not walking?" asked Amber, since it was customary to walk on a pilgrimage.

"We are," he said, handing her the reins. "I've had enough walking to last me a lifetime on the last pilgrimage. Besides, my wound is still healing. So, this time will be different." She saw him eyeing a horse at the other end of the stable and brought it over. It wasn't saddled, and she figured it would take a few minutes to do it. But instead of a saddle, he put already-filled travel bags on the horse and secured them into place.

"Let's go," he said, bringing the horses to the door of the stable.

"But aren't you going to saddle the other horse?" she asked.

"No need," he said, but nothing more.

"Where are you going with my horses?" asked Father Armand hurrying into the stables.

LUCAS JUST LOOKED the man in the eye and smiled. "My share," is all he said. Then he turned toward Amber. "Up you go." He hoisted her atop the horse in one swift movement.

"Nay! What are you doing?" she cried, kicking her feet and struggling in his arms.

"Stop that and get in the saddle," he instructed, moving his head as she almost kicked him in the eye.

"This isn't a lady's saddle," she protested.

"Then spread your legs and ride like a man."

"That's right," said Mirabelle as Sir Romney rode up with the whore latched on behind him on his horse. "Spread those legs, Sister Amber."

"Stop it," Lucas growled, and slapped Sir Romney's horse on the back end, sending them away from the stable.

"You're taking both of my horses?" complained Father Armand. "That will leave me with none."

"Then get used to walking," Lucas told him. "It's good exercise." He looked up at Amber struggling with her long robe, trying to get settled in the saddle. She had her bag in her hand and almost fell because of it. "Give me the bag," he said, snatching it from her hands. "What's in here anyway?"

"Not much. Just my prayer book, and a change of clothes really."

Nay, he thought. He was not going to have her praying the whole trip and neither was he going to let her have an extra robe of a nun. He'd already packed her velvet gown and jewels. He was so tired of seeing her hidden beneath that wimple, that it was the first thing he was getting rid of whether she liked it or not. All this time and he still had no idea of the color of her hair or if she even had hair at all tucked beneath that headpiece.

"Do you really need this?" he asked, holding up the bag.

"Yes, I do. Now please pack it with your things."

While she occupied herself with trying to get one leg over the other side of the saddle without getting too tangled in her robes, Lucas looked over to Father Armand.

"Get rid of this," he said in a low voice and pushed Amber's bag into the priest's hands. He saw the priest toss it behind a pile of hay as Lucas pulled himself up onto the horse behind Amber.

"What are you doing?" she squawked.

"Getting you settled," he said, putting his hands around her waist and lifting her up enough to get one of her legs over the saddle. "Give me the reins of John's horse," said Lucas to the priest, holding out his hand. He'd recognized the villein John's horse, as he had befriended the farmer years ago when he lived at the monastery.

"I'll expect these horses back in the same condition," Father Armand said, handing Lucas the reins.

"Expect what you want, but you'll not see John's horse again. I'm returning it to him on the way."

"That was part of his taxes since he couldn't pay," protested the priest.

"He'll never be able to pay if he doesn't have a horse to pull his plow to plant the fields."

"What's in those travel bags?" the priest asked suspiciously. "Is it grain?"

That's exactly what it was and the priest wasn't going to like it. "See you soon," said Lucas with a smile, urging his horse forward. Amber fell backwards into his arms as the horse moved. He liked the feel of her body pressed so close to his. Her veil lifted in the breeze, and he had to move his face in order to see where he was going. It took all his control not to rip the cloth from her head and throw it to the ground.

One thing at a time, he told himself, taking a deep breath and releasing it. But as soon as they got outside the monastery walls, things were going to be very different, indeed.

CHAPTER 7

Daughters of the Dagger

*A*mber was very aware of the fact that her body was pressed up against Lucas', and they rubbed together with each step of the horse. She felt that tingle on her skin again. And with her legs spread and riding in the saddle of a man, she felt so wanton.

She looked down and surveyed Lucas' arms wrapped around her as he held the reins and directed the horse toward the village. And just for one moment, she felt like this was right and the way it was supposed to be. Then she looked ahead of them and saw Mirabelle pushed up close behind Sir Romney, whispering in his ear and the both of them laughing. They seemed so happy, even if she was only a whore.

Amber, on the other hand felt sad, lonely, and confused. She hadn't laughed at all since she'd joined the Order, and neither had she really smiled. When she was at home and growing up with her sisters, they always had a happy time together. And though she was the most reserved out of all of them, her father went to extremes to make her laugh even if he had to tickle her to do it.

She missed that kind of interaction with people. The only

interactions she'd had lately, besides praying with the nuns and monks in church, were the conversations she'd had with Sister Ursula who seemed to be the only one who understood her. She thought she knew exactly what she wanted in life, but ever since the day Lucas had kissed her, she'd started having doubts that she should even be a nun at all.

"We'll stop here for a moment," Lucas called out to the knight and slipped off the horse from behind her with ease.

They were in the village, and she knew exactly where. They'd arrived at the small wattle and daub hut of one of the villeins who had a small plot of land that he farmed for his family. He also worked the lands of the monastery as well. His name was John. She'd often brought extra food to him and his wife and three children, since the man was very poor.

"Lucas? Is that you?" John ran out of the house, looking bedraggled and weary. His wife stood in the doorway holding a baby while her two toddlers gripped on to her skirt. They all looked hungry and Amber didn't like it in the least.

"John," Lucas said with a slight nod of his head. "I've brought you back your horse and grain to plant your winter crops."

She heard a gasp and then a slight cry of gratitude from his wife as she ran out with her children to greet them.

"Nay. I had to give my horse and grain to Father Armand since I couldn't pay the taxes, and as part of my tithes. Why are you bringing it back?"

"Because it was wrong of the priest to take it in the first place. Your family will starve to death without it."

"Thank you, Lucas," he said with a slight bow of his head. "But I can't take it."

"John," said his wife with her hand on his arm. "Please. We need it to make a living as we are barely getting by."

"If Father Armand finds out, we will be punished," he told her. "I have to protect you and the children and can't allow that to happen."

"He knows about it," Lucas assured him. "And when I return from my pilgrimage I will see to it personally that you will be protected as well as fed and clothed. Not just you, but all the villeins, so be sure to tell them."

"Thank you, Lucas. You were always good to us and this will not be forgotten."

"Give them some of our food as well," Amber said from atop the horse.

"What?" asked Lucas, looking in her direction.

"These travel bags are full, so I know we must have more food than we need. What is in here anyway?" She reached down to untie the bag but Lucas rushed over and grabbed her hand to stop her.

"It's not in there," he said, tying it back up quickly as if he didn't want her to see something inside. "I'll get it."

"Sister Amber, it is good to see you again," said his wife, Mary, with a slight smile. "Are you going somewhere?" she asked.

"I am going on pilgrimage to Canterbury," she relayed the information.

The woman looked over to the knight and whore next. "All of you?" she asked with a frown.

"Aye, this is Sir Romney and his . . . his friend, Mirabelle," she said in introduction. When she saw the woman's disapproval in her eyes, Amber added, "Mirabelle is a goose but is going to repent for her sins."

Mirabelle laughed at that. "It's Winchester Goose, Sister Amber. You are so cute when you make me sound like a fowl. Yes, I am going along. But I assure you, the purpose is not to repent for my sins."

"I will pray for you," Amber said.

"I've already received absolution from Father Armand, so your prayers are not needed," boasted Mirabelle.

"You did?" Amber asked, very confused as to why the priest

had refused to give her absolution in the confessional, but yet he freely gave it to a whore. She didn't understand it at all.

Lucas gave the family a loaf of bread and some cheese and they were ever so grateful. Sir Romney even gave them a coin from his pouch. Amber nodded her head in appreciation.

Then after a few more pleasantries, Lucas hoisted himself back atop the horse and they were on their way.

"That was a kind thing you did by giving them back their horse and grain," she said as they rode.

"'Twas theirs to begin with and they need it more than the church."

"But won't Father Armand just come and get it again once we're gone?"

"If he does, he'll have to answer to me."

She wanted to tell him she knew about his past, but not here, not now. It would wait until later. She had a lot to think about and it would take them a day or two to get to Canterbury. Blessing herself, she prayed aloud from atop the horse, hoping the others would hear and it would benefit them as well.

* * *

Lucas stopped as soon as they came to the first shrine along the road to Canterbury. He slipped off the horse, his ears burning and his head aching from listening to Amber praying the entire way. This was going to be a longer journey than he thought and he couldn't wait to stop for the night at a tavern and have himself a drink.

"Why are we stopping?" asked Mirabelle from the other horse.

"Sister Amber and I are on a pilgrimage," he reminded the whore. "We need to stop at every shrine along the way and it will take some time. So why don't you two just go ahead without us?"

He wanted to get rid of the whore before she said anything in front of Amber that they had been together. Mayhap this was the perfect opportunity to do it.

"Well, if you insist," said the knight from atop his horse.

"Nay!" shouted Amber, quickly trying to dismount on her own. Her robe got caught on the horn of the saddle, riding up her legs so everyone could see what was beneath it. Her legs were clad in black hose tied to her undergarments. Amber kicked her legs trying to reach the ground as she was hung up and her feet were in the air. Lucas eyed the shape of her long legs and the swells of her tight rounded cheeks beneath her braies. He felt himself becoming aroused and had to stop it quickly.

"Let me help," he said, reaching up and untangling her robe with one hand as he wrapped his other arm around her waist. He let her slip down his body to the ground and, unfortunately, she felt his arousal against her. Her eyes opened wide and she looked up to him. Then her tongue darted out quickly to moisten her dry lips and it about drove him mad. He turned away quickly.

"Don't leave," she called out to the knight. Amber rushed over to them and laid her hands on the horse. "I want to get to know you both," she said. "We haven't had time to talk at all. Please, stay with us on our journey. I will make certain to pray extra prayers for your souls if you do."

Lucas let out a small moan. Not more prayers, he thought. Just what he needed.

"Well, I suppose we can stay with you," said the knight. "After all, I feel horrible because you saw us coupling earlier. I think I need all the prayers I can get."

"Me, too," said Mirabelle with a giggle.

The knight dismounted and helped Mirabelle to do the same.

There was already a small crowd of people around the shrine of St. Augustine, and more pilgrims coming down the road. Lucas collected his bag of fake relics, knowing he could sell a bundle of them here.

"I need my rosary and prayer book," Amber said, coming to

his side. "Is it in here?" She reached for the bag containing her gown and jewels but Lucas' hand shot out and stopped her.

"I'll get it," he told her. "Why don't you just go to the shrine and start praying and talk to some of the pilgrims in the meantime?"

"Oh, all right," she said, joining the small group at the shrine, holding the hands of an old woman who looked up toward her with sad eyes. Amber was like an angel as she gathered around the pilgrims and monks that were there and led a prayer session amongst the people. She looked so holy in her habit. Lucas was going to have to do something soon to remove it.

He felt a knot in his stomach thinking what he'd promised Father Armand. He wanted this all to be over with and soon. He wanted his castle and would do anything to get it, even if it meant deceiving the beautiful angel who was so trusting of him that he hated himself for everything he was right now.

"What's in the bag, Sir Lucas?" asked Sir Romney as he came over to join him. Mirabelle had gone to use a bush, and Lucas was glad it was far from the shrine. That's all he needed was a whore pissing on consecrated ground. He certainly had his hands full with this challenge.

"I've brought relics from the monastery to sell," he said. "Would you like to buy one?" Lucas opened the bag and scattered the relics on the grass. "I have the hair of St. Edward the martyr, the blood of St. Thomas Becket, a piece of the cradle of Christ himself, and varied bones and teeth of saints, and even a shoe from the renowned St. Dunstan."

The knight picked up a bone, tossing it in the air and laughed. "This looks a lot like the bone from the leg of mutton that Father Armand gave me to eat last night in your refectory." He put it down and picked up a swatch of black hair wrapped in twine. "And this looks a lot like the tail of that horse you're riding. I think you're trying to pull off a guise here, Sir Lucas, or should I say Brother Lucas? You're not really a knight errant either, are you?"

"Why would you say that?" asked Lucas, hunkering down and quickly putting the relics back in the bag.

"Because Mirabelle told me you were naught but a mercenary. She also said you told her you were once training to be a monk."

There was no use denying any of the man's accusations. He'd been discovered. If he denied it, then the knight would probably make things worse for him.

"I used to be a mercenary, but I am certainly not a monk. And I would appreciate it if neither of you mentioned my past in front of Sister Amber. I don't think it would be proper."

"You mean you'll have no chance in hell of bedding her if she knows the truth about you, don't you?"

"You're speaking about a nun, if I must remind you."

"I've noticed the way your eyes devour her every time you look her way. And Mirabelle pointed out that lump beneath your tunic so don't try to hide the fact you lust for the wench as well."

"Only a whore would notice that," he mumbled under his breath.

"You're a fool if you think you're going to get anywhere with Amber even if she is just a novice. She'd never be interested in the likes of you. But I wish you luck in trying, as she is comely."

Lucas stopped loading the relics in the bag and looked over to Amber by the crowd at the shrine. She looked up just then and smiled at him and he felt like the loneliest man in the world. Sir Romney was right. Why would anyone as good and pure as Amber ever be interested in anyone with a soul as black as his?

"She may like me more if I really were a knight," he said.

"Then do something about it," suggested Sir Romney.

"Like what?" Lucas looked up to the man.

"Follow me," he said with a smile.

Lucas left the relics and did as told, joining the knight at his horse.

"Here," Sir Romney said, giving a rolled-up scroll to him. "This is the Code of Conduct for the knights. You can study it on the way to Canterbury, but I'll need it back when we get there. And if you want, I'll spar with you and that sword of yours in our free time. I could use a workout. I haven't practiced in a while."

"Why would you do this for me?" asked Lucas, taking the scroll in his hands.

"I don't know," said the knight. "I guess it's just because I like you. I have a sister but not a brother, and I always wanted one. Since I hear from Mirabelle that you were once almost a monk, mayhap you can be a Brother of a different kind to me." He laughed and hit Lucas on the back. "Sorry about that, but I couldn't resist. Besides, I am bored and I think watching you try to lure a nun to your bed will be quite entertaining."

"Thanks. I think," he answered, seeing Mirabelle coming back from using the bush. "Just try to keep her quiet in front of Amber, will you?" He regretted now ever bedding the Goose to begin with. And especially being well in his cups at the time and spilling his secret of almost becoming a monk and that he wasn't anything but a mercenary. This day was going from bad to worse.

"I'll try to keep her mouth occupied, if you know what I mean." Sir Romney smiled. "Actually, I am bringing her back to Canterbury with me because I enjoy her company, just like you enjoy being around the nun."

"Amber's a novice, not a nun," said Lucas, trying to feel better about his whole plan.

"Well, you'd better do something quick because your novice has just discovered your stash of fake relics."

"What?" He looked over to the bag of relics on the ground. Amber was on her knees going through them with a crowd of people around her. He rushed up to her, pushing his way through the crowd.

"What are you doing?" he asked, hunkering down next to her.

The crowd of people started picking up the relics and walking away with them.

"I'm giving out these relics that you brought from the monastery. They were to give to the pilgrims, were they not?"

"To sell! For money," he spat, trying to pull them out of the hands of the pilgrims. He reached over to a little boy with bare feet and torn clothes and dirt on his face. He grabbed hold of the horse tail relic in his hand.

"But these people have no money," she said, getting to her feet. "Give them the relics with no charge. Most of these people have loved ones at home that are sick and dying. If they bring back a bone or hair or even blood from a saint then their loved ones will be sure to be healed."

"Nay, they won't," growled Lucas, feeling frustrated by what was happening.

"Aye, they will. Holy relics have the power to heal."

"These aren't that holy." He let go of the swatch of hair and let the little boy have it. He was suddenly feeling horrible for his act of deception.

"When we return to the monastery, I'll contact my father," she offered. "He'll pay dearly for all these relics, I promise you. He is an earl and very wealthy."

"Take the relics. Take them all for free, I just don't care." Lucas picked up the old shoe that was supposed to be from a saint and hurled it through the air into the bushes.

"What's the matter, Lucas? I told you I'd pay for all these relics, so why are you so angry?" asked Amber.

"I can't let you pay for any of them, so just forget it." The pilgrims wandered away with smiles on their faces, holding their relics. Lucas knew that if naught else, he'd just given hope to these people who had nothing. Hope that a dying loved one may live after all, or that they'd be blessed and their souls would go to Heaven. Ironic, since he was the man with no hope, giving someone else the will to live.

"But they are priceless and certainly you must have paid much for them to begin with. I will see that you get what you deserve," insisted Amber.

"No need for that," he said, thinking how mad Father Armand would be when he returned with no relics and no money for them either. "I'm sure I'll be getting more than I deserve, mark my words."

CHAPTER 8

Daughters of the Dagger

$\mathcal{A}$fter visiting two shrines that day on the road to Canterbury, Amber was hot in her wool clothes, tired and ready for bed. Nightfall was setting in and she figured they would stop somewhere along the road and make a fire and spend the night there. But when Lucas directed their horse toward the Sinners Tavern and Inn, her heart beat wildly in her chest.

"What are we stopping here for?" she asked as Lucas slipped off the horse. Sir Romney and Mirabelle were right behind them. The inn was large, a two-story building made of stone and wood. It had an attached alehouse for making their own brew. Just past that was a detached kitchen. On the other side out back was a stable for housing the horses of the travelers on their way to Canterbury.

Amber had seen taverns and inns before while traveling with her father. This one probably counted on the nobles passing through and probably catered to them as well.

"We'll stay here tonight and continue on in the morning." Lucas held up his arms to help her down.

She looked over to the tavern, hearing music coming from within. The wooden sign hanging above the door swung in the breeze, creaking on the chains that held it. Above the entrance were branches and leaves. Amber remembered her father once telling her that that meant they served wine here as well.

There was laughing and foul language spewing out every time a patron opened the door. She caught glimpses of burly men in dirtied clothing as well as women in low-cut bodices inside. She would feel very uncomfortable in her habit walking into a place like this. She also knew she'd be reprimanded strictly for this by the abbess when she got back to the abbey.

"I can't go in there," she said. "It says Sinners Tavern and Inn. I am a nun!"

"You either go in there or stay out here by yourself all night," Lucas growled. "But I warn you, if you stay here, I'll not be around to protect you when the drunkards and thieves stumble out the door later on. I am hungry and thirsty and nothing is going to stop me from sleeping on a pallet instead of the hard ground."

"But . . . those pallets are probably loaded with fleas and lice."

"And you think there are no bugs out here in the woods?" he asked. "Now, are you coming or not?"

"Come on, Sister Amber," said Mirabelle, walking over and pulling the bodice of her gown lower to expose her cleavage. "It'll be fun."

"Not that much fun for you," said Sir Romney, walking over and pulling her gown back up to cover her breasts. "After all, I paid you for the entire journey and I'll not be sharing you with anyone along the way." He reached down and kissed her passionately. Amber realized this man seemed to have feelings for the whore. That made her feel even lonelier, as she wished someone would care for her in this manner as well.

"Well, are you coming or not?" Lucas grumbled. "I am not going to stand here with my arms outstretched all night."

"Well . . ." she looked back at the tavern and then over to Mirabelle who was giggling and still kissing Sir Romney. Then she looked down to Lucas with hope in his eyes and his arms outstretched just waiting for her to agree. She could be happy and giggling and kissing someone like Lucas if she wasn't a novice studying to take her vows. A little voice in her head told her not to go. But when she heard the cry of a wolf in the distance she didn't want to be alone in the dark out here in such a dangerous place.

"All right," she said, reaching down and putting her hands on Lucas' shoulders as his fingers encircled her waist. She felt the warmth of his touch as he slid her down his body and something inside her felt as if she wanted to reach up and kiss him the way Mirabelle was doing to her man. She looked up at Lucas and expected to see want in his eyes like she had in the past but, instead, she saw disgust.

"Take off that wimple already, will you? You're going to stick out like a sore thumb in there as it is with your black robe. At least if you're not wearing the headpiece, you might be less noticeable sitting at a table."

"Why should I?" she asked defiantly. "I am a novice and proud of it."

"Have it your way," he said, releasing her and going over to unfasten the travel bags from the horse.

"What are you doing?" she asked.

"In a place like this, you leave nothing outside that you want to see again in the morning. As it is, I'll have to pay the stable boy extra just to make certain the saddle is here as well as the horse come morning."

"Well, make sure you bring in my bag, too," she said. "Since I didn't have my rosary or prayer book all day, I'll need to pray extra tonight."

"Sure, you will," he grumbled, taking the bags and throwing them over his shoulder.

"I'll take the horses to the stable," offered Sir Romney. "You go on in with the ladies and secure some rooms for us for tonight."

"Fine," said Lucas handing over the reins to the knight and heading inside. Mirabelle hurried forward and grabbed on to one of Lucas' arms. He stopped and looked back to Amber. "Are you coming?" He held out his other arm to her. Without thinking, she rushed forward to take it.

LUCAS WALKED into the tavern with the travel bags over his shoulder, a whore on one arm, and a nun on the other. The music stopped when they entered, and every eye in the place was on them. He never felt more embarrassed in his entire life.

"Sir, there is an entry fee," said the bouncer at the door. The piece of wood he used to bounce the coins upon was under his arm and his grubby hand was outstretched.

"You're going to charge us to get into the tavern?" asked Amber innocently.

"You're a nun?" the man asked, eyeing her up and down.

"Yes," she said, raising her chin proudly. "I am a novice of the Sisters of St. Ermengild at Bowerwood Abbey and Monastery. I'm on a pilgrimage to pray."

The bouncer laughed heartily and lowered his hand. "And you're a whore?" he said, looking at Mirabelle.

"I am a Winchester Goose," she said, raising her nose proudly just as Amber had done.

"And I'm a knight," Lucas told him, knowing there was no entry charge for nobles.

The man laughed again. "It doesn't matter what you are, I'd let you in for free just to see what's going to happen. I've never seen a man enter with a nun and whore both. This ought to be good. Now go on in, and tell Dagmar at the drink board that the first round of drinks is on me."

"Why thank you very much," said Amber in her most polite voice. "God will bless you for this, good man." That only made him laugh harder as well as everyone else in the place.

"Come on," growled Lucas, pulling the girls over to a table. The room was crowded and every table was full. But when they saw him with the women, a group of men got up and gave up their seats, laughing.

Mirabelle leaned over as she sat down, showing everyone there her cleavage. The men called out to her and whistled, and the crowd became noisy. The music started up once again.

"Thank you, gentlemen," said Amber, lifting her hand and making the sign of a cross. "God will –"

Lucas pushed her down in the chair before she could continue. "Sit down already and, for God's sake, don't say a word until I get back." He threw the travel bags onto the middle of the table and looked at Mirabelle. "Neither of you say a word," he told her, hoping she wouldn't reveal any of his secrets to Amber while he was securing the rooms for the night.

He went over to the proprietor, grabbing a tankard of ale off a tray of a serving wench and tossing her a coin from the pouch at his waist. "I need some rooms for the night," he told the man behind the counter.

The innkeeper looked over to the girls sitting at the table. "You brought a nun in here?" he asked. "Are you mad? And you have a whore as well? I've never seen anything like it."

"The whore is with Sir Romney who is stabling our horses. And the nun – she isn't a nun, just a novice. She's yet to take her final vows."

"And you're going to do your best to see that she doesn't, aren't you?" he asked with a smile.

Lucas hated how everyone could see right through him. First Sir Romney, and now the innkeeper. He was only grateful that Amber hadn't noticed.

"Just give me the rooms and stop with the questions," he said. "I want private rooms, as we'll not be sharing a bed with half a dozen others. And send a wench over with some food and drinks to our table anon."

"I only have two private rooms left," the man said with a grin. "But then again, that's all you really want, isn't it?"

He felt like punching the man for saying that, but he knew the innkeeper was right. And the more that people pointed out his deceit to him, the more he hated himself. He never thought carrying out his plans was going to make him feel so miserable.

"I'll take the two rooms," he said, laying the money on the counter. Then he pulled out two more coins and laid them atop the stack. "And here's extra for a couple of baths sent up as well."

He was feeling dirty and sweaty from his travels. There was no way he wanted to be around Amber and all her purity while he felt like this. He had plenty of coin that he'd brought with him from the last relics he'd sold, so he paid for a bath for Sir Romney and Mirabelle as well. He was hoping he could buy their silence since he didn't want them spilling all his secrets to Amber.

"Of course, good sir," said the man, greedily scooping up the coins that were more than was required. "I'll have it sent up at once. You'll be in rooms number three and four."

"Thank you," he said, draining the mug of ale and placing it down on the drink board. "The bouncer at the door said to tell Dagmar the first round of drinks is on him."

"Well, the second round is on me," he said with a chuckle. "I think you'll probably be having many offers tonight to buy you drinks. This is more entertainment than we've had around here in a long time."

Lucas turned back toward the table but stopped in his tracks when he saw Amber digging through the travel bag that held her gown and jewels.

"What are you doing?" he ground out, making his way quickly toward the table.

"I'm looking for my prayer book," she said, digging inside and stopping when she realized what she'd just touched. "What is this doing in here?" she asked, pulling her velvet gown out of the bag.

"That is beautiful," said Mirabelle, taking it from her and

holding it up against her own body. "This is the gown of a noblewoman. Lucas, where did you get it?"

"It's mine," Amber said softly, her big, green eyes staring up at him. "Why do you have it, Lucas?"

A million lies ran through his head, but he couldn't bring himself to tell her a one. When he didn't answer, she dug back in the bag and brought out her mother's amber necklace and ring.

"You have these, too?" she asked in amazement. Then those big, green eyes were staring up at him again. "Lucas, did you steal all this from Father Armand?"

"Jewels?" asked Mirabelle, leaning over to see them with the gown still pushed up against her body. "Ooooo, let me try them on."

"Nay," he said, taking the jewels and pushing them back into the bag. "You keep flashing this around and we'll have a fight on our hands as these ruffians try to steal them."

His hand went to his wounded side as he remembered the last fight he was in, and aching from just the memory. He didn't want to feel the stab of a blade in his flesh again. He grabbed the gown from Mirabelle and shoved it back into the bag as well.

A wench came up and laid some food and drinks on the table. She put down a flagon of wine and four ceramic goblets and a big bowl of pottage in the center of the table. Then she threw down four spoons, but no additional bowls. "The drinks are paid for, and the meal is included in the price of the rooms," she relayed.

Lucas gave her a half-penny for her trouble. She shoved it into the cleavage of her bosom and walked away with a smile.

"Have something to eat and drink," he told the women. Mirabelle grabbed a spoon and started digging into the pottage, but Amber just sat there and glared at him.

"Aren't you going to eat?" he asked.

"Not until you answer my question. What are you doing with my things?"

"They're not yours anymore," he reminded her. "In case

ELIZABETH ROSE

you've forgotten, you gave them up when you entered the abbey." He picked up a spoon and leaned toward the steaming bowl in the center of the table and scooped up a bite.

"Well, they're not yours either, and I think you'd look a bit silly wearing them. So I ask you again, why do you have them? Does Father Armand know what you did?"

"Father Armand was the one who suggested I bring them," he admitted, which wasn't a lie.

"Why would he ever do that? You are lying."

"Nay," he said. "'Tis the truth. Now have something to drink." He filled a goblet with wine and pushed it toward her. Then he handed her a spoon.

She surveyed the bowl in the center of the table and shook her head. "I think there's meat in there. I gave up eating meat when I entered the abbey. And I don't partake of the drink either."

"You are not at the abbey now," he pointed out. "And this is what they are serving. So I suggest you either eat it or starve. Besides, if there is meat in this pottage, I assure you you'll have to look hard to find it. Now, you drink wine in church, so this is no different." He pushed the goblet closer to her, hoping she'd take a swig and loosen up already. If not, he was going to have one hell of a night with her, especially when she found out they were sharing a room.

"The horses are set for the night," said Sir Romney, sitting down to join them. "Did you get the rooms?" he asked, digging into the food hungrily.

"I did," he answered. "Your room is number four and ours is three." He looked at Amber. "I figured you'd like the number of the Holy Trinity."

"What?" Amber's head snapped up when he said it, but he just ignored her.

"I owe you some money," said Sir Romney.

"We'll call it even," said Lucas. "After all, you paid the stable boy, so don't worry about it."

"I can't wait to get out of these clothes," said Mirabelle, finishing off her wine. A serving wench came by and replaced the empty flagon with a full one. Lucas quaffed down his wine and refilled his cup. Sir Romney did the same.

"Did ye want more wine, too, Sister?" asked the wench, standing over Amber.

"Nay," she said, picking up her cup and finally taking a sip. Then to his relief, she picked up the spoon and reached over and started eating the food as well.

"Romney, sweetheart, will you be a dear and order me a bath?" asked Mirabelle. "I know how you like me to be clean before we couple."

"It's already taken care of," said Lucas, finishing off his food and laying the spoon on the table.

"A bath, too?" Sir Romney asked with a smile. "Well, I'd say someone is taking care of us for some reason, and I think I know why."

"No need to thank me," said Lucas. "I've ordered one for us as well."

He noticed Amber stiffen at those words. Then she slowly put down her spoon on the table and looked up toward him. "I will not be staying in a room with you tonight," she told him. "'Tis not proper."

"Oh, Sister Amber," said Mirabelle, "you need to relax a little. You'll feel better after a bath."

"They only had two private rooms left," explained Lucas. "It was either that or share a room and the same bed with a half-dozen drunken, lusty men."

"Then I'll stay with Mirabelle and you two men can sleep together."

"Oh, no. That'll never do," said Mirabelle. "Sir Romney paid for me for the entire trip and I'm obligated to service him whenever needed. I need to stay with him."

"Then you sleep in the stable," she told Lucas.

"I'm sleeping in a bed tonight and I don't want to hear another word about it," growled Lucas.

"Then I'll stay in the stable instead," she said.

Lucas was getting worried and had to do something fast, or she might do just that. He spied the serving wench coming with a tray loaded down with so much food and drink that she could barely see where she was going. He felt terrible for what he was about to do, but he didn't have a choice. There was no way he or Amber was going to sleep in the stable and he just had to make sure they both stayed together.

He quickly stuck his foot out and tripped the wench. She stumbled and dropped the tray of food and drink right on Amber. Lucas reached out and grabbed the woman just before she fell in Amber's lap.

"Oh!" cried Amber.

"You bastard, you tripped me," shouted the wench, squirming out of Lucas' arms. He looked over at Sir Romney who had a grin spread across his face obviously knowing what his intentions were.

The knight shot out of his seat and came to the girl's side. "Now, now, it was just a simple accident, no harm done," he said, looking over and winking at Lucas. "Here is a coin for your trouble, now try to calm down."

Lucas nodded his thanks slightly as the knight sent the serving wench away. Then he looked back at Amber who was covered from head to foot with food and drink. She looked so funny trying to hold in her anger that he wanted to laugh, but didn't dare.

"Are you all right, Sister Amber?" he asked, helping her from her seat.

"I . . . I . . ." She looked like she was about to cry. Lucas ushered her to the stairs and up them quickly.

"You are soaked and need to get out of your soiled clothes," he told her. "There is a bath prepared in our room. Go ahead and use it and I'll come up later."

He guided her to the room and closed her inside before she had a chance to object. Then he rested his head against the wood and closed his eyes. What was he doing? He had tricked a nun into getting undressed and into a bath. And now he planned on convincing her to sleep in the bed with him as well.

Changing his mind quickly about not believing in the devil, he started to wonder if he'd been named Lucifer for a reason – because he felt like the devil for what he'd just done.

CHAPTER 9

Daughters of the Dagger

Amber sat in the hot water of the tub still donned in her shift and braies. She'd only removed her shoes, hose, gown, wimple and veil. The hot water felt so good against her aching body. She wasn't used to being on the road and riding a horse all day.

Back home, she had ridden horses often, but she rode sidesaddle, not like a man – the way her sister, Ruby, rode. Now, she wished she'd taken Ruby up on her offer years ago of learning how to ride astride. If so, she wouldn't be feeling so sore now.

In the abbey, they were instructed to bathe in their shifts and underclothes as it was less temptation for one to pleasure themselves. She bathed this way now not only because of her training, but also because she didn't know when Lucas would be walking into the room, and she didn't want him to see her naked.

She couldn't stop thinking about that kiss he'd given her, nor the way she saw Mirabelle and Sir Romney rutting in the stable. Amber wondered how it would feel to make love to a man. Mirabelle seemed to enjoy it enough to make a living out of it. And though Amber did not agree with the girl's profession, she still liked her. Amber learned not to judge while at the abbey, though the subject of whores had never been part of her training.

She'd washed her hair and body and was now just soaking, as it felt so good and relaxing that she'd almost forgotten how upset she was with Lucas. Why had the man thought naught of sharing a room with her? Did he really think that she, a novice, would lie on the same pallet with a man who was known to be the devil?

She laid her head back against the tub and thought about the kiss she'd shared with Lucas. She could almost feel his soft lips on hers and his hand against the back of her head. She felt that tingling sensation again, and this time it was between her thighs. And when she opened her eyes, she saw Lucas standing there in the doorway staring at her. The light from the candles in the dim room made the whole atmosphere romantic.

"I thought you'd be done by now," he said, coming in and closing the door behind him.

She suddenly felt like a wanton woman for the thoughts she'd been having, and sank lower into the water in shame. "I . . . fell asleep, I guess. But I am ready to get out now. Just lay my bag with my extra clothes by the bed and leave and I'll get out and dress."

He threw the travel bags over the back of a chair and sat down and started to pull off his boots.

"Uh, I seem to have forgotten to pack your bag, so I guess you'll have to wear your velvet gown."

"What?" she sat up taller in the tub. "So, you're saying that I don't even have my rosary or prayer book? What am I going to do?"

"Sorry, Sister, but no praying tonight. And if you need to find something to do . . . I am sure I can come up with a few suggestions."

By the way he was looking at her, she had no question in her mind what those suggestions might be. And before she could answer him, he'd disrobed and was heading for the tub.

Her mouth dropped open at the sight of his naked body and she couldn't find the words to speak. He stepped into the water with her and she scooted backwards, sitting higher, trying to get away from him.

He looked at her with an odd expression upon his face.

"You're bathing in your undergarments?" he asked.

"'Tis the way we are taught to bathe in the abbey. 'Tis a way to resist temptation."

"Resist temptation? With whom? One of the monks?" He sat his naked body down in the water directly across from her, his knees touching hers though she was pulling her legs so close that they were nearly up to her chin.

"With ourselves," she answered. "And you can't come in the tub with me. You're . . . naked."

"That's the way most people bathe, my pure, little dove. Don't worry, I won't disturb you from being tempted by yourself."

"This is outrageous!" She stood to leave the tub, noticing his eyes settling on her breasts. When she looked down, she realized the shift was wet and transparent and there was naught left to the imagination. It clung to her swells, and the outline of her nipples showed through. Her hard nipples. She was so embarrassed. Sitting back down quickly, she sank down into the water until it covered her shoulders.

"Well, either you like the looks of my naked body or you were playing with yourself before I came in," he said with a smile.

"I do not play with myself," she spat.

"Ah, then I guess you don't hate me as much as you pretend. Your body doesn't lie."

"I might be a nun, but I'm not dead," she retorted.

"Good thing. I was starting to wonder." He took water in his hands and splashed it on his head, then leaned forward, dunking under the water, his face just above the juncture of her thighs. He came up slowly, very close to her, and she leaned back and looked off to the side.

"You know, this could be a very interesting position . . . that is . . . if you weren't a nun."

"I'm . . . not . . . yet," she said, her breathing deepening as a reaction of his naked body so close to hers. Feeling confused, she wanted to kiss him, yet she couldn't. She bit her bottom lip and didn't move as he came closer. His face was right in front of her now, their mouths so close together that she could feel his breath on her lips.

"I'm very attracted to you," he told her.

"I . . . like you . . . too." She couldn't stop thinking of the kiss they'd shared and she wanted nothing more at this moment than to experience it once again. His mouth came closer and she lifted her chin in anticipation. Her eyes closed as she prepared herself for the experience, and her heart thumped wildly against her ribs. Any second now, she'd feel his soft lips upon hers and mayhap even his tongue again inside her mouth. The idea scared her and excited her at the same time. The anticipation had her squirming beneath the water. She wanted this more than anything right now.

"Too bad you're ready to take your vows," he said, causing her eyes to pop open. He had pulled back and was scrubbing himself with the soft soap, rinsing his body as if nothing had almost just happened.

She felt disappointed and foolish at the same time. And very wicked. She would never be forgiven when she went back to the abbey and confessed that she sat in a tub with a naked man and wanted to kiss him. Nay, she had wanted to do more than just kiss. She felt the turmoil inside her and wanted to cry.

"You are an evil man to tempt me like that," she said.

"You are so modest. And don't think you are the only one being tempted." He stood in the tub and his waist was just above eye level to her. His manhood had grown enormously since he'd entered the tub and he obviously wanted her as much or more than she wanted him.

"Cover yourself," she told him, "or have you no decency?"

"I noticed you didn't turn your head this time. You like what you see, don't you?"

"I've had enough of this." She stood quickly and turned her back to him, meaning to exit the tub but slipped. He was there for her with his hands under her armpits catching her, his fingers very close to her breasts. She felt the poke of his hardened manhood at her back and a wave of heat passed through her body.

"Whenever you're ready, Sister, just say the word," he whispered into her ear, his breath caressing her like the stroke of a lover's hand. She straightened upward and turned her head to look at him. All she had to do was say yes and they'd be on the pallet coupling just the same as Sir Romney and Mirabelle were probably doing right now.

She felt her face redden and his essence called out to hers in a fit of passion that she'd never felt before. Mayhap she wasn't meant for the life of a nun after all. She was curious to know how it felt to couple and Lucas was giving her that opportunity.

She wanted to take it and just forget about the abbey and her vows and go back home to her father. But then she thought of her sisters and her mother and how tarnished their souls were right now. She needed to become a nun for them. To save them from the fires of Hell. It was up to her now, and she was their only hope.

She looked up into his beautiful, clear blue eyes and wondered how she could have ever thought they were the eyes of a devil. No devil would ask for her permission before he thought to touch her. Perhaps he was naught but an angel fallen from the heavens and he needed her to bring him back to the light.

"I can't," she said and pushed away from him and stepped from the tub. She would never forget the look on his face just standing there wanting to couple with her as she denied him. He looked so abandoned. It reminded her of the story of that little orphan baby left on the steps of the church.

She held back the tears she needed to let loose, grabbing for her soiled habit on the floor. He threw a drying cloth around his waist and then came to her with another cloth and wrapped it around her as well.

"Don't wear those," he told her. "They are dirty. Besides, I rather like being able to see your face without that wimple. I didn't even know the color of your hair until now."

He helped her to a standing position while a tear trickled down from her eye. He took his thumb and wiped it from her face, then reached up and ran a hand through her wet hair.

"Brown," he said. "I would have thought blond by the color of your eyes."

It felt so good to have him touch her, that another few tears escaped.

"I had long hair at one time, but had to cut it when I entered the abbey," she told him. Her hair didn't even touch the top of her shoulders. But at one time, it was down to her waist like her sister Sapphire's.

"I was a little worried that you'd be bald under that wimple like Sister Dulcina," he told her. He grinned and that made her laugh.

"Most nuns have their heads shaved under the wimples," she admitted. "Or at least very short hair. 'Tis because of the heat of the wool clothing that they do it. Besides, no one ever sees them without a wimple. How do you know Sister Dulcina is bald?"

LUCAS GAVE a deep sigh before he answered, knowing it was time to tell Amber the truth. "Amber, let's get dressed and sit down and have a talk. There are a few things you need to know about me."

"I don't have my bag with my extra gown, and now my undergarments are wet, too."

"Then wear this." He walked over to the travel bag and removed her velvet gown and held it up for her to see. She hesitated, and he knew she needed persuading. "It's either this or run around naked. But if you do that – I can't guarantee you'll still be a nun by the time you leave this room in the morning."

That did it. She grabbed the gown quickly and pulled it to her chest. "Turn around while I dress," she ordered.

"Of course." He went over to the bed and started to dress as well, looking over his shoulder to see her back turned toward him as she stripped off her wet undergarments. If he wasn't hot and bothered before, he certainly was now. She first removed her shift, and with her hands over her head he could see the sides of her bare breasts. The perfectly rounded swells of her buttocks drew his attention downward next as she bent over to remove her wet braies. Then she turned to get her gown, giving him full view of her dusky hard nipples and the thatch of hair between her thighs. She looked up and caught him, but he looked away quickly, mostly to hide the fact his arousal was back again.

What was he doing? He'd never sat in a tub naked with a woman before and not touched her. He could have her down on that pallet and be pumping into her, making her squirm and scream in a matter of minutes right now. He saw the way her body reacted to him. All it would take was a little coaxing.

Nay, he decided, he couldn't do it. Not only because she was a novice about to take her vows, but because Father Armand had ordered him to deflower her. The priest didn't want her becoming a nun, and neither did Lucas. But he couldn't take away from the girl the last thing she had left after the church had already taken everything else.

He knew what she was going through, because he had been in the same situation a few years ago. If he deflowered her now, she'd regret it and so would he.

"I'm ready to talk," she said, causing him to turn around. She stood there in her russet velvet gown with her wet hair hanging down to her shoulders. No more wimple and veil. No more black robe or prayer book either. In these clothes, it was going to be hard to keep away from her and not forget she was a novice in training to take her final vows.

"I want to see this on you, too," he said, going to the travel bag and pulling out the amber necklace and ring.

"Oh, no, I couldn't," she said, her eyes fastened to the pieces.

"Just try them on." He held them out. "I'm sure they'd look beautiful on you."

She meekly held out a hand to take them, then drew back and shook her head. "I've vowed to give up these pleasures in life."

"Well, I didn't, and I want to see how they look on you." He didn't give her a chance to say no again. He walked up behind her and fastened the necklace around her neck. From this position, he could see right down her bodice, and it was a wonderful sight, indeed. "Here, put this on," he said, handing her the ring and turning away quickly, trying to redirect his thoughts. The next time he turned back, she was standing there looking more like a princess than he had expected.

"You're beautiful," he said, not much louder than a whisper. He knew now he was only tempting himself, not her, by doing this as Father Armand had instructed.

"Thank you," she said, her hand caressing the necklace. Then she held out her hand to admire the ring. "These remind me of my mother. I miss her so much." Her face darkened and Lucas saw a sadness overcome her. "I can't wear them." She reached around the back of her neck and removed the necklace, then looked once more at the ring and removed it as well. Standing there with her arm outstretched she said, "Take them. Put them back into the travel bag, and please don't ask me to put them on again."

He did as instructed, then looked back over his shoulder. He felt awful for trying to trick her.

"Come, sit next to me on the bed," he said, walking over to the pallet. She hesitated, then walked over to join him. "Hold on, I'll be right back," he said, knowing she was never going to loosen up without some help.

He rushed from the room and down the stairs where he saw Sir Romney standing at the drink board paying for a flagon of wine. He had two goblets in his hand.

"I need that," he said, taking the flagon of wine and both the goblets.

"That is for me and Mirabelle," he said. "She is waiting for me up in our bed."

"I'll make good on it later, I promise."

"Oh, bedding the little nun, are you?" he asked with a smile.

"Well, she's waiting for me in bed also, but it's not what you think."

"Of course, it isn't," he said with a wink. "Go ahead, take it with no charge. You'll need the wine more than I will, I am sure. And good luck to you, my man."

Lucas hurried back up the stairs. Once inside the room, he locked the door.

Amber was sitting patiently on the straw pallet that was raised on a slight platform. Most inns just had thin straw pallets right on the floor, but this one had a few bedchambers that were slightly upscale since so many knights and noblemen passed through on their way to Canterbury.

"I thought we might want a little wine while we talk," he told her, sitting down next to her and pouring some into one of the goblets and handing it to her. He then poured one for himself and placed the decanter on the bedside table.

"I will have a little wine, but I don't drink in excess," she said, taking a sip and looking up to him as she did so. She must have noticed the lust in his eyes, because next she took a much bigger gulp and looked back the other way.

"I pulled off her wimple when she was sleeping," he said.

"Pardon me?" She looked up, and he could see the confusion in her big, green eyes.

"Sister Dulcina. You asked me how I knew she was bald. I was raised at the monastery and was always in trouble. When I was just a boy I decided one day that I didn't like her, and that I wanted to know what she looked like without her wimple. So, when she fell asleep in her chair saying her prayers, I snuck in and ripped it off. Now I wish I hadn't, because the sight of her bald head was scarier than the punishment I endured from doing it."

"Oh," she said with a small giggle. "No wonder you were worried if I had any hair."

They both laughed and it felt good. Really good. Oh, if only she weren't going to be a nun. He'd never found a woman who interested him as much as she did. And now, once again in his life, he was going to be disappointed since he could never have her.

"You don't sound surprised that I grew up in the monastery," he remarked.

"I'm not." She took another sip of wine. "Sister Dulcina told me about you before we left."

"She did? What did she say?"

"That you were an orphan abandoned on the steps of the church and Father Armand took you in and raised you. Also, that you were supposed to be a monk but backed out at the last minute and turned into a mercenary instead."

"Living a life of prayer and poverty, locked away from the rest of the world wasn't for me."

"I know what you mean." Her smile disappeared and she seemed as if she were in serious contemplation. He had no doubt that she was questioning her choice as well. Deep inside, he was glad.

"So, tell me about you and your family," he said. "I already know you are the daughter of an earl and have three sisters. You said you are all named after jewels, but you never told me why."

"That was the choice of my mother," she told him. "My mother was barren and wanted nothing more in the world than to give my father the children he desired. She'd heard of a superstition that if a woman bought a jeweled dagger from a blind old hag, in return, she would conceive a child."

"You don't really believe that?" he asked shaking his head.

"I do. My mother bought four daggers and she had four daughters."

"That is coincidence, nothing more." He refilled her goblet as she relayed her story.

"The blind old hag she bought them from also told her that if she named her children after the gemstones in the daggers that they would someday find their true loves."

"And did you all find your true loves as predicted?" he asked.

"So far," she said. "My sisters, Ruby and Sapphire, have, but Amethyst has yet to marry."

"How about you, Amber? Aren't you worried about finding your true love?" He bravely reached out and took her hand in his and, surprisingly, she didn't pull away. He thought mayhap this wine was relaxing her after all, as he'd intended.

"I found God," she said, looking down into her goblet of wine. "My true love is the love I have for God and the church. I'm sure of it."

"Are you?"

She looked up at him then and he saw the confusion as well as a newfound tear in her eye. "My mother did something terrible," she said. "That's one of the reasons I joined the Sisters of St. Ermengild in the first place. So I could help pray for her soul to be forgiven so she could make it to Heaven."

"Seriously, I doubt she did anything that bad."

"Nay, it's true." Amber took a good swig of wine.

"Please, I'm sure it's not like she killed anyone."

"Nay, that was my sister, Ruby."

"What? Your sister killed someone?" he asked being very surprised. "Really?"

"It was in self-defense."

"Then it's not a sin," he told her.

"Nay, it still is. And my sister, Sapphire, committed adultery." The goblet lifted to her mouth again, and he watched the movement of her smooth neck as she swallowed.

"She did?" My, her family was turning out to be very entertaining after all. Not at all the conversation he thought they were going to have.

"She was tricked into marrying an evil man who beat her."

"Well, then you can't blame her for what she did."

"And my mother . . . my mother," she said with her eyes going to her goblet of wine. Lucas reached out and poured her more. After another swig, she continued. "My mother tried to steal a fifth dagger, just after pushing away a beggar boy four times. Because of this, she had only daughters and was told she'd never have a son. She would also lose her true love. Mother did birth a son who had two different-colored eyes. It scared my father. All of us, actually. But both the baby and my mother died in childbirth. You see, she ended up losing both her son, and my father – her true love, just as the old hag had predicted."

"I'm sorry to hear that, Amber. I feel for your loss."

"My father discarded the daggers after that, saying they were the cause of my mother's death." She lifted the goblet and drank again. "'Twas only because my sisters' husbands found their daggers that they were able to find their true loves."

"So, you don't have your dagger?" he asked curiously, refilling her cup again.

"Nay. It's still lost as well as the dagger of my twin sister."

"Then I guess you'll never find your true love, will you?"

"That's not true," she said, lifting the goblet and drinking eagerly. She lowered it and smacked her lips. "I've already found it through my religion."

"I see," he said, putting down his empty goblet and laying back on the pallet. Then to his surprise, she finished off her third full goblet of wine, threw the cup to the floor and jumped off the bed and started undressing.

"Amber?" he asked, pushing up on the bed. "What are you doing?"

She stood before him naked now, the firelight from the candles in the room making her skin glow like the beautiful angel she was.

His head spun slightly from the wine as well, but he knew that she had no idea what she was really doing.

"I'm going to bed," she said, pulling back the coverlet and crawling underneath. He just lay there motionless and stared, not believing this was really happening.

"Well?" she asked. "Are you going to sleep in your clothes? I hope not, because I feel a bed is sacred and the dirt from the road shouldn't be brought into the clean sheets. Don't you agree?"

"I agree," he said, standing slowly and then quickly ripping off his clothes. He settled in next to her and she snuggled up under his arm.

"I really like you," she said, sounding as if she'd had too much to drink. "I'd like to know just once what it feels like to couple with a man before I take my final vows."

"What are you saying?" he asked, wondering just what to do.

"I'm saying I want to make love with you." She reached up and kissed him on the cheek.

"Amber, you have had too much to drink and if we do this, you'll regret it in the morning."

"Nay, I won't."

"But you've taken the vow of chastity," he reminded her.

"Then let's do everything but the actual act of consummation."

"I don't think that's the way it works," he said. But before he could object further, she reached over and placed her voluptuous lips upon his. He felt as if he'd died and gone to Heaven when her tongue shot out and entered his mouth. The beast within him could be held back no longer. He rolled atop her, kissing her as he straddled her naked body with his legs.

"I've seen naked men before but I've never touched one," she said with a giggle.

"Then tonight will be your first." He took her hand and wrapped her fingers around his arousal, sucking in his breath when she worked her fingers up and down his shaft.

"This is so interesting," she said.

"Keep that up and you're going to find something else interesting in your palm in another minute."

"Touch me, too," she said, her innocent eyes looking up at him from the bed, making him wish now that she was wearing the damned wimple after all. If so, he wouldn't be on the brink of pushing himself into her warm, soft body.

"I don't think I should, Amber."

"Then let me help you." She reached out and took his hand, placing it over her breast. He took a deep breath and closed his eyes, reveling in the feel of her warm, soft skin beneath his fingers. Then he opened his eyes slowly, allowing himself to fondle her, feeling guilty, especially when she started to squirm in pleasure beneath him. "I feel something happening," she said.

"So do I." He rolled off of her and dragged a hand through his hair in frustration, then rubbed his face in his hands.

"Give me your hand again," she said, reaching out to grab it and pulling it to her, placing it at the juncture of her thighs. "Touch me again."

He bit back a curse. "Amber, you're going to regret this come the morrow if we go any further."

"Nay, I won't. Now do it, please."

He struggled with what to do. If he denied her what she asked, he'd save her from being defiled and keep her virginity intact so she could still become a nun. But, like she said, she'd never know how it felt to couple with a man and she'd be sad and very lonely for the rest of her life, always wondering but never knowing. He didn't want to do that to her either.

She deserved a bit of happiness, he decided, slowly letting his fingers explore her womanhood, working his magic on just the right spots until she squirmed beneath him, throwing back her head with her eyes closed and arching her back. She seemed to enjoy it so much, and he wanted to make her happy. And when he slipped a finger inside her and continued to pleasure her, she screamed out in ecstasy beneath him, causing him to almost spill his seed.

She looked up to him then with hooded eyes, and smiled. She had the look of a woman who was fully sated. "I think I love you," she said in a sultry whisper.

That took him by surprise and he pulled his hand away from her, feeling his heart beating rapidly. No one had ever told him this before in his life, as he hadn't any parents and the only girls he'd ever bedded were whores. He didn't know how to react. "Nay, Amber you don't."

"I do. I think mayhap I've made the wrong decision and shouldn't be a nun after all."

This had been exactly what he'd wanted her to decide all along, but somehow her proclamation of wanting to leave the Order didn't make him happy. He felt as if he'd tricked her, luring her in with the pleasures of the flesh. He never thought this would make him feel so awful, but it did. She hadn't truly decided this on her own. He'd put the idea in her head and now he felt as if he'd taken away her free will by doing it.

He kissed her gently atop the head and hurriedly got out of the bed and dressed. He needed to get away from her before he defiled her further. He was very confused and needed to get some fresh air and think this over.

"Where are you going?" she asked in a sleepy voice.

"Get some sleep," he said, heading for the door. He had to get out of here and he had to do it now. If not, he'd be driving into her in another minute and contemplating the fact he'd just deflowered a nun.

He left the room quickly, knocking into Mirabelle who was coming out of the room next to him.

"Lucas, what are you doing?" She looked down and, of course, noticed his arousal pushing against his hose.

"Nothing," he said, trying to cover his groin with his hands.

"I can see that." She wrapped her arms around his neck and pulled him closer. "I can take care of that little problem in a minute."

"I don't want you to," he said, pulling her hands from his shoulders and pushing her away.

Then she looked back to the door of his room and her eyebrow raised. "Is the nun in there?" she asked.

"If you mean Amber, aye, she is sleeping."

"You want her badly," she said. "Don't you?"

"Nay," he lied, knowing how daft he sounded right now since she'd already seen the proof of it.

"You tried to bed her and she turned you away, didn't she?"

"Nay, that's not what happened at all."

"Then what?" She laughed. "I'm sure it's not like she tried to bed you and you turned her away." Her laughing stopped when Lucas didn't answer. "God's eyes, 'tis true, isn't it? The nun tried to bed you and you turned her away. Now that is the funniest thing I've ever heard."

"Mirabelle, you mustn't breathe a word of this to anyone. Not Sir Romney or Sister Amber tomorrow when you see her. She had too much wine to drink tonight and wasn't thinking clearly.

'Twas all my fault. But nothing happened – not really. So please, just keep your mouth shut."

With that, he hurried down the stairs and out into the cool air of the night. He headed to the stables to sleep where he'd be far enough away from that little temptress of a nun. Far enough from her, but not far enough from himself and his guilt for what he'd just done.

CHAPTER 10

*A*mber awoke the next morning, having had the sultriest dream she'd ever had in her life. She was naked and so was Lucas and they were rolling around together on the bed. Then she'd touched him and he'd touched her in return. She remembered feeling pleasure. Satiable pleasure and screaming out in passion, but she could remember nothing after that.

Her breathing deepened and she felt herself becoming hot just thinking of it. Then she opened her eyes and realized she wasn't back in her own bed in the abbey but at the inn. With Lucas!

She bolted upward in bed, seeing Lucas entering the room. Then feeling a breeze on her skin, she looked down to see her bare body.

"Nay!" She screamed and held the sheet up to cover her nakedness. Lucas entered the room and closed the door behind him.

"That scream sounds a lot like your cries of sated passion from last night. You do it again, and I swear before you're finished, I'll have my clothes off and be on top of you again, so you'd better stop it right now."

"Again?" she asked, feeling a sickening sensation in her stomach. "What do you mean by that?"

He sat down in the chair and rested his booted feet atop the bed.

"Now don't tell me you don't remember enticing me and asking me to touch you last night?"

"I did what?" She hoped he was jesting. But the more she thought about it, the more she realized the dream she'd had must have really happened.

"I've never seen a nun pull her clothes off so quickly. I think perhaps you had too much wine last night."

"Damn you!" she spat, then covered her mouth with her hand.

"Now, Sister Amber, is that any way for a nun to talk? First, you're pulling off your clothes and trying to bed me and now you are cursing. What's next? If you start dressing like Mirabelle, I'm really going to get worried."

"What happened last night?" she asked meekly. "Did we . . . did we do . . . it?"

"Do . . . it?" he asked. "That depends. What do you mean by *it*?"

"You know what I mean," she said, pulling the sheet off the bed and keeping it around her body, heading over to look for her habit.

"If you mean did we make love . . . would it bother you if we did?"

"Stop it," she said. "Just don't even speak to me about it anymore. I don't want to know."

She heard him chuckling from behind her as she frantically searched for her black robe.

"I told you that you'd regret it in the morning, but you assured me that you wouldn't and that you needed to know how it felt to couple with a man before you became a nun."

It was all coming back to her now and her actions appalled

her. "If you hadn't given me so much wine, none of it would have ever happened. I despise you."

"That's funny, because last night you said you loved me."

"I did not." She turned to face him and saw him smile and raise a brow. "Did I?" she asked meekly.

"Aye, my little dove, you did. And notice that I didn't call you pure anymore."

"God forgive me for what I've done. I am going to Hell."

"You didn't seem to be worried about it last night."

"Stop it!" she shouted, feeling embarrassed and foolish and disgusted by what she'd done. She couldn't remember everything that happened but, by the sound of it, they'd actually made love. This couldn't be. How could this have happened? She needed to think, as she had no idea what would happen to her now. "Where is my habit and wimple?" she asked him frantically. Mayhap if she could find them she'd feel better.

"They're gone," he said.

"Gone?" Sudden panic lodged inside her chest. "What did you do with them?"

"They were soiled too badly to even clean so I just got rid of them. Besides, I think you'll look much prettier in your velvet gown and without that ugly wimple. I burned them in the fire of the tavern last night." He held up her gown – the gown of a lady – and she rushed over and snatched it from him, almost losing her grip on the sheet that covered her. Tears welled in her eyes.

"They could have been cleaned. Or I could have just worn them dirty. How could you have done that?" she asked. "How could you take everything from me? First my prayer book and rosary, and now my robe and wimple. You have taken everything!"

"That's funny you feel this way because last night you were begging me to take your virtue, just carelessly throwing your vow of chastity to the wind."

"I want my undergarments," she told him.

"Those are gone, too, stolen by a servant most likely when I left them near the fire in the kitchen to dry. I guess you'll just have to go naked under your gown." He scratched the side of his neck as if this meant nothing to him at all.

Frustrated, she turned from him and dropped her sheet to don her gown, too angry to care that he was looking at her nakedness. She pulled the gown into place, too upset to confront him and too confused to cry. She rushed to the side of the bed and fell on her knees and blessed herself and started praying frantically.

"Amber, come on, stop it," he said, getting up from the chair and trying to pull her to her feet.

She brushed him off and squeezed her eyes tight and just kept praying.

"We didn't do it . . . not really," he told her.

"I told you, I don't want to know." She covered her ears with her hands and started praying out loud. "Hail Mary, full of grace –"

"We need to get going. Now, get up from there and pull yourself together."

"The Lord is with thee –" She opened her eyes to see him picking up the travel bags and throwing them over his shoulder.

"I said let's go," he growled.

"Blessed are thou amongst women –"

She was yanked to her feet and, before she knew what was happening, his lips were covering hers in a kiss that took her breath away. He pulled back, still holding on to her and looked her in the eyes.

"If that's what it takes to shut you up, I'll not bat an eyelid to do it every time." He released her and headed toward the door, leaving her standing there in shock. She should have slapped him. She should have reprimanded him for his bold and inappropriate action. But instead, she just quietly followed him out the door.

. . .

Lucas shouldn't have kissed Amber, but he had to do something to shock her and bring her out of her self-flagellation so to speak. She might as well have had a switch in her hand or be wearing a hair tunic the way she was beating up upon herself for something that didn't even really happen.

If he had known she was going to carry on like this, he may as well have bedded her last night and actually given her something to pray about.

He headed down the stairs quickly, only to find Mirabelle standing there waiting for him.

"I can't wait to see the little ex-nun," she said.

"Mirabelle, I asked you to be quiet about all this."

"Why should I? The way I see it, you still owe me for a night of service several months ago, so I can say anything I want."

"Here," he said, taking some coins from the pouch at his side and shoving them into her hand. "That's more than enough."

"What's that for?" Amber came down the stairs, surprising him that she'd even left the room at all. He cursed under his breath that she had walked up right at this moment.

"Lucas is just paying his –"

"Let's go," he interrupted, taking hold of Amber's hand and pulling her out the door with him. He walked out front to meet Sir Romney who had their horses ready and waiting.

"So, Sister Amber," said Sir Romney. "You're no longer a nun."

"Pardon me?" Her eyes shot upward toward Lucas but he just turned and secured the travel bags onto the horse. "Why would you say such a thing?" she asked.

"Because you're not wearing your habit, but rather the gown of a lady," answered the knight.

"Oh. I . . . I seem to have soiled my robe and wimple when the serving wench spilled food and drink on me yesterday and Lucas gave me this to wear."

"I'll bet he did," said Mirabelle, brushing past Lucas, her hand trailing across the backside of him.

He jumped up and glared at her. "Are we going to stand here and talk all day or are we going to take to the road?" He reached over to Amber and lifted her atop the horse. Just his hands on her waist had him thinking about her naked body underneath. It was going to be torture riding on the horse pushed up next to her. So he took the reins and started walking.

"Aren't you going to get on the horse?" asked Amber innocently.

"Nay, I think I'll walk for a while."

"But you said you never wanted to walk on a pilgrimage again and that's why you brought the horse," she replied.

So he did. But that was before he'd almost made love to a woman who was close to taking her final vows. He couldn't trust himself around her anymore. And he knew that, after tonight, he couldn't trust *her* in the matter of these issues either.

"I changed my mind," he told her.

"Well, I suppose changing one's mind is a good thing once in a while," she said.

He thought about how she had told him she'd changed her mind last night about becoming a nun. And then he thought about her announcement that she loved him. He didn't deserve her love. Not after all the deceit he'd had where she was involved. And now because of him, she wasn't thinking with a rational mind and he might have just ruined her life forever.

"It's not always a good thing," he said, wondering how much longer he could go without telling her what a rotten man he really was. And the next time she changed her mind, he was afraid it was not going to be in his favor.

CHAPTER 11

Daughters of the Dagger

Lucas sat with his back against the trunk of the tree with the parchment that had the knight's Code of Conduct written upon it in his hand. They'd traveled most of the morning and stopped at yet another shrine, enabling Amber to pray.

Sir Romney sat next to him with his arms crossed over his chest and his legs outstretched. He looked like he was thinking about a nap. And Mirabelle was hanging out near the shrine trying to get the men to talk to her, or in his opinion, trying to drum up business.

"Did you bed the wench last night or not?" asked Sir Romney with a yawn.

"Nay. But it wasn't from her lack of trying." He unrolled the scroll, admiring Amber's artistic handwriting upon it.

"Now that surprises me," he said with a chuckle. "I thought it would have been the opposite way around."

"I couldn't do it," he said. "Even if she was well in her cups and very willing. Something about it just didn't feel right."

"Well, I can't say bedding a nun would feel right for any man."

"I need to change," he said. "Amber is so good and pure and I have a soul blacker than the bottom of my boots. I don't deserve her."

"Well, then mayhap you should try a girl you do deserve. I am sure Mirabelle has a lot of friends who would be happy to oblige."

Lucas looked across the grass, seeing Mirabelle going up to one pilgrim after another. Each time, they just turned away from her. Then he saw Amber get up and put her arm around the girl and motion for her to join them kneeling in prayer. Mirabelle shook her head.

"What do you see in that whore anyway? I can't believe you're actually bringing her to Canterbury with you," said Lucas.

"I know what you mean, but I find her different than the rest of the Winchester Geese. She is truly happy to be with me. If I can bring a little happiness into her hard life, then so be it."

"The only thing hard in her life is what lies below the belt of every man she tries to coerce into her bed. She'll never be loyal to you. She tried to bed me last night."

"What?" He sat up straighter. "Did you?"

"Don't be ridiculous. Why would I want her when I have Amber?"

"Because at least with Mirabelle you can bed her without carrying the guilt of the world on your shoulders."

Lucas looked down at the parchment and shook his head. "At one time, I would have agreed with you. But since I met Amber, nothing in my life is the same. I constantly question every decision I make. I no longer know what to do."

"You are really smitten with the girl, aren't you?"

"She told me she loved me last night, but I know that was only the wine talking."

"Love you?" Sir Romney threw back his head and laughed. "Oh, Lucas, you do have a problem on your hands, and I must say I don't envy you in this position."

"That's why I want to know how to act like a knight," he said. "Suppose you can train me in what I need to learn?"

"Of course." Sir Romney nodded his head in thought. "Go on, read through the Code of Conduct and I'll explain anything you don't understand."

"All right." Lucas skimmed the words upon the parchment. "It looks like the first rule is that a knight should serve God alone and not let a person or object take the place of their affections."

"That's right," Sir Romney explained. "Your duty is to God."

"So that sounds as if I should have stayed a monk."

"I can't even imagine that."

"Now the second rule says that a knight should use God's name in honor and not in blasphemy."

"Aye, that's correct."

"God's eyes, I don't think I can do that."

"Obviously. Read the next one," said Sir Romney with a shake of his head.

"A knight needs to keep holy the Sabbath day by attending worship and not working, but rather relaxing and bringing joy to others."

"That should be easy enough," said the knight.

"Well, the latter part perhaps but I haven't attended a worship service since I left the monkhood."

"Then you'll have your chance tomorrow. We should arrive in Canterbury early in the morning and 'twill be the Sabbath. Canterbury Cathedral is one of the largest, most elaborate cathedrals in all of England. You'll have your opportunity to attend the service with Amber then."

"Aye, I will." Lucas had an ulterior motive for attending mass in Canterbury Cathedral. That was where the Regale ruby was displayed. He'd been instructed by Father Armand to bring the stone back to him. This would give him the opportunity to get near it.

He swallowed deeply. Somehow, he couldn't imagine being able to steal it with Amber at his side. He wasn't even sure he wanted to take it anymore. But he knew if he didn't, he would never have his own castle as Father Armand had promised in trade.

"Go ahead, read the next code," urged Sir Romney.

"It says that a knight shall honor and respect those in authority, especially his parents and also women. Well, that should be easy since I have no parents."

"You don't? Why not?"

"I was an orphan abandoned on the steps of the church," he relayed. "I was raised by Father Armand."

"Then I guess he is the one you need to respect and honor."

Lucas figured that was exactly what he'd be doing by stealing the ruby. Yet somehow, he didn't think the codex meant something like this. But at least he had a good start in respecting women. If not, he would have bedded Amber last night.

"The next says a knight shall protect the lives of others and those in need. I've already done that when I almost got killed on my last pilgrimage. So, moving on, the one after that says that a knight shall exercise sexual restraint, keeping chaste and pure and only having sex at marriage for the purpose of procreating." Lucas' eyebrows raised. "God's teeth, this sounds like the training of a monk all over again, I swear. I think this is only a variation of the Ten Commandments."

"Watch that blasphemy," the knight said with a chuckle. "And aye, I can't see you ever adhering to that rule.

"Really?" Lucas asked Sir Romney. "And you are the ideal knight to live by example I suppose. That is, with the way you drag your whore over the countryside as if she were naught but your workhorse."

Sir Romney's laugh stopped and he cleared his throat. "Well, it isn't like that . . . not really. Actually, this is the Code of Conduct, but in the knight's Code of Chivalry, I don't recall a rule like this. Now, just read the next code," he growled.

Lucas smiled to himself, glad to see that these codes were not always followed, thinking mayhap he had a chance of maintaining knighthood after all.

"This one says a knight shall remain honest and not steal." He felt the twisting of his gut reading this one, not able to stop thinking of his plans to steal the ruby. "The king himself condones pillaging after conquering an enemy, so I don't understand this. Let's move on to the next," he said hurriedly. "A knight shall not deceive or lie."

"That's right."

"What?" he growled, thinking of all the lying and deceiving he'd done lately, especially with Amber. There was no way he'd ever be able to live by this rule. "This is just too hard." He took the scroll and threw it on the ground.

Sir Romney looked at him and shook his head. "Tsk, tsk, no one ever said living the expected life of a knight is easy." He picked up the scroll and handed it to Lucas. "If you truly did almost become a monk then these rules and ways of life should be nothing compared to what you've been through. Now there's only two more, so read them."

Lucas took the scroll and looked over to Amber who was still on her knees in her good gown, leading a prayer session with a small group of people around her. Even Mirabelle was kneeling now. Lucas almost laughed, knowing that the only time she ever knelt was to use her mouth to pleasure a man. Amber must have gotten the whore to pretend like she was praying and this truly impressed him. Sir Romney was right. Lucas knew the life of rules and suffering that Amber was going through and this Code of Conduct was nothing compared to that.

"All right," he grumbled, running his finger down the parchment and reading the ninth rule on the list. "A knight shall have no desire for worldly gain and shall give away rather than to retain. They shall be happy with the simple things of life and not covet the wealth and goods of others."

"Well, that should be easy since you really don't have anything anyway," said Sir Romney.

"Aye, that's right." Lucas looked over to Amber who had just finished praying and was speaking with the other pilgrims, laughing and looking so happy. She even included Mirabelle in the conversations, getting the pilgrims and monks that were at the shrine to accept her.

This was her purpose of the pilgrimage. To pray and bring happiness to those who have nothing and to give them hope. His purpose of being here was quite different, indeed – to sell fake relics, steal a ruby, and his biggest goal which was to attain his own castle and lands. This didn't sound anything like the code of the knights. He almost felt ashamed of his greed and deceit. He shook his head to clear his doubts and read the last code on the list.

"A knight shall avoid temptations and not succumb to unlawful sexual encounters." He looked at Sir Romney. "Such as whores perhaps?"

Sir Romney squirmed uncomfortably. "She is a Winchester Goose, not a nun. And the archbishop has declared that her profession is legal, so that is different."

"I see." Lucas looked back at the parchment. "Mayhap the archbishop will make bedding a nun legal next." Then he continued reading. "And this finishes up by saying that a knight shall refrain from listening to, speaking of, or viewing anything that titillates his senses." He couldn't help but smile at that. "It is amazing that a knight ever has heirs at all if he follows these codes." He threw the parchment roll to the ground. "I should have just stayed and taken my final vows as a monk because this is no different than the rules of the Order."

"I highly suspect they may have been written by the church," said Sir Romney.

"Either that or when they were transcribed by monks they just added their own thoughts to it."

"Or perhaps transcribed by nuns is more like it. Now something else you need to know is that knights are expected to be courteous, humble, and to never turn their back on a foe, though he should show mercy. And he should never boast."

"What are you two talking about?" Amber came up to greet them with a serene smile on her face, making Lucas start questioning everything once again. Mirabelle was next to her brushing the dirt off her gown.

"Sir Lucas is just going over the Codes of Conduct of a knight," said Sir Romney getting to his feet.

"Really?" Amber looked at him with her eyes partially squinted.

"A knight?" said Mirabelle, still brushing off her skirt. "That is funny considering you were almost a monk."

"How do you know that?" asked Amber.

"Oh, I knew that months ago when I first met him."

"Time to go," said Lucas, grabbing the scroll and jumping to his feet. He took a hold of Amber's hand and dragged her to the horse.

"What's the hurry?" she asked. "I hoped we could get a bite to eat before we left."

"You can eat while we're riding," he said, trying to get her away from Mirabelle before the whore spilled his secrets. "I want to make it to our next destination by nightfall. And then we should be able to make it to Canterbury first thing tomorrow morning."

"Oh, I can't wait to get to Canterbury," said Amber, placing her foot in the stirrup to mount the horse. Lucas went over and helped her up.

"My sister's castle is in Canterbury," said Sir Romney, mounting his horse and pulling Mirabelle up after him. "Perhaps you two can join us for a few days before your journey back to Bowerwood."

"Oh, I would like that," said Amber. Then she looked down to

Lucas as he placed the scroll in his travel bag and secured it. "Can we do that, please?" she asked.

Her big, green eyes were begging him much like they were last night when she wanted him to bed her. He found a hard time denying her then and would not deny her now. He needed to get into Canterbury Castle and wait there for Father Armand once he stole the ruby. That was the plan and this was working in his favor.

"I suppose so," he said, climbing up on the horse behind her.

"Oh, thank you," she said with a sparkle in her eye. "This will remind me of home, and I do miss my home dearly."

It would remind him of home, too, he thought, but in a different way completely. Because although Sir Romney was inviting him to stay with them, none of them had any idea that if Lucas' plans worked out, in a short matter of time Canterbury Castle would belong to him.

CHAPTER 12

Daughters of the Dagger

*T*here wasn't an inn or tavern in sight when the sun started to sink. Lucas had suggested that they spend the night under the stars since the weather was fairly decent. He'd talked the rest of them into just building a fire and spreading their blankets on the ground to stay there for the night.

He'd pulled Sir Romney aside earlier and told him he didn't want to spend the night in the same room as Amber again. They both knew there was a tavern not ten minutes' ride up the road that had accommodations as well, but the girls didn't need to know that.

They sat around the fire finishing up the rabbit Lucas had caught, as well as the fresh bread and apples he'd brought from the inn they'd stayed in last night. Though Amber had said she didn't eat meat, she hadn't even paused this time when he offered her some. Sir Romney picked up the goatskin of wine he carried with him and passed it over to Amber.

"Would you like more wine, Sister?" he asked, handing it to her.

"Why yes, thank you." Amber reached for it but right before she took it, Lucas snatched it away.

"I think you'd do better with some ale," he said, handing her his goatskin container instead. "After all, it is less potent."

She glared at him and took what he offered.

"This rabbit is the best I've ever tasted," said Mirabelle licking her fingers seductively.

"Aye," added Sir Romney, throwing a bone into the fire. "How did you catch it without a bow and arrows?" he asked Lucas. "Are you sure you only used your dagger?"

"I used to hunt rabbit in the fields as a child," Lucas told him. "I learned to sneak up on them, probably from all the practice I had sneaking out of the monastery."

"Well, I can't wait to have a practice session with you with the sword," said Sir Romney. "I want to see how you handle that. Who taught you how to use weapons anyway?"

"No one," he relayed. "I taught myself out of desperation to be something other than a monk." He looked over at Amber when he said it and caught her eye. He wondered if she remembered saying she didn't want to be a nun anymore. Then he was sure she knew exactly what he was talking about when she couldn't even look at him, but rather glanced the other way.

"Well, I think it's time we get a little shut eye if we're going to get an early start to Canterbury tomorrow. I'll get the blankets out of the travel bags," Lucas offered.

"Aye, good idea. I'll help you," said Sir Romney, brushing the crumbs from his hands and following Lucas toward the horses.

AMBER SAT quiet as the men left, knowing Lucas was referring to her with his words about being something other than a monk. She hadn't forgotten she'd told him she might have made a mistake deciding to be a nun. And she also remembered earlier today telling him that she loved him.

"What's the matter, Sister? You look like you've been bitten by a Winchester Goose." Mirabelle came and sat next to her.

"Pardon me?" she asked, not knowing what the girl meant.

"That's what they say when a man gets a sexual disease from one of the whores," Mirabelle explained. "I don't really like the saying much though, as I am clean and careful."

"Oh," she said, not knowing how to respond to that. "Mirabelle, can I ask you something?"

"Of course, Sister, go ahead."

"Just call me Amber," she said, thinking how awkward it was for a whore and nun to be talking with each other.

"All right, Amber. Oh, that would be a great name for a whore if you ever decided to change professions."

"I don't think so," she said. "Actually, I wanted to ask you what makes a man love a woman?" It was bothering her that she'd been wanton with Lucas last night. But what was bothering her even more was that he said they hadn't coupled. Even after she said she loved him, it sounded as if he'd turned her away. Mayhap he didn't like her as much as she thought he did after all. If only she could change that.

"Hah!" laughed the woman. "Sweetie, you're asking the wrong person that question. Now if you want to know what excites a man, that I could answer."

"Well, tell me then. What excites a man?" She glanced over to Lucas who was conversing and laughing with Sir Romney over by the horses. She wanted to make him laugh, and she wanted to excite him even if it was wrong. She felt so undesirable at the moment and also like a failure. She'd basically thrown herself at him and he didn't want her.

"Well," said Mirabelle. "A man likes his woman curvy and willing, and able to please him in bed."

"Oh, I see." She'd been curvy and willing, but she obviously hadn't pleased Lucas in bed. "How does one . . . know what to do to please a man in bed?"

"Sister," she said with a laugh. "I find that an odd question coming from a nun."

"I was just curious," she said, drawing with her finger in the dirt, not able to look at the woman. "Just curious about the ways of the world."

"Don't tell me you're a virgin?" Mirabelle said it quite loud, and Amber noticed Lucas look up.

"Shhh," she said. "You don't have to tell everyone."

"So, he really didn't bed you last night, after all. He wasn't lying."

"What?" Her head popped up. "What do you mean?"

"Lucas. He said he didn't bed you and had the bulge under his tunic to prove it, but somehow I just couldn't believe it."

"He told you?" Her eyes shot over to Lucas who was still talking. She didn't think he could hear what they were talking about, but when he turned his head and saw her scowl at him she was sure he knew it was nothing good.

"Well, I saw him in the corridor last night and knew he hadn't been sated and needed some release. In my profession, we notice these things. After all, that's what I'm here for, to see to a man's release and pleasures." She smiled and leaned back on her arms with her legs stretched out lazily, seeming very pleased with herself.

Amber suddenly remembered the exchange of money between Mirabelle and Lucas earlier, and her heart sank. After she couldn't please him, he must have gone to Mirabelle to feel sated. This angered her and saddened her at the same time.

"You've had him, haven't you?" she asked.

"Who? Lucas?" She looked over toward the men and Lucas obviously must have heard his name because he looked up. Mirabelle waggled her fingers at him and he waved back. "Sure, I had him, and let me tell you he is a real tiger in bed."

"I don't want to hear about it," she said, but Mirabelle just kept on talking.

"He likes to do it in odd places, and you should hear the way he growls right before he's sated. Grrrrrr," she said shaking her shoulders and smiling and looking back toward Lucas.

"Mirabelle, that is enough," she told her, but her warning fell on deaf ears.

"And if you spank him and tell him he's a bad boy it really turns him on. He pretends like he doesn't like the name Lucifer, but call it out during coupling and it'll drive him wild."

"Stop it!" she cried, getting to her feet. She turned and ran through the woods in the dark. She didn't want to hear how the man she thought she loved had turned her away in bed only to run to a whore who knew exactly what he liked and how to please him. She would never be the type of girl he wanted and she knew now that being a nun was her only choice after all.

She ran through the woods in the dark, the branches grabbing at her clothes and hair. She needed to get far away from Lucas and her feelings for him. She needed to get back to the church and the abbey where she would be safe from the temptations that threatened to consume her.

Amber stumbled on a stump in the woods and tried to right herself. But in the dark, she couldn't see a thing. She fell, hitting her head on a rock and her world went black all around her.

CHAPTER 13

*L*ucas looked over toward the girls and realized Amber was no longer sitting by the fire talking to Mirabelle. He had thought at first that she'd gone to use a bush, but when it was a while and she didn't return, he knew something was wrong.

"Hold up," he told Sir Romney with his hand out, stopping the conversation. "Something is wrong."

"What could be wrong?" asked the knight.

"I don't know, but Amber seems to have disappeared." He rushed over to Mirabelle who was just lying there looking at the stars. "Where's Amber?" he asked.

Mirabelle sat up and brushed herself off. "I don't know. We were just sitting here talking and the next thing I know she jumps up and looks like she's going to cry and takes off into the forest."

"What did you do to her?" he snapped.

"Nothing," she said.

"Well you must have said something to upset her," added Sir Romney.

"I don't think so."

"Mirabelle," said Lucas, gritting his teeth and trying to hold back his anger, "what were you two talking about?"

She sighed deeply and seemed to be thinking. "Let me see. She was asking about men and I was giving her advice."

"Bid the devil, you've got to be jesting," said Lucas glancing up toward the woods, wondering where she went.

"Nay, I'm not. She asked what excited a man, so I told her."

"And that caused her to run away?" asked Sir Romney.

"Well, we were talking about you, Lucas."

"God's bones, don't tell me you told her we coupled?"

"You did?" Sir Romney asked, seeming as if it bothered him.

"She's a whore," Lucas ground out. "Don't act so surprised."

"You never told me you coupled with Lucas," said the knight.

"I thought you knew," said Mirabelle. "That's where I got the idea to couple in the stables with you, as Lucas likes to do it in odd places."

"Please don't tell me you told that to Amber." Lucas was doing all he could to keep from hitting the woman.

"Well, I was giving an example to her question so she could learn. Just like when I told her how you growl like a bear and like to be spanked and called a bad boy –"

Lucas didn't give her the chance to finish. He pulled her up by her shoulders and shook her so hard he swore he could hear her brain rattle. It was all he could do not to hit her, even if she was a woman. Damn the Code of Conduct, he no longer cared. "You fool. You don't tell that to a nun!"

"Let her go," shouted Sir Romney, grabbing him from behind. Without thinking, Lucas' survival skills kicked in and he turned around and swung his fist, hitting Sir Romney in the jaw. The knight stumbled backwards and righted himself, pulling his sword. "Mayhap this is the time to see just how good those fighting skills of yours are," he threatened.

"Put away the sword," warned Lucas. "I have no desire to fight you." He turned his back on the knight and heard him rushing toward him. In one motion, he grabbed his sword from his side and turned to block what could have been a devastating blow.

"Stop fighting," screamed Mirabelle, but neither of them listened.

Lucas could see the anger in the knight's eyes and did all he could to ward off the man's blows without hurting him.

"Don't hold back, you bastard," Sir Romney said in challenge. "Or is this all you're capable of doing since you're really not a knight?"

"I'm not looking for a fight. Now put down your sword."

"Never," called out the knight, picking up the intensity of his blows. Lucas had to stop this, or someone was going to get hurt. He'd been holding back, but he would do so no longer.

He fought like a wild man, letting loose with all his pent-up anger. Swords clashed as he met with every one of Sir Romney's blows. Then in one swift move, he twisted the tip of his sword around the knight's weapon and flipped it out of his hand and up into the air. Sir Romney fell backward onto the ground and Lucas lunged forward and held the tip of his sword to the man's throat. He heard Mirabelle screaming from behind him.

"I might not be a knight, but don't forget I was a mercenary. I could kill you right now if I wanted to with just a flick of my wrist."

"Then, why don't you?" asked Sir Romney.

"Because I have no quarrel with you, nor do I have time for this." He placed his sword back into his scabbard and reached out his hand and helped Sir Romney to his feet.

"I misjudged you," said the knight. "Because with the way you fight and your chivalry to offer me your hand, you truly are a knight after all."

"I've got to find her," said Lucas, ignoring the man's compliment, and turning and running into the forest. "Amber," he called, but heard no answer. "Amber, where are you?"

He searched for a good amount of time in the dark, not

understanding how she could have gotten so far away so quickly. He had just turned around and was heading back to camp when he saw her in the moonlight bent over as if in prayer on the ground.

"Amber," he called and rushed toward her, but she continued to pray. Then as he approached, he realized his mistake. She wasn't praying at all, but was slumped over on the ground with her head lying on a rock. There was a gash above one eyebrow and blood trickling from it.

"Nay!" he shouted and hunkered down and gently turned her body over. "Amber, talk to me. Please, my little dove, please don't die." He felt for a pulse at the side of her neck, and breathed a sigh of relief when he found it. Then he gathered her up into his arms and headed quickly back to camp.

* * *

AMBER STIRRED and opened her eyes, feeling a throbbing on her forehead. It was night, and the full moon was above her as well as a splatter of stars across the vast, dark velvet sky. It took her a moment to realize where she was, then she remembered. She had fallen and hit her head after running through the woods, being upset by what she'd heard about Lucas.

She felt a heaviness across her chest and when she looked down, she saw Lucas' arm lying protectively across her. He was sleeping at her side and holding on to her as if he really cared. She touched her head and felt the binding wrapped around it and realized he must have found her in the woods and tended to her wound.

That still didn't make it right that he'd bedded a whore after refusing her. She gingerly picked up his heavy arm and slipped out from under him. Getting up, she went to sit at the fire. That's when she noticed Sir Romney sleeping at the far side of the fire and Mirabelle nowhere in sight.

"He really cares about you," came a woman's voice from behind her.

Amber turned so fast that she became dizzy and swayed. Mirabelle was there and reached out for her, taking her by the arm.

"Sit down before you fall over." She guided Amber to a sitting position.

"Please don't touch me," said Amber, reaching down and settling herself on the ground.

"Why not? Because I'm a whore?" she asked.

"Nay, I didn't mean that. I'm sorry. I'm just upset that Lucas bedded you when he didn't want me."

"I think we need to have a little talk." Mirabelle sat next to her. "First off, you need to realize that when a man beds me it has nothing to do with feelings. I am naught to any man but an answer to the bulge that keeps him awake at night. I know that and I accept it."

"But Sir Romney cares for you . . . doesn't he?"

"I wish I could say yes." She eyed him from across the camp still sleeping on the ground. "But even if I thought it were true, it would never go anywhere. A knight and a woman of my profession can never be together."

"And do you think a nun and a man like Lucas could be together?" she asked.

"Well, you've got a point there," she answered with a smile. "I guess we have more in common than we thought."

That made Amber smile and she started to see a side of Mirabelle that wasn't so different than her.

"I'm sorry. I just got jealous when I heard Lucas turned me down and ran to you."

"What?" asked Mirabelle. "Is that what you think?"

"I saw him paying you. And you said he'd been with you."

"That was months ago," she said with a smile. "He finally got around to paying me, the bastard." She held a hand over her mouth. "Oh, sorry about the language."

"You mean . . . he didn't sleep with you last night?"

"Nay. I offered, but he turned me down. Whether you realize it or not, the man only has eyes for you, Amber."

Her heart skipped a beat and she really wanted to believe it. But yet it didn't make sense that he'd turned her away. "I don't know why he'd refuse me when I was so willingly trying to give myself to him."

"You are a nun, Amber. Or almost one, anyway. Don't you think that made a difference in his decision?"

"I don't know. I guess I never thought of him as having a conscience."

"Most men don't," she said with a giggle. "But sometimes they surprise you."

"I'm sorry I judged you before, Mirabelle. I knew I was going to like you the moment I found out you had the same name as my late mother."

"I like you, too, Amber. It's not just anyone who can get me to kneel in the dirt . . . not to pray, anyway. It felt nice," she admitted. "Mayhap I misjudged you as well."

"Then let's start over and be friends." Amber reached out and took the girl's hand in hers. "I haven't any real friends since I decided to enter the abbey, and it would feel nice to have one."

"Are you going to stay with your plans of becoming a nun?" she asked.

"I'm not sure. Are you going to stay with your plans of being a Goose?"

Mirabelle laughed. "That sounds so funny coming from you. And to answer your question . . . I don't know either. Do you think you can get me signed up at the abbey to become a nun instead?"

. . .

Lucas awoke to the sound of laughing and opened one eye to see Amber and Mirabelle sitting by the fireside like they were old friends. He blinked, trying to clear his sight, thinking it was naught but a dream. Then he realized it was real, and groaned and turned over the other way. If Mirabelle was giving Amber pointers on how to seduce a man again, it was going to be a long ride to Canterbury in the morning.

CHAPTER 14

Daughters of the Dagger

The next day was Sunday and Lucas awoke early, anticipating the task of stealing the Regale ruby from the Canterbury Cathedral as soon as they arrived. He paced back and forth and ran a hand through his hair, thinking about the knight's Code of Conduct. Rule number seven, to be precise. The rule that states a knight does not steal. And rule number eight and nine saying a knight shouldn't be greedy or deceitful or want worldly goods for himself.

"God's eyes, this is impossible!" he spoke to himself, then squirmed inwardly. Rule number two, he reminded himself, knowing he'd never be able to drop the habit of cursing.

Habit. Just that word reminded him of Amber and the fact he'd told her he'd burned her habit when, in fact, he'd had it cleaned. Another rule broken. It, along with her undergarments, were neatly folded and sitting in his travel bag right now. He couldn't burn them, though he'd wanted to. It just didn't seem right to burn the robes of a nun, even if she was only a novice.

"Good morning," he heard Amber say, and turned to greet her. But then he realized she was talking to Mirabelle, not him. She looked so alluring in her velvet gown. Her hair was pulled up and tied back with a piece of twine. She'd removed the binding from her wound, and her gash seemed to be healing nicely.

His hand went to his own wound. His side was still sore, especially after fighting with Sir Romney, but it was healing as well. He'd taken out his stitches with the tip of his dagger last night, since they were starting to pinch.

Visions of Amber standing naked before him and the feel of her soft skin against his hand had him aching to hold her once again . . . and drive himself deep between her legs. Rule number ten, he reminded himself, as these thoughts were definitely titillating.

"Well, at least I have number six under control," he said aloud thinking how he'd had sexual restraint around her though he really didn't want to.

"You broke the rule last night of never refusing a challenge from a rival, as well as never turning your back on a foe." Sir Romney walked up to him, strapping on his sword as he spoke.

"Sorry about the punch," said Lucas, seeing the bruise staining the man's jaw. "I got a little out of control last night, but I was really worried about Amber. Besides, I don't consider myself equal to you, nor are you my foe so I didn't break those rules. And if I must remind you, we did fight after all. Even if I initially turned away."

"You pack a good punch," said the knight, rubbing his jaw. "I'm surprised I can move my mouth enough to talk this morning. You handle your sword with the expertise of a well-trained knight as well. I'm impressed."

"When I feel attacked, I lash out," explained Lucas. "It's the only way I survived after I left the Order."

"I never should have pulled my sword on you. A knight doesn't draw his weapon unless he intends to use it."

"You could have fooled me. You had intent in your eyes."

"I only intended to scare you," he admitted. "But when you

started fighting like that, I had no choice but to fight back if I didn't want to get killed."

"Mayhap so, but I didn't kill you, nor would I have even considered it. I think of you as a friend."

"I do as well," said Sir Romney, holding out his hand. Lucas clasped it and they hit each other on the back in a gesture of making up. "How is Amber?" he asked. Concern painted his words.

Lucas looked across the campsite where Mirabelle and Amber were cackling like a couple of hens. "I'd say she's feeling better, wouldn't you?"

"Sure looks like it. What happened between those two anyway?"

"I'm not sure, but I'm just happy to see Amber smiling again."

"I feel the same way about Mirabelle. I don't think I've ever seen anything like this. A nun and a whore as best friends."

Lucas turned and tugged on the strings of the travel bags, finishing packing for their journey. "Never try to understand a woman," he said, causing them both to laugh. "It's time to go," called out Lucas, and both of the women came forward. He reached out and lifted Amber up atop the horse. But when he started to climb up after her, she stopped him.

"I think I'd like to ride with Mirabelle the rest of the way to Canterbury," she told him.

"Mirabelle rides with me," said Sir Romney, reaching out for the girl.

"Nay," said Mirabelle, stepping away and hoisting herself up onto the horse in back of Amber. "Today I'll ride with my new friend."

"You can't," protested Lucas. "Where am I going to ride?"

"How about with Sir Romney?" Amber looked back to Mirabelle and they both smiled.

"Aye," agreed Mirabelle, "I think you two will look lovely together."

Amber reached down and took the reins from Lucas and then spoke to Mirabelle over her shoulder. "Hold on," she said. "I haven't felt the wind in my hair in a long time and I intend to feel it today." She reached up and released the twine holding up her hair and let it fall to her shoulders. Then with a kick to the horse, she sped away leaving both the men standing there staring after them.

"I can't believe she just did that," said Sir Romney.

"Neither can I," said Lucas in admiration. "I didn't even know she could actually ride. Or not in that saddle and with a rider on back at least."

"I also can't believe you will be riding with me now."

"I'm not, so get that idea out of your head right now."

Sir Romney mounted his horse and turned a half-circle looking down to Lucas as he spoke. "Then I guess you'll be walking and it'll take a lot longer to get there. I don't plan on waiting for you, so you're on your own."

Lucas didn't want Amber out of his sight that long. He also had to make it to Canterbury in time for mass so he could scope out the best way to steal the ruby.

"I ride in front," he growled, putting out his hands to pull himself up into the saddle.

"Like hell you do." Sir Romney wouldn't budge, causing Lucas to settle in behind him. "Now, if you don't want to fall off you'd better hold on."

"Never."

"Have it your way." Sir Romney took off at a good clip, making Lucas almost fall off the horse since only one person really fit in the saddle and he was sitting directly on the horse's back. His arms shot out and he grabbed on to Sir Romney to keep from falling.

"God's teeth, man, don't do that again," warned Lucas.

"Rule number two," Sir Romney reminded him as they sped away, making Lucas start to hate the Codes of Conduct almost as much as he'd hated his training to be a monk. Either way, they were one and the same as far as he was concerned.

* * *

AMBER SLOWED DOWN as they passed the tavern that also served as an inn just up the road from where they'd camped last night.

"Look at that," said Amber. "There was an inn right here and yet the men made us sleep on the ground. Do you think they knew about it?" she asked Mirabelle who was clinging to her on the back of the horse.

"Sir Romney's sister lives in Canterbury. He's traveled these roads many times and knows, I am sure," said Mirabelle. "My guess is that Lucas just didn't want to sleep in the same bed with you last night."

That's exactly what she was thinking and she was bothered by this thought.

"Well, I don't care," she lied, knowing she'd have to confess it later. "Do you see them behind us yet?"

"Let me check." Mirabelle turned and looked over her shoulder. "Aye, here they come like a bat out of Hell and I have to say they don't look happy."

Amber waited until they rode up next to her, holding back her laughter. They looked so silly riding together. Lucas dropped his arms from around Sir Romney's waist when they approached, and she could see him nonchalantly lay his hands atop his legs.

"Amber, stop already and let's ride the way we did yesterday," he shouted.

"I don't know," she answered, looking straight ahead when she spoke. "It may not be as satisfying for you as you'd like by riding with me. Mayhap riding with Sir Romney will be to your liking more, so enjoy it."

With that, she took off quickly and darted away. Looking over her shoulder, she saw Lucas lurch backward and curse as Sir

Romney took off after them. He reached out and clasped his arms around the man's waist in order not to fall off.

"This is the most fun I've had in a long time," said Amber.

"Me, too," agreed Mirabelle. "That is, except for the time I made love atop a horse."

"You're jesting, aren't you?" Amber said over her shoulder.

"Not at all. You should try it sometime. It's dangerous but very exciting."

Thoughts ran rampant through Amber's head of her and Lucas naked atop a horse doing just what Mirabelle suggested. She picked up the speed, trying to blow that idea right out of her mind, wondering if she'd ever be able to don the robes of a nun again.

CHAPTER 15

Daughters of the Dagger

They arrived in Canterbury early that morning, way ahead of schedule because of the way Amber was riding. Lucas quickly took his hands from around Sir Romney's waist and jumped from the horse when they rode into a crowd of people. He hoped no one had noticed. He felt so embarrassed.

The bells of the cathedral rang out. Noblemen and women, servants, villeins, and even beggars flocked through the iron gates, making their way to mass.

"This is beautiful," gasped Amber, dismounting. Mirabelle followed. "I've never seen such a wonderful house of worship."

Lucas looked up to the cathedral, three times the size of any of the churches he'd ever seen. Several tall steeples rose up to the sky, leading to a very high bell tower just above the main stairs. Many windows framed the building, all of them in colorful shards of stained-glass, depicting the life of Christ, as well as many of the saints. Arches lined the cloistered walkway all around the church, and in the walls were stone-carved various angels, saints and designs of many kinds. The sight took his breath away.

"This is Canterbury Cathedral which also houses the shrine of

St. Thomas Becket," Lucas pointed out. "There is a lot of wealth here, and it shows." He thought of all the money and items Father Armand had collected in greed back at Bowerwood. They looked like naught more than a pittance compared to the ornate décor and display of grandeur of this cathedral and the grounds surrounding it as well.

The crowd grew larger. Lucas walked over and grabbed the reins of the horse from Amber. He didn't like the fact there were so many people here. How was he supposed to steal the ruby and not get caught with all these eyes upon him?

"What the hell is going on around here to draw this kind of a crowd?" asked Lucas.

"Lucas, please refrain from cursing while in the presence of such a holy place." Amber blessed herself, all the while staring in awe at the terrific sight.

"It looks to me like the archbishop is here and saying mass today," stated Sir Romney. "We're in luck."

"Aye. Such luck," Lucas grumbled, feeling his luck suddenly changing. Could it possibly get any worse?

"I'd like to meet the archbishop after services," said Amber in awe.

"I'm sure that'll be impossible with all these people," said Lucas, not wanting to get anywhere near the man. Not when he was about to steal the most coveted icon in the whole country.

"Not so." Sir Romney dismounted. "I can get us in to see the archbishop personally, as he is my uncle."

"Your uncle?" Lucas shook his head. Yes, it could get worse. Now when the jewel was reported stolen, the archbishop himself will have seen the robber's face, being able to identify Lucas and have him beheaded.

"I'm going inside," said Amber anxiously, picking up her skirts and hurrying across the road.

"Me, too," said Mirabelle, following after her.

"What just happened here?" asked Sir Romney, watching the

whore race toward the cathedral as if it were a ship of lust-filled men returning from war. "Is she really planning on going into the church?"

"Well, if the walls cave in when she enters, you'll know she wasn't jesting."

"Give me the horses." Sir Romney grabbed the reins. "I'll find someone we can pay to watch them while we're inside."

"Nay, I'll do it. You go find the girls and keep them out of trouble." Lucas took the reins back and Sir Romney headed toward the church. Then, once more, Lucas looked up to the towering cathedral.

The sight was intoxicating, and the sound of the clanging bell echoed in his brain. He thought of his reason for being here and his stomach twisted in a knot. If the walls of the place were going to cave in, it would be when he entered, not Mirabelle.

He almost changed his mind about the whole mission, until he glanced the other way and saw Canterbury Castle rising up and taunting him in the distance. The sun reflected off the turrets in the morning sun. It was the largest, most impressive castle he'd ever seen, besides the castle of the king himself.

This could all belong to him soon. All he had to do was steal one little ruby, and then he'd be Lord Canterbury and ruler of the castle, a fief, and probably several pieces of land as well. Mayhap he'd even own a whole forest as a part of this sweet deal. He was so close to attaining everything he ever wanted in life that the anticipation was driving him mad.

He wanted it so desperately that he could almost taste it. But the Code of Conduct kept pushing its way into his head, almost like a little voice warning him he shouldn't do it.

"Hell with the Code of Conduct and living like a pauper," he spoke to himself. In just a few short hours, he would have the key to unlock all the treasures and titles he'd always wanted in life. And if there was one last thing he had to do before he died, this was it.

He headed away with the horses, wondering how he was going to explain all this to Amber if she ever found out. Then, he decided, he wouldn't tell her, and just deny it if he had to. Otherwise, it would only give her one more reason to hate him. He wanted her to give up being a nun and stay at Canterbury Castle with him. He'd be saving her from a life she didn't really want anyway. Aye, he thought, though she would never understand, he was actually doing this for her just as much as for himself.

* * *

AMBER ENTERED THE CATHEDRAL, pushing past the crowds of people, straining her neck to see the shrine of St. Thomas Becket off to the side of the main dais and altar.

"There are too many people," she said, wishing now she still had her habit. Dressed like a nun would get her to the front of this crowd, she was sure.

"Why do you want to see the tomb of a dead man anyway?" asked Mirabelle coming up behind her.

"Because Thomas Becket was Archbishop of Canterbury several decades ago, and also a martyr," Amber explained. "He was very rich and a threat to King Henry II. They did not see eye to eye and Thomas refused to do the king's bidding. Therefore, the king sent four knights to kill him. His brains were scattered from his head right here in this cathedral. And people who have touched any of his relics since then have claimed to have been healed."

"Oh, he was murdered," said Mirabelle making a face. "I'm feeling a little uneasy about all this now, so I think I'll wait for you outside."

"Nay," she said holding on to the girl's hand. "If you want to impress Sir Romney, you should stay for mass."

"Who said I was trying to impress him?" she asked. "I don't even know if I'm allowed to stay."

"As long as you don't take communion, it won't matter," she said. "Now, come and let's take a seat, as I believe the service is about to start."

* * *

Lucas entered the cathedral just as the mass started. He stood in the vestibule of the church, almost running into the processional as taper bearers and altar servers, as well as the archbishop himself passed right by him.

The archbishop wore an alb, or long white robe, representing purity, with his shoulders covered with a stole. The purple cloth was circular in shape with a hole where his head stuck out in the center. He had strips of cloth with embroidered scenes of the last supper around the sleeves at his wrists, and a cincture, or cord with a tassel around his waist. A long strip of cloth hung around his neck all the way to the ground, and he wore a small cape on his back as well.

On his head was a skullcap, and atop that a miter, a tall, ornate pointed hat with a cleft in the center. A large gold ring with a diamond sparkled on his right hand, and in his left hand he held a crosier, or tall staff, carved of ivory with a curved shepherd's hook atop. He also wore a pectoral large gold cross on a chain around his neck.

He busily blessed people as he walked, and didn't notice a small child crawling on the floor and stopping directly in his path. He turned to take a step, and Lucas rushed forward and grabbed the man by the elbow.

"Your Excellency," he cried out. The man jerked backward. There were several soldiers standing around who rushed forward with their hands on the hilts of their weapons, thinking he meant to harm the archbishop.

Lucas quickly let go of the holy man and raised his hands in the air to show them he meant no harm. Then he stooped over and scooped up the child from the floor. The baby's mother rushed over and took him from Lucas.

"Thank you, my son, as that would have been disastrous if I should have tripped on the child. Bless you," said the archbishop, making the sign of the cross.

"Anyone would have done the same." Lucas felt as if he didn't want or deserve the blessing.

Then the archbishop smiled and said, "God will reward you, my son," and headed on his way down the aisle with music from the gallery being played on flutes and harps as the monks chanted out their haunting tune from the choir.

"That was noble of you," whispered Sir Romney, coming up behind him. "Just like a true knight. You should feel proud of what you've done."

Lucas couldn't take all this praise and being revered and honored. Especially coming from the archbishop – one of the holiest men in the world who held almost as much, or perhaps more, power than the king himself.

"What are you doing out here?" Lucas grumbled. "I thought you were going to find the girls."

"They are saving seats for us on the bench and I came out to find you at Amber's request. She wanted to experience this mass together with you."

"How wonderful," he said, letting out a slow, frustrated breath. He had planned on scoping out the surroundings during the mass and hopefully sneaking back into the sacristy to figure out a way to come back and steal the ruby after the mass was over and the crowd cleared out. Now he would have to sit there and listen to Amber pray the entire time which was only going to make this whole thing harder on him. He felt a sense of doom overwhelm him and he just knew this was not going to end well.

Lucas sat through the mass with his traveling party, not able to concentrate on a word since his mind was elsewhere. His eyes were fastened to the ornate casket of Thomas Becket that was raised up on a dais and surrounded by an iron fence. Right next to it was a wall of homage with a large iron cross attached to it. All around it were rosaries and pieces of cloth and ornate trinkets that pilgrims had attached to the wall and left in honor of their martyred saint. And high above the casket was a tall iron holder displaying the prized and honored Regale ruby.

He was going to have a hard time just getting close to it.

He looked over and saw Sir Romney dozing off. Mirabelle, who he knew could not understand a word of the mass since it was in Latin, was biting her nails and fixing the bodice of her dress to expose more cleavage. She was obviously getting ready to solicit a few of the wealthy noblemen as soon as she stepped foot outside the church.

Amber, instead of sitting on the bench like most people, decided to kneel on the stone floor for the entire mass, obviously in some form of self-inflicted penance for the night she'd spent with him.

His toe tapped nervously on the ground and Amber gently reached out and touched his foot to still it. What was he doing? he wondered. What were any of them doing here right now?

He surveyed his party next to him and felt like they were some of the most mismatched people to have entered the cathedral today. One fallen knight who didn't really live by the rules expected of him, one bold whore who probably never followed a rule in her life if it didn't involve men and money, and one very confused woman who couldn't decide from one day to the next if she was a nun or a strumpet.

So where did that leave him? He was the worst of the whole lot. He was a man who once lived by the strict rules of a monk, then lived by his own rules of being a mercenary, neither of them satisfying him in the least. And now he struggled and flipped back and forth between following the rules of the knights or the rules of greed and deceit laid down by a man who had raised him and served as his surrogate father.

He'd admired Father Armand his entire life, respecting him like the fourth rule of the Code of Conduct instructed. But now, he basically despised the man, since he was asking him to do something that no real parent would ever ask of their child.

The mass finally ended and Lucas blessed himself, thankful it was over. He had work to do and needed to get up to the front of the church and survey this ruby he was supposed to steal.

"Let's make our way up to the front of the church," said Amber. "I want to meet the archbishop."

"He won't be here long," Sir Romney told them. "Instead, follow me, and I'll take you around the back and we'll be able to stop him before he leaves."

"Aye, let's do that," said Lucas, knowing this is right where he needed to go. Sir Romney was going to be a bigger help than he knew.

They followed Sir Romney through a narrow passageway and then around the back of the church in a dusty corridor that looked like it was never used.

"This looks like a secret passageway," surveyed Amber. "How did you know about this?"

"Uncle Simon – I mean the archbishop showed me once when he was trying to quit the crowds and get home for dinner," explained Sir Romney. "This is also used as an escape route should anyone try to kill him. Ever since Thomas Beckett died here over two centuries ago, they are very careful that nothing like that ever happens again."

They waited in a small, enclosed room at the back of the church. Then, to Lucas' surprise, he saw a small shrine attached to the room with lit candles inside it.

"What's that?" asked Lucas.

"Oh, that's another private shrine to Thomas Becket," said Sir Romney. "It's where the real Regale ruby – Canterbury's prized possession is kept for safety."

Lucas' heart about beat from his chest. Only one man guarded the room, and he sat on a bench and looked to be dozing off.

"So what is that shrine out in the church?" Lucas asked. "A fake?"

"Nay." Sir Romney shook his head. "That is his real tomb. His scalp as well as pieces of his bloodied robe and other relics are displayed for the public to see. Sometimes the people are allowed to touch or kiss them but only under supervision. The pilgrims get so desperate to take a relic home that they often try to bite off a piece when they put their lips upon it."

"Unbelievable that anyone would even think of trying to steal from a church," gasped Amber.

"Aye, unbelievable," echoed Lucas. "So, Sir Romney, tell us more about this ruby."

"Well," said the knight, "the Regale ruby is just too valuable to put out on display, especially when there is such a big crowd. So they keep it back here and display the fake ruby instead. They only bring out the real one on special occasions, such as if the king were to visit. Actually, my uncle doesn't want to even bring it out on special occasions anymore, because he said he's had a holy vision that someone is going to try to steal it. So, having it hidden here ensures its safety, and thieves won't know that they've stolen a fake instead."

"Aye, I can see your point," said Lucas, his pulse racing as he realized this would be easier than he thought.

"I want to go in there and pray." Amber started to head over to the room like a bee attracted to a flower.

"Here comes my uncle," said Sir Romney. "Wait and meet him first, and I'll get the permission for us to go in there."

The archbishop entered the room with several taper bearers and altar servers around him. "Romney?" he said, walking forward, almost gliding across the floor. "It that really you, Nephew? I haven't seen you in years." He nodded to his entourage, and they headed away to the sacristy, the room adjoined to where they stood, that housed the things needed to conduct the mass.

"Uncle Simon – I mean, Archbishop, how are you?"

"I am well, but I am saddened by the death of your sister Helen's husband. May God guide him to Heaven and also be with you all in this trying time," he said, making the sign of the cross in the air with his hand.

"Thank you, Uncle."

"It seems he left the castle and his lands to the church. I'll have to find a noble knight to give it to," continued the holy man.

"I'm sure you will find one," Sir Romney assured him with a smile. Lucas knew the knight was hoping his uncle would give it to him. He wouldn't be surprised if that was the whole reason that Romney had come to Canterbury in the first place.

"Did your parents come with you as well?" asked the archbishop. "I would like to visit with your mother."

"Nay," he answered. "I am sorry to say your sister is not here. Or not my mother, anyway, but your other sister has arrived at Canterbury not long ago, I hear."

"Veronica?" he asked. "I didn't know she was back from overseas, as she hasn't come to visit me. Please tell me she is doing better."

"She is not doing well," he said. "Helen sent word in a missive that Aunt Veronica still is very saddened and has never married nor had any children. I am afraid she will die soon if she doesn't find a reason to live."

"I'll come by in a few days and talk to her," the archbishop told him. "Perhaps a blessing is in order to heal her heavy heart."

"Sir Romney?" Amber interrupted in a meek voice, reminding him that she was there.

"Oh, Archbishop, I would like you to meet some friends of mine. This is Mirabelle," he said putting his arm on the whore's shoulder. The bishop raised his hand and placed it on Mirabelle's head. Her eyes widened in surprise.

"I absolve you of your sins, my dear and I hope to see you start a new path in life," he told her.

"That's the second time in a matter of days I've been absolved of my sins," she relayed with a smile.

"I am Sister Amber, and I am so happy to meet you." Amber didn't wait for her introduction, and Lucas' heart went out to her as she knelt on the ground in front of the man, reaching out and kissing the ring on his hand.

"Bless you, dear," he said. "But please stand. I am only a vassal of God and not the deity Himself."

She stood quickly, her smile bigger than Lucas had ever seen.

"If you are a nun, where is your habit?" the archbishop asked curiously.

"She is a novice, and her clothes became ruined on the trip here," Lucas answered for her before she started telling the man what really happened.

"You are the man who saved me from tripping on that child in the vestibule before mass," the holy man said, nodding toward Lucas. "What is your name? I will have to reward you kindly."

"No reward necessary." Lucas looked down to the ground, not wanting to tell the man his name.

"His name is Lucas," Amber answered for him, repaying the favor he'd just done by answering for her, he supposed.

"Lucas," he repeated. "You seem familiar. Do I know you from somewhere?"

"He was raised by Father Armand as a monk at Bowerwood Abbey and Monastery," Amber blurted out before he could stop her.

"Father Armand," the archbishop said with a nod. "Yes, I know the man well."

Lucas doubted that, as he was sure he knew nothing of Father Armand's ways or he would have him removed from the church altogether.

"Are you a monk then, in a civilian's clothing as well?" he asked.

"Nay," answered Lucas.

"A knight perhaps? As you were so valiant and honorable the way you acted in the vestibule."

"Nay, I am not a knight either," he told him.

"Well, then mayhap you should be knighted, and soon. I will see to it personally, as you are the perfect example of what a knight should be, Sir Lucas." The archbishop chuckled, calling him Sir.

Lucas looked over to the room with the ruby, knowing that having a title bestowed upon him by the archbishop was an honor. But being a landless knight without a castle wasn't what he wanted. He felt like the devil for even thinking of what he was about to do. It was going to be the least honorable thing that no true knight would ever consider doing in a million years.

"Just call me Sir Lucifer," he said, knowing that today was the day he would truly earn his title of being the devil.

CHAPTER 16

Daughters of the Dagger

*L*ucas paced back and forth impatiently, waiting for Amber to finish praying in the secret shrine as he idly made small talk with the guard outside the door. The archbishop and his entourage had left, and he'd already sent Sir Romney and Mirabelle to collect their horses. He'd have only a short window of opportunity to steal the ruby before they returned. But Lucas would never be able to accomplish the feat with her in there. He also had to think of a way to distract the guard.

"Amber, darling," he called to her. "Are you finished praying yet? We need to get going."

She looked over her shoulder, then blessed herself quickly and hurried over to where he stood with the guard.

"That was amazing," she said to Lucas. "Especially the ruby."

"That ruby was sent from France as a present to England by King Louis VII," relayed the guard.

Lucas suddenly had an idea and hoped Amber's ability to chat would work into his plans.

"Sister Amber here knows a little about gemstones," he told

the guard. "She and her sisters at one time all had jeweled daggers."

"How nice," said the guard not at all interested.

"Tell him about it, Amber."

She took the bait and started telling the man the whole dagger story involving her mother. The guard gave a blank stare and nodded with boredom. This was Lucas' opportunity. He slipped away into the shrine and pretended to pray. Actually, he was eyeing up the ruby that was displayed on a pedestal atop the dais, surrounded by statues and candles, just out of arm's reach. If he stood atop the dais, he could reach it with no problem.

He quickly looked back over his shoulder, hearing Amber rattling on. The guard was watching her instead of him, and his back was partially toward Lucas.

Lucas quickly stepped up onto the dais and reached up toward the ruby, his fingertips skimming the surface of it. Then, stretching just a bit more, he curved his fingers around it, knowing that Canterbury Castle was as good as his right now.

"Lucas?" Amber walked into the room, and he had no choice but to release it. "What are you doing?" she asked.

"I'm just . . . trying to receive a blessing by holding my hand in front of the ruby, that's all," he lied.

"Come on. Mirabelle just came in and said Sir Romney has the horses and is in a hurry to get to the castle to see his sister."

Damn. He was so close. He stepped down from the dais defeated, taking one last look at the biggest ruby he'd ever seen in his life glittering in the candlelight of the room. It teased him, mocked him, and made him want to scream.

He turned to find Mirabelle giggling, talking with the guard, keeping his attention. He should have used her instead for the distraction and that ruby would be in his pouch right now instead of taunting him from atop the pedestal.

"What's the matter?" asked Amber. "You look as if you have just lost your best friend."

He glanced back at the ruby as they exited the room. Aye, he felt as if he'd not only lost his best friend but his best and only chance of ever having a castle to call his own.

* * *

Amber was in awe as they rode over the drawbridge of Canterbury Castle right behind Sir Romney with Mirabelle clinging to the back of him.

She rode in front of Lucas. One of his arms was wrapped around her while he held the reins in his other hand. She admired him for always putting her in front and allowing her to sit on the saddle, instead of behind him the way Mirabelle had to sit when riding with Sir Romney. Lucas had been acting more like a knight lately, too, she realized, ever since studying the Code of Conduct. Mayhap there was hope for him yet. He seemed to be changing, and acted more chivalric than the devil of a man she'd first met in Bowerwood.

She found herself thinking about her sisters lately and how happy they were now that they were married. And though she was happy being a nun, she wondered what it would be like to spend her life married to someone like Lucas. She only wished her sisters were here now so she could confide in them about how she was feeling.

"This castle is huge," commented Mirabelle.

Amber agreed. "Even my father's castle is not this large, and he is an earl."

"I told you, this is Canterbury and where the archbishop lives," explained Lucas. "This is a very wealthy area."

The castle towered over them, bathed in a golden hue from the morning sun. Four round turrets made up the corners, and in the center was the square keep. Atop the battlements were crenellations, rectangle openings atop the parapets where archers could shoot arrows toward an attacker. Long, amber-colored banners fluttered in the breeze with the heraldry of an orange rampant lion upon them. There were several black banners as well, depicting that the lord had died and the occupants were in mourning. A moat surrounded the castle with ducks floating atop the dirty water, calling out to each other as they swam. Amber considered that a good omen.

"Are those banners black because of the death of the lord of the castle?" asked Mirabelle.

"Aye, they are still in mourning over the death of my brother-by-marriage, as his accident happened not long ago." Sir Romney spoke as they rode through the gates and into the courtyard.

"What happened to him?" asked Amber curiously.

"He had an accident while practicing the joust," said the knight. "His horse lost its footing and he was thrown and hit his head. My sister is so distraught that I thought my being here might help her recover."

"So what will happen to the castle?" asked Lucas.

"Well, like the archbishop told us, it was left to the church. They were newly married and hadn't yet the chance to have heirs." Sir Romney dismounted as soon as they entered the courtyard. A herald with a straight trumpet blurted out a few notes to announce them.

"Sir Romney and . . ." the herald looked at the whore and raised an eyebrow.

"And friends," said the knight, with a wave of his hand to include all of them.

"And friends," finished the man and once again raised the horn to his mouth. Sir Romney's hand reached up and stopped him. "That's enough," he said.

"Brother, you are finally here!" A young woman ran out of the keep with her handmaid right behind her. She had dark hair coiled atop her head and wore a black mourning gown with a veil to match. Amber thought she looked similar to a nun in this attire.

The young woman threw herself into Sir Romney's arms and started crying.

"Helen," he said. "I am here now. You needn't cry, though I feel your pain. I know you are distraught over your husband's death and I pine for you. But I have brought guests with me that you need to greet."

"I'm sorry," she said, wiping her eyes on the long tippet of her sleeve. "I would like to meet them."

"This is Sir Lucas," he said, nodding toward them, and surprising Amber by using the fake title.

"Pleased to meet you, Lady Helen." Lucas got off the horse quickly and rushed over to kiss her on the hand.

It was an innocent and required act but, for some reason, it still bothered Amber.

"I am Amber," she introduced herself, wasting no time in dismounting the horse.

"*Sister* Amber," Lucas pointed out, and she almost wished he hadn't called her that in front of everyone. It was odd to be thinking this way. But since she'd been wearing her velvet gown instead of her black robes and veil, she had started to feel like she was back living at home again as a lady of a castle. A woman of wealth to be respected by titled men. She'd been getting too used to it, and knew she had to remember who she really was now.

"Aye, *Sister* Amber," she repeated, more for her own benefit to remind herself she needed to start thinking and acting like a nun again. She let out a deep sigh and Lucas looked over to her and smiled.

"Why aren't you wearing the required robe and wimple of the Order?" asked Helen.

"Aye, Lucas," Amber said looking at him. "Would you care to explain?"

"Because she is only a novice," he told Helen.

Amber nodded, knowing he wouldn't say what happened to her clothes.

ELIZABETH ROSE

"And she prefers to act like a lady instead of a nun," he continued.

"That's not true," she said, giving Lucas a daggered glance.

"Who is that atop your horse?" asked the girl, perusing Mirabelle.

"Oh," said Sir Romney, "she's no one. She is just a –"

"She is a traveling companion of ours," broke in Amber, not wanting the man to call her a whore in front of everyone. "Her name is Mirabelle. Lady Mirabelle," she said, glancing over to Lucas who was opening his mouth to most likely object. "Isn't that right, *Sir* Lucas?" Lucas shut his mouth and Romney didn't dare say a word. Mirabelle smiled back at Amber and gave a small nod of thanks.

Lucas leaned over and spoke to her in a low voice. "I'm just pointing it out, but I believe that is called a lie. Not an admirable trait of a nun the last time I checked."

"It's also number eight in the knight's Code of Conduct," she pointed out to him in return.

"Number seven," he said from the side of his mouth.

"Eight. I copied the parchment, I'd know. Seven is not to steal." His head turned sideways and his eyes opened wide, but he didn't say a word. That shut him up for some reason.

However, Amber knew he was right when he said she wasn't acting like a nun. She found herself wondering how that lie sprang so easily from her lips and she felt no remorse for saying it. But she wanted to make Mirabelle feel welcome here because she liked her and considered her a friend. Aye, she only did it to make her feel better about herself and save her from embarrassment. Still, she did lie and knew she would have to confess it soon.

"How is Aunt Veronica?" Romney asked his sister.

"No better," she said sullenly. "Her state of sadness has gotten worse over the years. She spends too much time crying. I am just glad she has come back from overseas, as now we can watch over her."

"Oh, my, what is wrong with her?" asked Amber. "Perhaps I can console her and pray with her in her time of grief."

"She still suffers from the fact that she lost both her husband and her newborn baby years ago. She never remarried or had more children," said Sir Romney.

"That's right," agreed Helen. "She just can't seem to overcome it."

"Then bring me to her," said Amber, picking up her skirts and heading toward the keep. "I am trained to help people in need." She stopped and turned back. "Perhaps you can join us in prayer for your late husband, Helen."

"I would like that very much," she said, then looked up to Mirabelle. "Would you like to join us in prayer, Lady Mirabelle?"

"Me?" Mirabelle slid off the horse. "Nay, I think I had enough prayers for one day. I was hoping to take a walk around the castle." She looked over the courtyard and up toward the battlements. "Where is your garrison?"

"You'll stay with me and not go near the soldiers," said Sir Romney. Amber almost laughed at his possessiveness over her.

"Sir Lucas?" Amber called out. "I am sure you'd want to join us, as you were trained in helping those in need as well."

"Aye, that is a trait of a knight," agreed Sir Romney.

"Or a monk," she added.

"Enough with the talk," Lucas grumbled. "Fine, I'll go, but just for a short visit, as I have a lot to do."

CHAPTER 17

Daughters of the Dagger

𝓛ucas didn't want to be rude to Sir Romney and his sister, or he would have refused to go see their addlepated aunt. He didn't have time for this. He had a ruby to steal.

Father Armand was going to be arriving in a few short days and in order to claim the castle, Lucas needed that ruby to give him in exchange as part of their deal. He decided he would just stop in and pretend to care about the old bitty and then he'd head on out and plot his next attempt.

He followed the group into the keep, through the great hall, and down another corridor. Mirabelle had decided to come with them rather than stay in the courtyard alone. For some reason, she seemed to cling to every word Sir Romney said and she obeyed every order he gave her. She certainly didn't learn that from keeping company with Amber.

"She's in here," said Helen in a low voice, pushing open the door to a room slowly. "The smallest things make her cry for no reason at all, so try not to do or say anything to startle her."

They walked into the room quietly. Lucas saw a woman sitting in a chair with her head down and her body slumped over. It was dark and he could only see her silhouette.

"Aunt Veronica?" asked Helen softly. "Some people are here to see you."

"I don't want to see anyone," the woman mumbled.

"It's me . . . Romney," said the knight, walking up to her and laying a hand on her shoulder. She jerked backward and held up her hand to shield herself.

"Let me try," said Amber, moving forward slowly. "I am a nun," she told the woman. "My name is Amber, and I'd like to pray with you."

"I don't want prayers!" she shouted, startling all of them. "Don't mention prayers again."

"My, she is temperamental," commented Mirabelle, causing the woman's head to snap up as she tried to see her in the dark.

"What is the Goose doing in here?" she asked, surprising Lucas that she even knew what a Goose was, let alone was able to see her in the dark.

"I'm leaving," said Mirabelle, her voice sounding shaky. Sir Romney put a hand out to stop her, but she continued to pull away. "I'm not going to sit here and be insulted by a crazy woman."

"What did you say?" The woman's voice sounded angry and Lucas thought she was going to cry out in rage again.

"This is ridiculous," he said. "We're all standing in the dark and walking on eggshells. Woman, if you're going to sit here and feel sorry for yourself then you deserve to be left alone."

"Lucas, don't say that," warned Amber, but he'd had enough of this nonsense and wasn't going to be a part of it anymore. He turned to leave, but stubbed his toe on something in the dark. Angered, he shot across the room and ripped open the shutters on the window. Sunlight filled the room and a bright beam shot out and hit the woman in the face. She turned her head, raising her hand to block it and cried out as if she'd been struck and was in pain. Amber turned to Lucas with fire in her eyes and her hands went to her hips. He'd never seen her look so angry.

"Stop it, Lucifer!" she shouted. Lucas knew she was more than upset with him or she wouldn't have called him by his devil name.

"Lucifer?" The woman lowered her hand slowly, the sunlight filling her piercing, pale blue eyes. She wasn't as old as he'd thought, though she was a good twenty years his senior. She grabbed hold of the arms of the chair and sat upright, staring at Lucas. "Are you Lucifer?" she asked. Lucas saw what he thought was fear in her eyes.

"I'm not the devil," he ground out. "So you needn't worry that I'm here to take your soul."

"My soul's been gone for years now," she said, probably because of the husband and baby that Romney told him she'd lost.

"Look, I feel your pain, Lady Veronica, but forgive me if I won't stand here and cater to your fits of depression," Lucas ground out.

"Mayhap we should go now." Amber grabbed Lucas by the arm and started for the door.

"Wait!" They turned back to see the woman standing.

"She hasn't stood without help in years," said Helen.

"Aunt Veronica, sit back down before you fall," urged Romney.

"What do you know about my pain?" she asked.

"What?" asked Lucas, confused by her question.

"What do you know about a hard life and pain and losses?" She started crying and Lucas shook his head and sighed.

"Now you've done it, Lucifer," Amber said again, still very angry with him "You need to apologize."

"I'm sorry I made you cry," he told the woman. "But no one's life is as miserable as mine so I cannot say I feel pity for you, if that's what you're looking for."

"I think we all should go now," said Sir Romney, and they headed for the door.

"Nay!" Lady Veronica shouted out. "Tell me, Lucifer, have you ever lost a loved one?"

"I can't say I have," he admitted. "Because I had no loved ones in my life – ever. And I rather like it that way as it keeps my head from becoming clouded. Forgive me for saying, but you need to forget about your past and move on, Lady Veronica. If not, you are going to lose whatever you have in the present."

With that, he turned around and rushed from the room, hearing her voice whisper, "Lucifer. You've come to get me after all."

CHAPTER 18

Daughters of the Dagger

Lucas sat on the wooden bench near the fire in the great hall, not wanting to sit next to Amber during the meal since she was still angry with him for the way he'd talked to Lady Veronica earlier. He, himself, was so upset by the turn of events since they'd arrived in Canterbury, first with the ruby and now with this, that he couldn't even eat.

"What's the matter, Lucas?" asked Sir Romney, sitting down next to him.

"What isn't the matter?" Lucas took a last swig of his ale and banged the metal tankard down on the trestle table.

"Don't worry about the incident with Lady Veronica. She's been like that ever since I've known her. I guess the incident happened just before my older sister, Helen, was born. My aunt moved overseas many years ago, I think trying to escape her memories. I thought when she'd returned that she had been healed of her inner wounds, but I was wrong. There is nothing anyone can do about it. We just learn to live with it, that's all."

"I don't know how you put up with such nonsense," he told him. "I certainly wouldn't."

"Well, mayhap we won't have to anymore," said Romney, staring across the room.

Lucas looked up to see Lady Veronica enter the room with Helen right behind her. She looked beautiful, dressed in a long taupe gown that hugged her at the bodice and trailed down her thin waist to the ground. Her golden hair was pulled upward in a half-braid and she wore an airy, short, veiled headpiece attached to the metal, jewel-embedded circlet on her head. Lucas swore she looked ten years younger than she had looked while sitting and sulking in her room.

Her eyes scanned the area, and Amber noticed and jumped up, running to her side. They conversed for a moment, and then Amber pointed in his direction and started leading the lady toward him.

"God's eyes, they are coming over here," Lucas grumbled. "I just want to be left alone."

"Remember the Code of Conduct," Sir Romney reminded him. "Try to act respectful like a knight and mayhap she won't start crying again."

Lucas didn't really care about acting like a knight nor did he care about ladies crying right now. All he wanted was to be left alone to think. And Amber bringing the addlepated woman right to him was the last thing he needed.

He got to his feet, intending to leave, but Amber called out to him. "Lucas, Lucas, wait!"

Well, at least she wasn't calling him Lucifer anymore. He bit back an oath and tried to smile, though he was really ready to dart out the door.

"Thank you, Lucifer," said Lady Veronica, coming to join him. The woman actually had a smile on her face and Lucas didn't know if she was happy or just about to have another crazy fit.

"My name is Lucas," he snapped.

"It is?"

"He likes to be called Lucas but his real name is Lucifer," Amber intervened. "Have you ever heard such an odd name?"

"Just once before," the lady said, her eyes burning into Lucas, making him even more uncomfortable. "But that was a long time ago, and I never thought I'd ever hear it again."

"Well, if I have anything to do with it, you won't," he assured her.

"It's the most wonderful name I've ever heard," she said with a smile.

Now Lucas knew the woman was mad. No one ever thought his devil name was wonderful.

"Was there something you wanted?" he asked, wishing to be done with this quickly.

Helen rushed up to join them then and Mirabelle was with her.

"My aunt has seemed to have had a miraculous recovery and she said she has you to thank," relayed Helen.

"I'm named after the devil, not God," he told her. "I don't do miracles so you don't have me to thank."

"Oh, yes I do," the woman said. "Before you came to me, I thought I had no hope of ever being happy again. But now I know I can be happy. You were right when you said I need to forget about the past and live in the present and that's exactly what I intend to do."

"That's wonderful," he said. "I'm happy for your revelation. Now, if you'll excuse me, I need to be on my way."

"We haven't even had time to get to know each other. Please stay. I have so much I want to tell you."

"No disrespect, my lady, but I doubt you'd have anything to say to me that could possibly hold my interest. Now if you'll excuse me, I bid you a goodnight."

He turned his back on her, meaning to go to the chamber Sir Romney had given him to use during his stay, but stopped dead in his tracks when he heard her reply.

"I once had a child I had to abandon on the steps of the church. His name was Lucifer."

Lucas' body stiffened. He felt a course of anxiety wash through him. Could this woman be his mother? After all this time, could he finally have found the woman who abandoned him three and twenty years ago, leaving his life in the hands of Father Armand? He wanted to know, and at the same time he didn't. He didn't need a mother who abandoned him in his time of greatest need coming back to him now. He had his life planned and he was about to get everything he'd ever dreamed of. With one last task, he'd be able to attain the wealth, the title, and the castle, and live the rest of his days the way he wanted. Why did this have to be happening now?

"I'm not your son, if that's what you think." He didn't turn around, and she came up and lightly touched his elbow.

"Were you found on the steps of Bowerwood three and twenty years ago and taken in and raised by a priest named Father Armand?"

"He was," Amber answered for him excitedly.

The anger inside him grew stronger. All the loneliness, the suffering, and the hope of her someday coming back to claim him year after year welled up in his chest and threatened to choke him. She hadn't returned for him, and if he hadn't come to Canterbury Castle, she still wouldn't have sought him out. She knew where she left him, and she couldn't take the time to collect him again after all these years. So why should he even care about her now?

"I think you have the wrong man," he ground out. "My mother abandoned me on the steps of the church and paid the priest to take me." He turned and stared into her eyes – the eyes that were birdlike and light blue and looked a lot like his. Her hair was blond as well, and he didn't want to admit she could be his mother. "I hate my mother for not coming back for me and I hate her even more for leaving me with a priest who thought to raise me as a monk. So if you really are my mother, then you were best left in that dark room feeling pity for yourself. Because, I swear to God, I want nothing to do with you!"

He rushed out of the great hall feeling dazed and confused and very angry. As he ran down the hall to his bedchamber, he heard the woman who'd called herself his mother crying once again.

CHAPTER 19

Daughters of the Dagger

$\mathcal{A}$mber helped Lady Veronica sit on the bench, apologizing for Lucas' bad behavior. The woman was crying hysterically, causing a ruckus in the great hall.

"Get her back to her room," Sir Romney ordered his sister, Helen. "And someone go talk some sense into Lucas and tell him he needs to apologize to her at once to make her stop crying."

"I'll go talk to Lucas," Amber offered, hurrying down the hall and stopping in front of the door that was his chamber. She took a deep breath and then released it, not knowing what she was going to say to him. Her heart went out to him because she knew how hard it was to be raised without a mother. She wished more than anything that her mother could have somehow returned to her. But now Lucas had a miraculous thing happen to him and he was going to throw it all away.

She'd felt his pain of abandonment and seen the hurt in his eyes when Lady Veronica told him she was his mother. He was confused, and she couldn't blame him for being angry. She didn't know the woman's reasons for abandoning him all those years ago, but it did seem that if the woman was a noble, she could have come back to get him. If she loved him, she would have.

That meant to Amber, and she was sure to Lucas as well, that the woman hadn't loved him. Lucas needed love and understanding right now, and Amber decided she was the one who was going to give it to him.

She straightened her stance and threw open the door and barged in, not giving him the chance to deny her entry.

Amber stopped and looked around the room, but didn't see Lucas anywhere.

The door slowly swung closed on its own, and there was Lucas standing behind it with his arms crossed and his back against the wall.

"I knew you'd follow me," he ground out. "I'm warning you now, I don't want your prayers, I don't want your scolding, and I definitely don't want –"

She grabbed him by the front of his tunic and pulled him to her, fastening her lips upon his in a forceful kiss. Then she let go of his tunic and he fell back against the wall with his arms splayed out on either side of him.

"I didn't expect that," he said, looking more than shocked.

"Well, would you rather have me reprimanding you for what you did?"

"I highly expected that. Why did you kiss me?"

"I don't know," she said, shaking her head, tears welling in her eyes. "Probably for the same reason you ran out of the room when you discovered Lady Veronica was your mother."

"Because you hate me?"

"Nay, because I am just as confused as you. But one thing I do know is that I love you, Lucas. I just couldn't bring myself to admit it before."

"You did admit it, the night you got drunk and tore off your clothes."

"That was the wine talking, but I'm sober, now," she explained. "I am tired of living in fear. Fear that my family is going to go to Hell if I don't sacrifice myself for them by becoming a nun. Fear that I'll never find my true love, or ever know what it feels like to make love with a man. Fear that –"

It was her turn to be surprised now, as he reached out and pulled her to him and fastened his lips roughly upon hers in a punishing kiss. Then he released her just as quickly.

"What was that for?" she asked, her fingers going to her lips which were now burning with passion.

"Just for being you."

She reached back up and kissed him again and, this time, his hands closed around her waist. As he slowly slid them downwards, he gripped her hips.

"Make love to me, Lucas. I need to know how it feels," she begged him.

"Don't tempt me, my little, pure dove, because I just might do it."

"I want you to. Please. I don't want to be pure anymore."

"You've begged me for this before, and then the next day you've changed your mind and despised me."

"I could never despise you, Lucas. When I saw the pain in your eyes when you found your mother, I realized that you are the strongest man to walk the earth."

"I walked away from her," he pointed out. "That was being a coward."

"Nay, just the opposite. It takes a strong man to stand up for what he believes."

"I don't believe in anything, so you are wrong."

"You believe in yourself, don't you?" When he didn't answer, she continued. "I believe in you, Lucas."

"Well, don't. Because you might end up sorely disappointed."

"I know you have had such sorrow in your life and you don't deserve it. You have every right to hate your mother for what she did, and every right to never speak to her again if you so choose."

"I have never felt the love of anyone in my life, Amber. I am not about to start now. Not with a mother, not with you. I don't need love in my life. I've survived this long without it and I've learned to accept it. Do you understand me? If we couple tonight, it doesn't mean I love you or that I ever will. Let's make that point perfectly clear right now before we go any further."

She felt a tear drip down her cheek, as she understood him perfectly now. He was just as frightened as her. About coupling with her, and about the subject of love in general. But that was all going to change. She wanted to give him the happiness he deserved and find the answers she sought as well, even if he never said he loved her in return.

"Hush up and make love to me," she said, noticing the surprise in his eyes.

"You don't sound like a nun, Amber. If you do this with me, there's no going back."

"And neither do I want to. It's not my fate to become a nun, and I've realized that now. I think you knew it all along."

"I knew it from the moment I kissed you in the infirmary. You have just as much need and passion repressed inside of you as I do."

"Then let's not be repressed any longer. Couple with me, Lucas, please."

He grabbed her by the shoulders and turned her quickly, pinning her against the wall. His face was close to hers and his knee parted her legs as he pushed his groin against hers.

"Do you feel how hard I am?" he asked her. "You'd better not be toying with me and you sure as hell better not be changing your mind as soon as you become scared, little girl. Because whether you know it or not, you're doing naught but tempting the devil."

"I thought you didn't believe in the devil," she said boldly, looking into his eyes that were filled with lust and tinged with anger. She did feel scared right now, but she wouldn't back down, not for anything. This is the night she would lose her virginity, and this is the man she wanted to take it from her.

"I didn't believe in the devil. That is, not until you told me to believe in myself."

"You're not the devil, Lucas," she told him, feeling her body starting to tremble from the anticipation.

"You might change your mind about that in the next day or so," he said, almost sounding as if there were something he wasn't telling her.

She felt his need for her growing beneath his braies, and she bravely reached out and untied his hose. His hands loosened the grip upon her and he backed up slightly. Then, all the while staring into his piercing blue eyes, she slowly slid her back down the wall, pulling his braies and hose with her as she went. His freed arousal was right in front of her face now, as she fell to her knees on the ground before him.

"With a bold move like that, you'd better be planning on doing something other than praying right now," he warned her.

She felt her body trembling, and didn't answer. She'd heard how to do this, and she was curious, but it scared her to death. She reached up and took a hold of his form, then closing her eyes, she parted her lips, opened her mouth, and bent forward.

He gasped and his legs almost gave way under him. She didn't really know what she was doing, but she got the impression she was doing it correctly by the sound of his labored breathing.

"Bid the devil, how the hell does a nun know how to do that?" he asked.

She pulled away long enough to tell him. "I've been talking to Mirabelle," she explained, resuming her position but, this time, sliding forward down his shaft. She felt his knees bending slightly and his hand came around the back of her head and he growled like a bear just like Mirabelle had said, pushing himself into her so far that she almost choked. Then he moved away from her quickly, breaking the connection.

"Dammit," he cursed, and then dragged a hand over his head, his fingers gripping at his hair in frustration. "Amber, come here," he said in a low voice. He reached under her arms and pulled her to a standing position, still pressed up against the wall. "Tell me right now that you really mean what you said and that you're not just toying with me. Because if you are, I don't think I can take it."

"I don't want to be a nun, Lucas. I promise you it's true." Her voice trembled as she answered. "I want you. I want to spend my life with you. And if you don't want that, then I'll respect it, but I want you tonight either way."

"No changing your mind?" he asked. "This is the last time I'm going to ask. By the rood, Amber, you'd better be sure. Because once I start, I won't be able to stop."

"No changing my mind," she said, feeling her body becoming aroused.

He came down on her like a man possessed, kissing her like there was no tomorrow. "I've wanted you for so long," he said, his hands caressing her breasts right through her gown. Then he reached behind her and took hold of the cloth of her gown roughly, and almost ripped her clothes right off of her in the hurry to undress her.

Since she had no undergarments, she now stood there naked. His eyes glowed with the intensity of a man about to take a woman to his bed, the desire within them so vibrant and alive that she found herself scared but, at the same time, very aroused.

He lowered his head, nipping at her collarbone as his hands squeezed her breasts.

"Oh!" she cried out, her legs becoming weak beneath her. This felt so good that it was sending a shiver of pleasure dancing across her skin. Then he looked at her and took her hands in his, placing them on the front of his tunic, closing her fists until she gripped the cloth.

"Rip it off of me, Amber," he commanded.

"I . . . I can't," she said, her labored breathing making the rise and fall of her chest more pronounced. She wanted to oblige, but it felt so wanton and so wicked that she just couldn't bring herself to do it.

"Do it!" he ordered. "If you really mean what you say, then show me you are willing to drop your guard and veer away from your pious ways."

She thought she'd already shown him that by attempting the little trick with her mouth that Mirabelle had told her men love. She hesitated, and when she did, he used his own hands over hers, and pulled. The sound of tearing cloth filled the room, and with his guidance, she ripped the tunic from his body. He now stood there naked as well.

"Oh, my!" she gasped, realizing what had just happened.

"I have waited so long, and I will wait no longer."

He pulled her to him in a tantalizing kiss, his tongue reaching out to part her lips and enter her mouth. She felt herself suddenly vibrating between her thighs, realizing that a part of him was inside her body. Then he reached out and cupped her breasts, bringing her nipples to rigid peaks. She arched her back in elation while he covered one breast with his mouth, then pushed them together and buried his face between them.

He was hungry and rough and she found she liked this dangerous, dark side of him, though she never thought she would.

Both of them let out all their pent-up emotions. She was making noises of passion that she never knew were in her.

"Let me show you what you would have missed out on by being a nun, sweetheart. He slid his hands down the front of her, suddenly hunkering down and tasting her very intimately in her most private spot, the way she'd done to him.

She gasped as he worked his magic with his lips and his tongue, knowing exactly what he was doing. She cried out as she felt herself finding that release she needed so desperately. Her legs opened farther and she gripped at his hair to keep from falling over.

"Lucas, I never knew it could feel . . . so good."

"You haven't felt anything yet, Sister," he said, about driving her wild with his words.

He picked her up, spreading her legs for her to hold on around his waist as he made his way to the bed. Laying her down upon it, he straddled his naked body atop hers and kissed her so passionately she thought she would burst. The anticipation was maddening, the excitement beyond control. She, the virtuous one of all her sisters, the one who was going to be a nun and give up the chance of coupling forever, was finding out that she would have been making a very big mistake.

"Lucas, I need you inside me. Please. I need to know how it feels."

"Oh, you will, my little dove, you will."

He positioned his manhood at her door, just dangling himself above her.

"I'm not gentle, I warn you. I hope this doesn't scare you."

"Nay," she said. "I told you, I want to know everything there is to know about making love."

"Everything? All in one night?" This is the first time she'd seen him grin since she'd entered the room.

"Is there much to know?" she asked, being very innocent of the act.

"Well, just put it this way, sweetheart. I am so looking forward to being the one to teach you. And I assure you, one night will not nearly be enough time to learn."

With that, he lifted her legs up around his waist and pushed himself into her. She felt the barrier of her innocence give way as he took her maidenhead and made her a full-fledged woman. He used his hands to make her hips rock back and forth, thrusting into her at the same time. And wanting to learn, she continued the movement on her own, getting a slight nod of approval from him.

She closed her eyes, reveling in the glorious feeling, now

knowing what she'd been missing. Then she felt her passion climbing again, and as their mating dance continued, they were both brought to their peaks.

Tonight, she had let loose with all her fears and inhibitions, and found a side of her that had been ignored for much too long. She would be there for Lucas, and love him, even if he never loved her in return. And she knew now why she'd joined the abbey. It wasn't to atone for her family's sins, or to live a life in secluded prayer within its cloistered walls. Nay, it was fate bringing her to him. Lucas was the reason she had to be there. God had guided her to the abbey, but really guided her to find Lucas. And after today, things would never be the same again.

CHAPTER 20

*L*ucas leaned over and gently kissed Amber atop her head, then picked up his travel bags and headed toward the door. Thankfully, he'd had another tunic in his pack, because after that wild night he never could have worn the shredded one again. It was early in the morning, and the sun hadn't yet started to rise. Father Armand was going to be arriving any day and he needed to find a way to steal the Regale ruby before the cathedral was filled with people again.

He'd had the most wonderful night of his life coupling with Amber and sleeping with her snuggled up in his arms. This is what he'd wanted since the day he'd met her dressed in that silly habit. She'd never be a nun now. Although he should be happy he got what he wanted, it was like a stab to his heart with a sharp knife.

He looked at her lying there, sprawled out naked across the bed, tempting him to take her again, but asleep and oblivious of the fact she affected him like no other woman ever had. She wasn't a pure, little dove anymore, and he felt like the devil for being the one to take her virginity from her.

Though she'd begged him to do it, he shouldn't have done it.

He didn't deserve anyone as good and as loving as her. God's eyes, she even told him she loved him! That only made matters worse, because as soon as she found out he stole the Regale ruby, she would be back to hating him again.

But he had to steal it, he tried to convince himself. He'd lived a life of sacrifice and pain, and he refused to go back to those ways. He had no one his entire life except the man who raised him and, right now, he hated Father Armand almost as much as he hated himself for what he was about to do.

But after today, none of that would matter. Once he supplied the priest with his end of the deal, he'd have a castle and lands to go with the title of knight that the archbishop said he was going to bestow upon him. Father Armand had said he could claim Helen, the lady of the castle for himself, but he didn't want her. The only woman he wanted was Amber.

A knot twisted in his stomach. He didn't deserve any of this. Who was he kidding? He hated Father Armand for expecting him to do his evil bidding, and he hated the crazy woman named Lady Veronica who claimed to be his mother. He didn't want to believe it was true but, deep in his gut, he knew that it was. He should go talk to the woman, but he couldn't bring himself to do it.

Deep down, he didn't want to know why she'd left him on the church doorstep and not returned for him after all these years. No reason could be so important that it justified abandoning a baby. For this, he wouldn't even give her the chance to try to explain. As soon as he was Lord of Canterbury Castle, the first thing he'd do is throw her out and abandon her the same way she'd done to him.

He turned and laid his hand on the door to open it, hearing Amber's sweet, angelic voice coming from the bed.

"Lucas? Where are you going so early?"

"I have something to attend to," he told her without turning around.

"Let me come with you." He heard her starting to get off the bed.

"Nay!" he said sharply, turning to see the startled look in her eyes as the light from the nearly extinguished bedtime candle reflected in her big, green orbs.

"Why not?"

He couldn't even pretend he didn't hear the hurt in her voice.

"I'll be back later," he told her, hurrying out of the room before she had the chance to try to make him change his mind.

Amber's heart fell at Lucas' refusal to take her with him. She didn't understand where he was going so early and why she couldn't go with him. After the night they'd spent together, she thought she'd broken through the walls that Lucas put up between them.

What they'd shared was wonderful, and though he said he would never love her, she thought, over time, she could change his mind. She walked over to the wall where Lucas had undressed her last night and picked up her gown and donned it. She had a feeling something was really troubling him and it had nothing to do with her.

It could be that he was still upset about his mother, but she had a feeling it was more than that. Last night when she'd told him he wasn't the devil, he'd said something odd that confused her. He told her that she might not think that way in the next day or so, which led her to believe there was something going on that she didn't know about.

Something dangerous perhaps, or immoral or illegal. If not, why would he think that she'd ever consider him the devil?

"I've got to follow him and try to find out what he's up to," she said aloud, pulling on her shoes. Lucas would be upset if he thought she didn't trust him, and also angry that he'd told her to stay here and she didn't obey. Still, she didn't care. She'd seen the tension on his face. Something was bothering him immensely and she had the feeling he was in trouble. And if he was in trouble, then she wanted to be there to help him in any way possible.

* * *

Lucas sneaked into Canterbury Cathedral just as the sun had started to rise on the horizon. He had planned on being done with his little task and out of here before the sun rose, but he'd overslept. He'd been so exhausted from making love with Amber so many times last night that he could barely move this morning.

He'd had the best night of his life, and never thought the little dove would be such a frolicking vixen in bed. She had more stamina than half the whores he'd slept with throughout his life. But she wasn't a whore. She was a lady. A lady who used to be a pure dove before last night, no thanks to him.

She'd said it was her free will that made her want to couple with him but, somehow, he still felt guilty. She'd been so virtuous and pious before she'd met him. That was one of the things that had attracted him to her in the first place.

Well, after the lessons he gave her in lovemaking last night and her willingness to learn and try everything he could throw at her, his pure, little dove was gone for good. This saddened him in a way. Although he didn't want her to be a nun, neither did he want her spoiled for whatever man she ended up marrying.

She said she loved him, and he had feelings for her as well, but they could never be married. She was still the shining example of morals, goodness, charity and inner strength in his eyes. He, on the other hand, was deceitful, greedy, lustful and about to become a thief. He'd sold his soul to the devil ever since the day he'd decided to leave the monastery and become a mercenary. He killed men for money, and he paid women to sleep with him. He lusted after what he didn't deserve, and now he'd even turned away his own mother.

He didn't know who he was anymore, but the one thing he did know was that Amber deserved someone better than him. He'd never be able to live like a knight by the Code of Conduct. And he'd never be able to tell her he loved her, though in his heart he felt that mayhap he did.

Still, he refused to love or be loved, that's all there was to it. Love only made a man weak, and gave him reasons to sacrifice things in order to make a woman happy. He had a plan and, dammit, not even Amber was going to ruin it.

If she knew what he was about to do, she'd talk him out of it and make him confess the intention, probably to the archbishop himself. Then he'd land himself in the dungeon and probably be sentenced to death. He'd go to his death never having had the chance to live the life he wanted so badly that he'd do anything to get it.

Nay, he wouldn't change his mind about this. He'd do the job he came to do and then live the life he had planned for himself. And if Amber happened to be a part of it, then all the better. But either way, he would never be able to let her know what he'd done. Because although she said she loved him, he could guarantee she wouldn't love him anymore when she discovered the man he truly was, after all.

By the rood, the last thing he wanted was to become weak and tell her he loved her and then end up abandoned again when she decided to walk out of his life forever. Nay, he wouldn't give her the chance to do that. He would never fall prey to love. He would never give anyone the opportunity of walking away from him again. Nay, he'd never again feel the burning pain of being abandoned if he had anything to do with it.

He crept down the long, secret hallway that Sir Romney had taken them down the day before. It led to the back of the sacristy and the small room that held the holy vestments and things used for the mass. Just beside it was the secret shrine to Thomas Becket that housed the Regale ruby.

He walked softly and silently and stopped in the shadows, scoping out the situation. The door to the room with the ruby was closed and outside it, sleeping on the chair in front, was a guard.

His heart raced and the blood pumped through his veins excitedly. This was going to be a lot easier than he thought. He took a step forward, his travel bags over one shoulder, but stopped suddenly when he heard a noise from the sacristy in the adjoining room and a clang of something metal hitting the floor. There was a voice that followed of someone grumbling but he couldn't make out what they were saying.

He didn't dare breathe, as he was standing right next to the guard who stirred and repositioned himself on the chair at the sound of the noise. Thankfully, he never opened his eyes and, in a minute, he was snoring again.

Lucas carefully reached out to open the door but, to his dismay, it was locked. He was trying to think of a way to pick the lock when he noticed the key hanging from a piece of twine tied to the belt of the guard.

He looked around quickly, hoping whoever was in the sacristy wouldn't emerge. Then taking his dagger from his side, he carefully cut the twine and gathered up the key. Replacing his dagger, he put the key in the lock and turned it, gaining entry into the room.

He heard another noise from the sacristy and quickly closed the door. It was dim inside the small room, but there was one nearly extinguished candle in an open jar that was burning in honor to the late saint. As he lifted his eyes upward, he saw the glimmering Regale ruby sitting like a king on its throne atop the pedestal on the high shelf. He wasted no time admiring its beauty, though he could have stayed there all day looking at it. Instead, he put a toe on the dais and raised himself up and gingerly touched the ruby in its metal holder.

He took one more look at it glittering in the light of the fire, and the thought of keeping it for himself and not giving it to Father Armand flitted through his brain. But he could never do such a thing, though it was probably worth more than a castle. So before he was tempted again, he closed his fingers around the ruby, getting ready to lift it from its holder. Instantly, he saw Amber's disappointed face in his mind. He froze in mid-motion.

Was this all worth it, he wondered? If Amber ever found out what he did, she would not want him. He felt a knot in his gut thinking about living without her. He released his hand slowly. Then the thought of Father Armand and how the man was sure to make Lucas' life miserable if he didn't do his bidding entered his mind. He closed his fingers around the ruby again.

Then he thought of last night with Amber and how much she meant to him. She'd given up being a nun for him. He released the ruby. But without a castle and lands, what kind of life could he possibly have, not able to give Amber all she truly deserved? He grabbed the ruby and snatched it from its holder to examine it. The inner struggle battling inside his brain was driving him mad. He no longer knew what to do.

He stepped down from the dais to the floor, holding up the ruby in the light of the candle and, for the first time in a long time, he prayed.

"Help me know what to do," he whispered. "God, please send me a sign."

The sound of a man's voice from behind him startled him, as he heard the words, "Well, Lucifer, are you going to steal the ruby or not?"

CHAPTER 21

Daughters of the Dagger

Amber hurried down the corridor and out toward the garden, having seen Lucas heading for the stables when she looked out the bedchamber window. If she cut through the gardens, it would save her time getting to the stables. She'd have to borrow a horse somehow to keep up with him if she was going to know where he headed this early in the morning.

She might have been able to do that if she hadn't spotted Lady Veronica sitting on a stone bench inside the castle gardens, weeping softly. She was going to turn around and sneak away rather than to be slowed down right now, but the sound of her weeping was so sad that she couldn't leave a woman in need.

Her training as a nun took over, and she found herself going to talk to Lady Veronica instead of following Lucas. She must have sat there for an hour with the woman, trying to comfort her before she actually got her to speak.

"Don't cry, my lady," she said, once again. "Perhaps you can tell me what has made you so sad."

The woman wiped her eyes in a hand cloth she pulled from her sleeve. The first rays of the morning sun hit her face and Amber noticed her piercing blue eyes that reminded her a lot of

Lucas' eyes. Finally, her attempts paid off as the woman decided to speak to her.

"Oh, Sister Amber, I am so happy you are here. I looked for you late last night in the great hall, but I couldn't find you anywhere."

"Please, just call me Amber," she said, knowing that after last night she was the furthest thing from a nun. Thoughts of the outrageous things she'd done with Lucas were stuck in her mind. Even though she had liked it, she found herself feeling a little wanton and guilty this morning. "I am here now," she told the woman rather than to explain where she'd spent the night. "How can I help you?"

"I want to talk to Lucifer," she said. "But he doesn't want anything to do with me, though I can't say I blame him."

"Mayhap, if you'd like him to warm up to you, you can start by calling him Lucas, as he despises the name Lucifer."

"I will," she said with a large nod. "Of course. Lucas," she repeated.

"Lady Veronica, if you don't mind me asking, why did you abandon Lucas in the first place?"

"I had no choice," she explained. "I was young and foolish and made some wrong choices by letting a man talk me into going to bed with him. I wasn't married, and I became pregnant. So when the baby was born, I had to give him up."

"So you were never married, nor did you lose a husband?"

"Nay."

"I don't understand. Why didn't you just marry Lucas' father?"

Her head snapped up and her eyes opened wide. "I couldn't do that."

"Why not? Was he already married with a wife, perhaps?"

"Nay, that wasn't the case."

"Did you love him?"

"I loved him, but not in the way you think."

"I am so confused, Lady Veronica. Was his father a warlord

perhaps? Or just a peasant and that's why you couldn't marry him?"

"Please, Amber, do not ask me about Lucas' father because that is something I cannot discuss with anyone. I haven't been able to for the past three and twenty years and won't be able to for the rest of my life."

"Do you love Lucas?" she asked boldly.

Her hand reached out and closed around Amber's. "I have loved Lucas since the day he was born and I held him in my arms and he looked up at me and smiled."

"He smiled?" she asked, thinking it was probably the only time he'd done that in his life, or near to it anyway. "Why didn't you go back to get him from the monastery?" she asked. "Surely, you must have known that Father Armand never found a family to foster him."

"I paid Father Armand to keep him there." She looked down and folded her hands on her lap. "That was probably the worst decision I ever made, but I had honestly hoped to go back someday and bring him to live with me."

"Why didn't that happen?"

"Because Father Armand decided he would keep the boy and raise him as a monk instead."

"I don't understand. Why would he do that? How could he do that, if the child was yours?"

"Sister Amber, I have kept a deep, dark secret inside me for many years concerning the identity of Lucas' father. I've lived in fear every day by how people would be affected if I were to reveal this information to anyone. I thought I was doing the right thing, and even refused to marry because I knew I didn't deserve to have other children after I abandoned the one I had. But I have been so miserable all these years, and now my own son hates me because of my decision. I need to tell someone, Sister, as I believe it is time. I hope I can trust you with my secret."

"Of course you can trust me," she said, patting the woman's

hand, thinking that Lady Veronica would be more shocked with knowing what Amber, a novice, had done with her son last night. "I am sure it isn't as bad as you think."

"It is," she said. "You see, Lucas' father is –"

Just then, the church bells from Canterbury Cathedral clanged frantically in the distance. People started to appear from nowhere in the castle courtyard, wondering what was going on. Even Amber stood up and looked toward the cathedral in the distance.

"What is that?" she asked.

"Those are the warning bells of Canterbury," said the woman, getting up and rushing toward the courtyard. "Hurry," she said. "Something horrible must have happened."

They ran to the courtyard where people were buzzing around in confusion. Helen ran up with Sir Romney. Mirabelle was right behind them.

"What has happened?" Helen asked.

"We don't know," answered Amber.

"Those are the warning bells," relayed Lady Veronica. "Something must have happened in Canterbury."

Just then, a messenger rode in atop a horse, and Sir Romney ran up to greet him. He conversed briefly with the man as the rest of them followed him.

"What is it?" asked Amber. "Is something wrong?"

"Aye," answered Sir Romney, turning to them with a sullen look on his face. "It seems as if the warning bells are ringing because someone has stolen the Regale ruby."

CHAPTER 22

Daughters of the Dagger

"The ruby's been stolen?" Amber could not believe what she was hearing.

"That's right," said the messenger. "It seems someone broke into the room that houses the true ruby and took it early this morning. Not many people knew that the ruby in the main part of the church's shrine was a fake and that the true one was guarded behind the sacristy. So whoever stole it knew what he was doing."

"Where was the guard when this all happened?" asked Sir Romney.

"Aye, he would be able to identify the thief, wouldn't he?" asked Amber.

"He was sleeping at the time," said the messenger. "And the archbishop is not happy about it."

"I can't imagine he would be," answered Helen.

"Well, it's a good thing we got to see it before it was stolen," said Mirabelle.

"Yes," Amber answered, suddenly remembering that she had caught Lucas with his hand on the Regale ruby yesterday. She had thought nothing about it then, and mayhap wouldn't question it now, except for the fact that Lucas had been acting odd this morning when he left with his travel bags earlier. "Sir Romney, have you seen Lucas at all this morning?"

"Nay, I haven't, why do you ask?"

"There he is now," said Mirabelle, pointing toward the entry gate.

Amber looked up to see Lucas riding into the courtyard. He hopped off his horse quickly and handed the reins to the stable boy. She ran over to greet him.

"Lucas, where have you been?" she asked. She wanted to throw her arms around him and give him a kiss, but since everyone still thought she was a novice, she decided not to do anything like that. Besides, she didn't know how Lucas would react after last night either.

"I went out for a ride," he commented, throwing the travel bags over his shoulder. As he did so, she caught the scent of incense clinging to his clothes. He turned and headed for the keep. "Why? Is something the matter?"

She ran to catch up to him, wondering where he was going so quickly. "Haven't you heard the warning bells of Canterbury Cathedral? It seems someone has stolen the Regale ruby. Do you know anything about it?"

He stopped in his tracks and turned to her. "What are you saying? Because you almost sound as if you are accusing me of stealing it."

"I didn't say anything of the sort. I was just wondering if you heard anything when you stopped by the cathedral this morning?"

"Who told you I was at the cathedral?" he asked, his eyes narrowing in the process. "Were you following me?"

She didn't like the way he was acting. Something wasn't right. He seemed distracted and jittery. She'd never seen him act this way before.

"No one had to tell me. I can smell frankincense on your

clothes. That's the same scent I smelled in the cathedral during the mass the other day."

"You think since you're a nun you know about these things but you don't. Now, please, just leave me alone." He marched past his mother and the others without saying a word, and headed into the keep.

"What's the matter with him?" asked Mirabelle, shaking her head.

"Aye. He's acting like he's angry," said Sir Romney. "Amber, did something happen between you two last night?"

All eyes were on her, and she suddenly felt as if she were standing there naked and they were about to judge her for what she'd done. Something had happened, indeed. But she wasn't going to tell them. And what happened, in her opinion, was a happy thing, so she had no idea why Lucas was acting so very angry.

"I'll see if I can find out what's bothering him," she said. She ran into the keep and to the bedchamber, opening the door and walking in without knocking.

Lucas was on his knees looking at something inside his travel bag and shoved it back in quickly when he saw her.

"Don't you ever knock?" he growled, taking the conjoined bags and throwing them over the back of the chair.

"I didn't think I had to," she answered. "After last night."

"Forget about last night. I told you how I felt before we did anything."

Her heart dropped. "What do you mean?"

"I hope you're not getting your hopes up about us."

She didn't like the way this conversation was going. She'd given of herself freely last night. Although he said he'd never love her, he didn't say he was going to hate her in the morning either.

"It almost sounds like you're trying to say goodbye."

"Mayhap that would be best."

Amber felt as if she were going to cry. How could this be

happening? They'd just had a wonderful night together and now he was acting like it meant nothing to him.

"I gave up being a nun for you," she said. "I gave up my virginity as well. I know you said you would never love me and I am not asking you to. But dammit, Lucas, I will not stand here and take this abuse from you. I don't deserve it."

She saw the sadness in his eyes then, and he walked over to her and held her in his arms. She couldn't help it, and she started crying and put her head against his chest.

"Don't cry, my little dove," he whispered and placed a kiss atop her head. "I wish things could be different. I hope someday you'll understand that I was only trying to make a better life for myself. A life that would hopefully include you."

"We can do that," she told him. "Let me help you. I want to be a part of your life."

He held her at arm's length and looked into her eyes. She felt fear and sadness within his gaze and also the fiery shadow of anger and hate.

"You'd be better off without me, sweetheart. Don't you understand that? I don't deserve you. You are too good for someone with a blackened soul."

"Lucas, what is bothering you? I've never seen you like this. Please, talk to me."

"I'm sorry, Amber, but I can't."

"Is it something I did? Because if so, I am sorry."

"This has nothing to do with you. Now please stop asking me questions."

Just then, the sound of the straight trumpet was heard and Lucas ran to the window. Amber followed, looking out into the courtyard to see the visitor who was being announced.

"Father Armand from Bowerwood graces us with his presence," announced the herald.

"Father Armand?" asked Amber, seeing the priest riding into the castle surrounded by several monks, half a dozen guards and, to her surprise, the abbess. "Sister Dulcina is here, too? I wonder why?"

"I'm sure they're just passing through," said Lucas, heading across the room and out the door before she knew what had happened.

She eyed the travel bags hanging over the chair and then looked back out the window. This whole thing was odd. Lucas did not seem surprised in the least to see Father Armand. She hadn't remembered hearing that anyone from the abbey would be traveling to Canterbury anytime soon, and this concerned her. There was something Lucas wasn't telling her, and she was going to find out just what it was.

She raced over to the bags he'd brought back with him this morning, ripped one open and stuck her hand inside. There was something in here he was hiding, she was sure of it. She pulled out a black cloth that was folded neatly into a square, and when she did, something white came out with it and fell to the ground.

"My wimple?" she picked it up from the ground and shook her head, realizing Lucas had been lying when he said he had burned it. Then, looking back to her hand she discovered she was holding her black nun's robe as well. It felt a little heavier than it should, and she carefully unfolded it to see what else Lucas was hiding.

She moved away the last fold to expose the item inside and gasped. There in her hand, winking in the sunlight was none other than the stolen Regale ruby!

CHAPTER 23

Daughters of the Dagger

Lucas was very nervous and afraid that Father Armand would know he was up to something. He greeted the man with a nod, and the priest slipped off the horse and threw his arms around him in a pretentious hug.

Lucas stiffened under his touch. The priest whispered into his ear. "I hope you have what I sent you here to get."

"So nice to see you as well, Father," he said and tried to smile, though he wanted to punch him right now. "It's in my travel bag," he whispered back to him. "But there are too many people around. I'll get it and meet you outside the cathedral."

Lucas didn't give the priest a chance to answer as he turned quickly, meaning to go back up to the room since he'd left in such a hurry that he'd forgotten the bag. But he stopped in his tracks when he saw Amber standing there – wearing her habit.

"Amber?" he asked, eyeing her in her black robe and wimple once again. It was odd seeing her dressed in her habit after what they'd done last night. Especially since she'd told him she no longer wanted to be a nun. "Why are you dressed like that?" he asked.

"She is a novice, and always dresses that way," said Sister Dulcina, waddling over to greet Amber.

"Not anymore," Lucas mumbled under his breath. "Sweetheart, where did you get those clothes?" he asked, already fearing her answer.

"I found them in here," she said, bringing her hand from behind her back and holding up his travel bags. "Do you want to know what else I found in here as well?"

"Amber, stop it," he said under his breath, stepping forward and retrieving the bags from her. He quickly looked inside to make certain the ruby was still there.

"So now you know that I've discovered your little secret," she continued. "Do you want to be the one to tell your mother, or should I? Lady Veronica, please come join us."

His mother stepped out from the shadows and came to her side, followed by Helen. Sir Romney and Mirabelle ran up to see what was going on.

"Hello, Father Armand," said Lady Veronica. "It's been a long time."

Father Armand turned as white as a ghost. "Veronica, what are you doing here?" he asked. "I thought you were in the south of France."

"I've returned, and I told Lucifer he is my son," she said. "I only regret that I didn't fight harder to take him from you all those years ago when you decided to keep him."

"We can talk about this later," said Father Armand, putting his hand on Lucas, intending to leave.

"Nay, why don't we talk about it now?" Lucas pushed the priest's arm off of him. "I'd love to know the whole story."

Father Armand climbed atop his horse. "I guess it was a mistake to come here after all." He reached down and snatched the travel bags from Lucas and turned and took off, riding like the devil out the castle's gate.

"I won't let you get away with this," shouted Lucas, grabbing the reins of his horse from the stable boy and taking off after him.

Amber watched the men riding out of the castle gates and she now felt as if she had done a terrible thing.

"What is going on?" asked the abbess.

"Oh, Sister Dulcina, Lucas needs our help," cried Amber. "I still don't understand everything, but after what I just saw, I think I've misjudged him."

"What do you mean, Sister Amber?" asked the abbess.

Amber pulled off her wimple and handed it to the woman. "First of all, let's get something straight. My name is just Amber, not Sister Amber."

"I don't understand."

"As of last night, I am no longer a virgin and no longer a nun."

Sister Dulcina gasped and put her hand to her mouth, but Mirabelle started clapping and so did everyone in the courtyard.

Amber looked over to Lady Veronica next. "I coupled with your son, Lady Veronica, and I am proud to say that I enjoyed it."

"Sister Amber, please, hold your tongue," cried the abbess, blessing herself and grasping on to the metal cross hanging around her neck.

"I told you, Abbess, I am no longer a novice, and I will speak as freely as I please. Lady Veronica, I love your son. And while I know it seems he hates you, 'tis only because he has never known love from anyone and is frightened of the notion. I know if he just took the time to get to know you that he would accept you into his heart. But he is very troubled and confused, and needs our help. Today, inside Lucas' travel bag, I discovered the stolen Regale ruby."

Gasps went up from the crowd. Sir Romney stepped forward and pulled his sword from its sheath. "I will find him and bring it back," he offered.

"He didn't do it of his own accord," said Amber. "I know it now. And I have the means to prove it."

"Then let's go get them before they get away." Sir Romney jumped atop his horse. "Helen, tell your guards to follow. We have to stop them and bring the ruby back to the archbishop."

"I'm coming, too," said Amber, rushing over and mounting a horse.

"Don't go without me," said Lady Veronica.

"Give me your hand and you can ride with me." Amber took the woman's hand and helped her mount the horse.

"I like you, Amber," said Veronica. "I can see why my son would want to be with you. Now, let's go find him because there is something very important I need to tell him that I should have told him the moment I saw him."

"What is that?" Amber turned the horse and headed after them.

"I am going to tell him the identity of his father."

CHAPTER 24

Daughters of the Dagger

Lucas rode his horse hard, right on the tail of Father Armand, knowing that if he didn't catch the man, all his plans would be ruined. He needed to get him to the cathedral and in front of the archbishop, but he was heading in the opposite direction.

Lucas had spent this morning confessing every sin he ever had to the archbishop, right after the man caught him trying to steal the Regale ruby. He'd told him about his greed to attain Canterbury Castle and the deal he'd made with Father Armand.

When the archbishop heard Father Armand's name mentioned, he'd shaken his head and smiled. Lucas was shocked to hear that the archbishop had once been best friends with the priest, and even more surprised to know that for over the last two decades they'd been arch rivals.

Lucas discovered that when the archbishop kept getting promoted and Father Armand was left as only a parish priest, all the trouble had begun. Father Armand was insanely jealous of the archbishop, and that jealousy was what forced him to turn to the ways of the devil. He wanted to attain the wealth and titles of the man that was once his best friend, no matter who he hurt or betrayed in the process.

So when the archbishop heard it was Father Armand who talked Lucas into stealing the ruby and promised him a castle and lands that he couldn't have given him anyway, he'd forgiven Lucas and said he wouldn't bring him to trial.

Lucas was thankful for the absolution, but even more furious with Father Armand. He had been a pawn his entire life, being trained to do the man's bidding just to get back at the archbishop for attaining more wealth and power than he had. But after today, that would all change. Father Armand was about to be confronted and, at the very least, his sentence would include being excommunicated from the church. But that was never going to happen if the plan they devised to bring this all out in the open didn't work.

Lucas was gaining on Father Armand, and just about to reach over and grab the travel bags from him when a group of the archbishop's soldiers rode up and surrounded them. Lucas rested his hand atop his lap and stopped his horse.

"Well, good morning," said Father Armand to the guards, stopping just in front of them. "What can we do for you, gentlemen?"

"We are the guards of the archbishop," said one of them.

"I know who you are. I can see the archbishop's crest on your chests," growled the priest. "What do you want?"

"There's been a theft this morning of the Regale ruby from the shrine of St. Thomas Beckett," relayed the guard.

"Really?" asked Father Armand. "What a shame."

"Do either of you know anything about it?"

"Nay. I just came into town," said the priest. "We don't know anything about it at all." He looked over to Lucas in a silent warning not to talk.

"Then you won't mind if we check your bags, Father, will you?"

"I am a man of the cloth. You have no right to accuse me of anything."

"We didn't accuse you, 'tis our duty," said the guard. "We need to search everyone on the road and find the ruby. Those are our orders from the archbishop himself."

The priest slowly handed the attached bags to the guard. "This is not mine, mind you, but the man next to me who owns it. I was only transporting it for him and have no idea what's inside."

"I believe that is a lie," said Lucas. "I have never seen it before in my life."

"Well, let's have a look." The guard reached inside and pulled out the ruby and held it up for the other men to see. "We found it," he said. "Take them both to the archbishop anon."

"You have no right to treat me this way," complained the priest as they grabbed the reins of his horse and led him away. "I am a man of the cloth. I am a vassal of God."

Lucas stayed silent and followed the guards, knowing that now their plan was set into motion.

* * *

AMBER FOLLOWED SIR ROMNEY, stopping when they got to the church. There was a group of the archbishop's soldiers leading both Lucas and Father Armand up the steps into Canterbury Cathedral.

"Wait!" she cried, jumping from the horse and running up the stairs. "You can't arrest him. He isn't guilty."

"Amber, what are you doing?" Lucas growled.

"Lucas, I know you didn't want to steal the ruby. I know you were put up to it."

God's eyes, she was going to ruin all the plans. He had to stop her from talking.

"Amber, just be quiet. Please."

"I figured it out, Lucas. I know exactly what's going on."

He pulled her to him and kissed her just so she'd shut up. It worked. She pulled back and looked at him.

"You don't hate me?" she asked, looking up to him innocently with those big, green eyes.

"Nay, my little dove, I don't hate you. I could never hate you."

"Lucas, I can't let them arrest you and take you away from me."

"Amber, do me a favor and go back to the castle."

"Nay, I'm not going to leave you."

"Then just keep your mouth shut and trust me." He looked deep into her eyes and the begging she saw there made her understand that she needed to do what he asked.

The guards brought both Lucas and Father Armand into the church and Amber followed. It wasn't long before Sir Romney and Lady Veronica were at her side.

The archbishop was standing atop the dais, wearing his miter hat and holding his crosier cane. He descended the steps as the party approached.

"What is this?" he asked.

"Archbishop, we have caught the thieves who stole the Regale ruby." The guard brought the ruby forward and held it up for him to see.

"Hello, Father Armand. I should have known you'd try to pull something like this on me," said the archbishop.

"Simon, you know I wouldn't do something like stealing from the church. Especially a priceless ruby. I am a man of the cloth," Father Armand tried to convince him.

"Aye, that's true, you wouldn't," agreed the archbishop.

"Lucifer is the one who stole it," shouted the priest. "Arrest him and throw him in the dungeon at once."

Amber knew that the priest had been behind the theft. She was sure of it. Yet, Lucas just stood there and didn't say a word to try to defend himself, and she really didn't understand why.

"Nay, don't arrest my son." Lady Veronica rushed forward, kneeling in front of the archbishop.

"*Your* son?" The archbishop raised an eyebrow.

"Aye, Brother, Lucas is my son," confessed Veronica. "He is the baby that I said had died years ago."

Amber walked forward to hear the conversation better. She was reminded by the woman's words that she was, indeed, the sister of the archbishop.

"Lady Veronica, you are addled and everyone knows it. Now someone take her away," commanded Father Armand.

"She is my sister, and she should be able to speak her piece." The archbishop helped her to her feet. "Continue, Veronica. Tell me why you kept this a secret all these years. You know I wouldn't have ever judged you."

"I did it to save the family from embarrassment. I gave away my only child." She looked at Lucas. "I gave up the son that I loved in order to keep you, Brother, from possibly losing your position of archbishop."

"That makes no sense," he said. "Why would my position be threatened because you had a baby out of wedlock?"

"Because I was tricked into it by a very deceitful man. A man who claims to be holy and honest but, in fact, is naught more than a liar and a thief. He wanted you to suffer and that's why he took me to his bed. He used your own sister against you, trying to bring out your anger and get you to strike out at him so your title would be stripped and he would win after all. He knew that you wouldn't be allowed to be archbishop because of the shame I had brought to the family name."

"Who are you talking about, Sister? Tell me this man's name."

She turned then, and looked at Lucas. Tears fell from her eyes. "I am so sorry, Lucas, for everything I did to you. I never meant to hurt you and I only hope someday you can forgive me. But I have to tell you that your father is none other than . . ." she turned her head and looked at the priest, ". . . Father Armand."

CHAPTER 25

Daughters of the Dagger

Lucas felt all the air leave his lungs. He had never thought he'd be hearing these words coming from his mother's mouth.

"Nay!" he cried out, feeling the blood rush to his head. The pounding in his ears was louder than drums and he fell to his knees and hid his head in his hands. Amber rushed to him and covered him with her body, but he stood up and glared over at the priest, wanting to strangle the life out of him with his bare hands. "How could you do this to me, you bastard?"

"Lucifer, you are in a church. You'd better watch your language or you may be struck down by the hand of God," Father Armand warned him.

Lucas gently pushed Amber to the side and took two steps toward the priest, his hands balled in fists, his body trembling as he walked.

"All these years of pretending you took me in as an orphan and that you didn't know either one of my parents. All these godforsaken years of putting me through a life of hell just to get your revenge on a man who used to be your best friend. You coveted everything he had and you wished you owned it and would do anything to try to get it."

"Lucas, please," said Amber, touching his arm, but he continued forward toward the priest as the man took a few steps backwards. Father Armand moved toward Becket's shrine and the wall of homage, the standing wooden partition with the huge ornate cross hanging upon it.

"You were the one to name me Lucifer, you told me. Now I understand why. Because you wanted me to be the pawn that you could shape into your minion, and do all your dirty deeds for you. You made me sell fake relics and, in the meantime, you were stealing blind the villeins and keeping all the tithes for yourself rather than giving them to the poor. You took their food and their coin and even their seed to grow crops. You are a miserable, deceitful, despicable man and I hate you for trying to turn me into you!"

"I didn't steal from the villeins, I assure you." He looked over to the archbishop. "I gave all the tithes to the church and to the poor."

"I can vouch that that is a lie," said Amber. "I saw the wealth in your personal room. You even kept my dowry for yourself."

"They're lying," said the priest. "They're lovers and that's why they're saying this. They're protecting each other."

"I saw the wealth in his room as well, Archbishop." Sister Dulcina walked forward, and Lucas hadn't even seen her come in. "Thanks to the tip Amber gave me before she left on pilgrimage, I went to your room when you were out one day, Father Armand, to find it locked. Since I am the abbess, I have all the keys. I let myself into your chamber. I was stunned in disbelief by what I saw. That was the reason I accompanied you on this journey. Because I came to tell this to the archbishop myself. I am only too ashamed of myself that all these years I let you have control of not only the entire monastery but me as well." She looked back to the archbishop. "Everything they say is true. Father Armand is the one to blame, not Lucas."

"Why, Father, did you name me Lucifer?" asked Lucas, his jaw clenched and throbbing. When the man didn't answer, Lucas shouted out, "Tell me, dammit!"

"You were named Lucifer because I was overtaken by the devil," the priest ground out. "He was the one to make me do these things and he was the one to make me lay with Lady Veronica in the first place. The devil is to blame and you are naught but his spawn. Aye, that is why I named you after him, Lucifer."

"Stop calling me that name! You know I hate it."

"Lucifer, Lucifer, Lucifer," the priest taunted him and Lucas felt the rage inside him swell and he could no longer hold back his anger. He reached out and punched the man hard on the jaw, sending him stumbling backwards into the wall of homage in front of the shrine of Thomas Beckett. The large iron cross attached to the standing wooden partition rattled as he fell against the wall. The cross banged against the rosaries and trinkets that pilgrims and worshipers had left attached to the cloth covering the partition in honor of the patron saint.

Then Lucas pulled the sword from his side and probably would have stabbed Father Armand through the heart if his mother hadn't called out his name.

"Lucas, my son, don't do it." He stopped with his arm raised and just looked down at the frightened eyes of the priest looking up at him. "Do not spill blood on sacred ground." His mother came forward and touched him gently on the shoulder. "I love you, Lucas, and don't want you to live with the guilt of killing your own father, even if he is naught but a deceitful liar and a thief. Put down the sword and let's go home," she told him. "I want to stop living in the past and live in the present just like you said. I have much to make up to you. I have regretted abandoning you every single day of my life. Please, Lucas, don't do it. I love you, Son."

In that moment, something happened to Lucas to change his idea of never wanting to be loved. It felt good to hear his mother say she loved him, and also that she'd called him son. She was right. Although he wanted more than anything to kill the bastard, he wouldn't. He understood now why his mother abandoned him as a baby and, though he didn't agree with it, it was behind them now. He wanted the chance to know his mother and, dammit, he was going to get it.

"You're not worth the time or energy of sticking my sword through you, though there is nothing else I'd rather do right now," he told the priest, throwing his sword to the ground. It clattered against the ornate marble floor, echoing loudly throughout the cathedral. "You are the one going to Hell for what you did. You'll be the one that is excommunicated and sent to rot in the dungeon if you're not beheaded first for all the crimes you've committed – not me."

He turned then and gathered his mother up into his arms, hugging her tightly to his chest. She cried and kissed him and hugged him back. For the first time in his life, he'd felt the love of a mother. His mother.

"Lucas, behind you!" cried out Amber. Lucas raised his eyes to see Father Armand lifting the sword and rushing to stab Lady Veronica in the back.

"This is all your fault for speaking up, bitch."

Lucas threw his mother to the side for her safety and stepped in front of the priest to protect her, jumping out of the way of his own sword, but getting nicked in the arm in the process. He heard Amber scream his name from behind him and also the weeping of his mother. He lunged forward and threw his body into the priest in anger, managing to get him to drop the sword. They both went crashing into the wall of homage, falling to the floor.

From his position on the floor, he could see the wall wobbling, and the iron cross wavering back and forth from the impact. Then the wall toppled over under the weight of the heavy cross. As it came crashing down upon them, Lucas rolled out of the way just before it covered Father Armand's body.

"Guards, get that off of him, quickly," shouted the archbishop.

Lucas pushed himself up to a sitting position, his hand covering his wounded arm that was bleeding profusely onto the cathedral floor.

It took half a dozen guards to remove the wall of homage from Father Armand, and when they did, the huge iron cross was atop him. They pulled it away to reveal the large gash across his forehead. His eyes were opened and bulging out. Lucas didn't have to wait for the guard's announcement to know that Father Armand – his father – was dead.

CHAPTER 26

"Lucas, are you all right?" Amber rushed over to him and helped him to his feet. His arm was wounded and he was bleeding everywhere. She didn't hesitate to rip off the bottom of her black robe into a strip and tie it around his arm. "Looks like I'm going to have to stitch you up again."

He reached out with his good arm and laid it over her shoulders. "Thank you, sweetheart." Then he looked over to his mother. "Are you all right, Mother?"

Lady Veronica walked over and reached out and kissed him on the cheek. "I have waited a lifetime to hear you call me Mother. And yes, I am fine since you risked your life to save me."

"The Regale ruby is safe," said one of the guards, holding it up for everyone to see.

"The Regale ruby was never in danger," the archbishop relayed to the crowd.

"I don't understand," said Sir Romney. "Lucas stole it and the priest almost escaped with it, so how could it not have been in danger?"

"Lucas?" The archbishop looked over at Lucas and motioned toward the ruby. "Would you care to have the honors?"

"I would love to." Lucas walked over to the guard and took the ruby in his hand. He held it up high for all to see, then threw it to the ground, smashing it into a million pieces at his feet.

Shouts went up from the small gathering and a few of the bystanders talked amongst themselves.

"Lucas what have you done?" cried his mother.

"Don't worry," he told her. "That was never the real ruby in the first place." He pointed to the stand that usually held the mock ruby by the visitor's shrine, high atop the tomb of the saint. "There is the true Regale ruby, right where the archbishop and I placed it this morning."

"Lucas, I don't understand," said Amber. "So then . . . you never stole the ruby in the first place?"

"I thought about it," he answered. "A lot, actually. But decided against it in the long run. I had it in my hand and had just decided to put it back and walk away when the archbishop walked in and caught me." He walked over and took Amber's hands in his. "Amber, I could not bear the thought of living without you, and that's why I never stole it. Even if it meant giving up everything Father Armand promised me for stealing the ruby and bringing it back to him, I couldn't do it. You mean more to me than any possession."

"But why did he want you to do it in the first place?" she asked.

"Because he wanted to hurt me," relayed the archbishop. "We were once friends but his jealousy of my good fortune caused him to do many evil things trying to attain what he wanted."

"I am one of those evil things," Lucas told her.

"Nay, don't ever say that," said Amber. "You are not a devil like you think, but rather just a fallen angel. I love you, Lucas, and I hope someday you can learn to love yourself as well."

"Amber, you have taught me so much about myself since I've met you. Though my thoughts were at one time misled, I am starting today to make decisions of how I want to live the rest of my life. And I want you by my side, no matter if I have a castle and lands or just a hovel of wattle and daub. Would you accept that, sweetheart?"

"We both have lived with nothing, having given up everything when we were training for the Order," she told him. "So this will be nothing we're not already used to. I have all I need as long as you are by my side, Lucas. That is all I will ever need." She reached over and kissed him then.

"Amber, I have something I want to ask you with everyone in this cathedral as my witnesses. Will you marry me and be my wife, my little dove? I . . . I love you."

Lucas had never thought he'd say these words to anyone but since meeting Amber, he'd learned a lot about love, as well as a lot about himself.

"That would make me the happiest girl in the world," she replied. "Yes, Lucas, I will marry you and be your wife."

Congratulations were exchanged with everyone. Then the guards prepared to take Father Armand's dead body from the cathedral.

"Ironic that the thing that killed him was a cross," said Mirabelle. "And he was a priest. Mayhap I shouldn't be in here at all."

Sir Romney laughed, "Aye, we may all be in danger of the walls coming down."

"Father Armand was killed by God for the things he'd done," said Lady Veronica, as they all viewed his dead body as it passed by them.

"Nay," said Lucas feeling the guilt about to consume him. "I killed him."

"How can you say that?" asked Amber. "It's not true."

"I'm the one who pushed him into the wall in the first place or the cross never would have fallen."

"You did it to save me," his mother reminded him.

"I should be dead as well. That wall was meant to fall on me but I moved out of the way. I am only glad this didn't fall and break in the process." Lucas stepped over the iron fence surrounding the shrine, and stood upon the dais to reach up and grab the true Regale ruby. He stepped back over the fence and held the ruby out to the archbishop. "I think it should be placed back in its secure spot before anyone gets the idea to steal it again."

"I agree," said the archbishop. "I'll have to assign another guard to the secret shrine, as you've showed me it wasn't safe to begin with. Lucas, will you do me the honor of putting it back?"

"I would love to." Lucas felt good that the archbishop trusted him enough to ask him to do this, after he was the one to almost steal it in the first place. He was sure the archbishop asked him in front of the others to prove his trust and so that they would trust him as well. He was a changed man now. The archbishop's actions showed everyone that he'd forgiven Lucas for his sins.

Lucas made his way through the narrow passageway that led to the secret shrine in back of the sacristy. He nodded to the guard who sat watch, and pushed the door open and entered, closing it behind him.

Candles burned brightly, lighting up the small room. He stopped suddenly in surprise to see an old woman kneeling in front of the shrine in prayer.

"Oh, I'm sorry," he said. "I didn't realize anyone was in here."

"Come in," she said without turning around. "You obviously have a reason for being here."

"I do," he said, walking up to the dais. "I've been instructed by the archbishop to replace the Regale ruby back where it belongs."

"Let me feel it," she said, holding out her bony fingers.

Lucas thought at first that perhaps she was going to try to steal it, but then he saw her clouded eyes and realized she was blind.

He held it out for her to feel, and she ran her fingers across it.

Then she ran her hand up his arm, feeling the piece of Amber's robe tied around his wound.

"You are injured," she said.

"Aye." He took the ruby and stepped up onto the dais and replaced it in its proper holder.

"That is the robe of a nun tied around your wound. Someone loves you very much."

He looked at her and shook his head, wondering how she could know that cloth was part of a nun's habit. "That's right," he said. "Amber loved me enough to give up being a nun."

"Amber?" she asked. "That is an odd name."

"Her mother named her after the jewel in a dagger."

"A dagger like this, perhaps?" She pulled a dagger from the folds of her cloak and held it up in the firelight for him to see. It had an etched, ornate design upon the two-toned metal with a large amber gemstone in the center of the hilt.

"Why, yes," he said reaching out for it. "That looks like the exact dagger she described to me."

The old woman pulled it away from him quickly. "Do you love her as well?" she asked.

"I do," he admitted. "Although I never thought I'd love anyone in this lifetime."

"Prove it to me," she challenged him.

"What?" he asked, not knowing why the old woman would even care.

"Tell me one thing you've done that proves you love her."

Lucas looked up at the ruby, thinking of everything he'd been through. He'd given up everything he'd always wanted by not stealing the ruby. He could have gone ahead with the plan and attained many treasures just by living the life Father Armand wanted him to live. But he'd given it up because he knew that Amber was all that mattered to him and all he really wanted after all.

"I cannot prove the love I hold for her. Neither do I deserve her. I have a tarnished past that I am not proud of, but Amber's love has shown me that riches and wealth are nothing if you hold no love in your heart. She is all that matters to me, and if I had known her years ago, I am sure I would have lived my life differently."

"Spoken like a true knight."

"I do love Amber. More than life itself. And I would give my life in a split second to secure that she'd be taken care of and happy for the rest of hers."

"That's good enough," she said with a nod of her head and handed the dagger to him.

"Why are you giving me this?" he asked.

"It is to ensure she gets that true happiness you just spoke of. Now, go to her and never stop loving her for as long as you live."

Lucas turned the dagger over and over in his hand, looking at its beauty. He couldn't get over the fact this old woman would just give him such an expensive gift. He walked toward the door slowly, then realized he hadn't thanked the old woman for the dagger. He turned back to thank her – but she was gone.

His heart jumped. The door to the room was still closed and he was standing in front of it, so he didn't know how she'd disappeared so quickly or, for that matter, where she'd gone.

He ripped open the door and looked at the guard. "Who was that old woman and where did she go?" he asked.

"What are you talking about?" asked the guard.

"The old woman who was praying in the shrine. Who was she?"

"No one's been in there all morning. That is, no one but you."

"That's not true. She was here, I saw her. She gave me this dagger."

"I'm sorry, but I don't know what you're talking about."

"Is there a secret exit in the room? Another way that someone could get in and out?"

"Nay. If there was, I'd think you'd be the first to know, as you were the one trying to steal the ruby in the first place."

Lucas headed out to the main part of the church, staring at the dagger in his hand as he walked.

Amber spotted him from across the room and came running over. She looked down to his hand and squealed.

"You found my dagger!"

He reached out and gave it to her. "Aye, Amber, and I want you to have it."

"Where did you find it?" she asked.

"A blind old hag gave it to me . . . but then she disappeared. I don't know," he said, shaking his head. "Mayhap I am going crazy."

"Nay," she said with the biggest smile covering her face. "She has a habit of disappearing, as I've heard that same story from both of my older sisters. This is the dagger my mother gave me as a child. This proves to me, Lucas, that we were meant to be together."

"I don't understand."

"Don't you see?" Her eyes lit up and her whole face seemed to glow. "Lucas, finding my dagger again proves to me that you are my true love."

CHAPTER 27

Daughters of the Dagger

Amber and Lucas were married a sennight later in the Canterbury Cathedral by the archbishop himself. Amber's father and sisters and their husbands had come to Canterbury for the wedding and they all celebrated now in the great hall of Canterbury Castle.

Amber had made sure to invite all the nuns and monks from Bowerwood Abbey and Monastery, as well as Mirabelle who had come back to the castle with all her things. It seems Sir Romney had taken such a liking to her that he asked her to stay with him. He was staying at the castle, as well, by invitation of the new Lord of Canterbury – Lucas.

"I still can't believe that the archbishop gave me the castle and lands to go with it," said Lucas, as they all celebrated in the great hall.

"You deserve it, Husband." Amber reached up and kissed him on the lips.

"Don't step on your train," her twin sister, Amethyst, reminded her, acting as her maiden of honor and pulling the edge of her gown from under her feet. Amber wore a gold gown made of the softest silk, with long tippets made of lace trailing from her elbows all the way to the floor. Her hair was loose and held down by a circlet of fresh flowers entwined with colorful ribbons that trailed down her back. And around her waist was a gold belt that held her special amber dagger.

"You look so beautiful, my wife, that I can hardly wait until we share our wedding bed," Lucas whispered into her ear.

"Do you mean there is something else you need to teach me?" she asked. "I can't even imagine more."

"Have you made love atop a horse yet?" asked Mirabelle, overhearing their conversation. The Winchester Goose hung on to the arm of Sir Romney who proudly displayed her to the rest of the castle – in a gown meant for a lady instead of a whore.

"Mirabelle, please," said Amber, feeling embarrassed by the suggestion. But when she looked up at Lucas, he was grinning devilishly.

"I've always wanted to try that," he admitted in a low voice.

She drank in his manly beauty, as he'd donned special clothes for the wedding as well. He was dressed all in pale blue, as he refused to wear dark clothes, saying he wanted to get away from his devil image. His hair flowed down around his shoulders like a golden halo of an angel. And his piercing, iridescent, blue eyes made her feel as if he were undressing her right there in front of her family, causing her face to blush.

"Amber, I am so happy for you." Her eldest sister, Ruby, walked up and leaned over and gave her a kiss. Her sister's husband, Lord Nyle Dacre, was right next to her. Ruby held their young son, Tibbar, in her arms and when she leaned over, he grabbed the ribbons of Amber's headpiece.

"Let go of that, you little rabbit," said Nyle, taking the boy from her arms. "Ruby, did you tell your sister the good news yet?"

"What news?" Amber looked at her sister. Ruby's long, blond hair was so light it almost seemed white. It was in a long braid down her back. Tibbar leaned over trying to tug it from his position in Nyle's arms. He giggled as he did so.

Ruby smiled and nodded with her head to her stomach. Amber's eyes went downward, and she realized she'd been so busy with the wedding that she hadn't even noticed the new bulge.

"You are having another baby?" she asked. Amber knew how hard this must be for Ruby as she had birthed a stillborn baby boy with her first pregnancy not that long ago. It reminded them all of what happened to their mother and they'd been worried that Ruby could have lost her life in the process. Having Tibbar had helped her through the hard times but, still, Ruby was feeling the need to birth a child of her own.

"We are," said Ruby, smiling up at her husband.

"Oh, Ruby, I am so happy for you. I am sure this time things will be just fine."

"I hope so," she answered. "Little Tibbar needs a playmate."

"I hope it's a girl so she'll be able to play with Mirabelle," said her sister, Sapphire, coming to join them with her newborn baby girl in her arms. Her husband, Lord Roe Sexton, walked up behind her and wrapped his arms around his family. Amber had been so happy to see the baby when they'd arrived, as it was a newborn and she was surprised they'd traveled with it. Her sister, Sapphire, said she wouldn't have missed Amber's wedding for anything in the world.

"Your baby has my name," stated Mirabelle happily. She looked up to Sir Romney and smiled.

"She was named after our mother," Sapphire told her.

"Congratulations to all of you," said Lucas. "I hope someday we'll be able to join you in having children of our own."

"Do you really mean that, Lucas?" Amber looked up, feeling very excited. When her sisters had arrived in Canterbury for the wedding, Amber had told Lucas she wanted children, too, but he had never responded. "You know, I want lots of children, just like my sister, Sapphire, desires as well," she warned him.

"I know," he said. "Mother, will you join us please?" he called across the hall.

His mother was talking with Amber's father, Earl Talbot of Blackpool, and they both came to join them.

"Son," she said, "I have had the nicest conversation with Amber's father."

"As well as I have had with your mother, Lucas." Amber's father guided Lady Veronica with her hand on his arm. Amber smiled to herself, wondering if some romance was blooming between them. They were both unmarried and lonely, and she thought this might be beneficial for the two of them.

"Mother, Amber tells me she wants many children," said Lucas. "We might need help in watching all of them and I'd like to know if you would stay at Canterbury Castle to help us raise them."

Tears welled in Lady Veronica's eyes and she threw her arms around him in a hug. "I missed out on your childhood, Lucas, and I vow I will not miss out on the childhood of my grandchildren as well. You will not be able to get rid of me if you try."

Amber smiled at the new relationship that was forming between a mother and a son. This was the best gift Lucas could ever give his mother. That is, to be here to be a part of their children's lives, and to be able to love and help raise the babies to make up for what she'd missed out on when she had to give up Lucas years ago.

Ever since the day they'd buried Lucas' father – on unconsecrated ground, she had seen a closeness developing between the two of them. Lucas was warming up to his mother, although Amber realized it would take him some time to overcome the abandonment that affected him for his entire life. But because of what Lucas had lived through, he was going to be the best father to their children that there ever was.

"Congratulations, Lady Amber," said Helen, walking up to

greet her with Amber's friend from the monastery, Sister Ursula, at her side.

"Thank you, Lady Helen," Amber replied. "I wanted to say I know how hard this must be for you since you were once lady of this castle."

"It was at first," Helen agreed. "But since talking with Sister Ursula, I've decided to join the Sisters of St. Ermengild."

"Really?" asked Amber, very surprised by the announcement.

"That's right," said Sister Ursula with a giggle. "She's going to be taking your place, Amber. I am happy to be gaining another friend at the abbey."

"Are you sure about this, Helen?" Amber asked her. "You know there is no going back if you change your mind."

"Unless you're a novice with a man determined to make you forget your vows," added Lucas with a smile.

"Lucas, please," she said, looking up for her father's reaction. But to her relief, he was busy staring at Lady Veronica and hadn't heard him.

"I lost my husband and, without him, I feel an emptiness that I think will be filled by my dedication to the church and God," said Helen.

"Then I wish you the best," said Amber.

"Sister Ursula," called the abbess from across the room. "Bring the new novice here so I can instruct her."

"Watch out for her," Amber said with a chuckle.

"Whatever you do, don't pull off her wimple, or you'll be shocked for the rest of your life," warned Lucas, causing them both to laugh.

"What?" asked Helen, not understanding their private jest, as Sister Ursula pulled her away across the hall.

"He just means, congratulations on your decision," called out Amber, looking over to Lucas with a smile.

"Lucas," said Amber's sister, Sapphire. "Would you like to practice by holding the baby?" She looked up to him with a playful smile, her blue eyes sparkling and her long, mahogany hair pulled up and twisted into a knot atop her head, making her look very regal.

"I think I'll wait," he said, pulling Amber into his arms. "I'm still getting used to being married. One step at a time."

"I'd like to hold her," said Lady Veronica anxiously. With that, Sapphire and her husband as well as Lady Veronica walked away to talk. Lucas' mother cradled the baby gently in her arms, smiling all the while.

"Amethyst, you are so quiet," said Amber. "You do realize you are now the only sister not married, don't you?"

"That's right," broke in her sister, Ruby. "I think mayhap it's time for Amethyst to find a husband as well."

"I have other plans," Amethyst told them. "I want to travel first, the way I did with Uncle Clement when I was growing up."

"He never settles down," Ruby reminded her. "He is a Master Mason. You don't want a life like that."

"I would love to build a castle," Amethyst told Ruby with excitement in her eyes.

"Then you'd better find a rich man to marry," said Amber with a giggle.

"Nay, that's not what I mean. I want to actually . . . build a castle, the way Uncle Clement does for the king and the rich barons and earls."

"What do you know about building castles?" asked Ruby.

"I learned a lot by watching him," Amethyst said. "I also asked lots of questions. We write each other all the time, and I know everything he's doing."

"That is a man's trade," Lucas reminded her. "You'd be better off sticking to something more suited for a lady."

"Lucas and Amber," broke in Sir Romney. "My uncle, I mean, the archbishop, is headed over to congratulate you as well."

The archbishop walked over with his long robes sweeping the floor.

"Congratulations once again," the holy man said. "Now Lucas, I will expect you to take good care of Canterbury Castle."

"Thank you for your generosity," said Lucas. "I will do my best."

"There is one more thing I've yet to do. If you are to be lord of the castle, you must also be a knight. Now bow before me and hand me your sword."

Lucas quickly handed him the sword at his waist and knelt before the bishop with his head bowed.

"Do you promise to uphold the standards of a knight and put God before all else?"

"I do," said Lucas.

"And do you vow to protect the weak and respect all women, as well as fight for the welfare of your king and your country?" asked the archbishop.

"I do," answered Lucas reverently.

"Then by the power invested in me as Archbishop of Canterbury, I dub you, Sir Lucas." The bishop touched the sword to each of Lucas' shoulders, then reached out and blessed him with a hand atop his head.

Everyone clapped and crowded around them. When Lucas got to his feet and collected his sword, Amber saw the tears in his eyes.

"You are a knight now," said Sir Romney. "Mayhap we'll have to go over the Code of Conduct one more time."

"Aye, both of us," Lucas said with a laugh, watching Mirabelle as she ran her hand up and down the man's arm.

"Archbishop," said Amethyst. "I was mesmerized by the beauty of Canterbury Cathedral. I have always been interested in the construction of a church or castle and would love to explore it more and perhaps tour the cathedral at your side."

"I would be happy to show you the cathedral as well as the grounds," answered the archbishop. "You and your whole family," he said with a wave of his hand to include everyone.

"Thank you," she answered with a huge smile.

"My twin sister has always been fascinated by castles and their construction," said Amber. "She never misses a chance to travel and see as many as she possibly can. She even traveled with our uncle for a year, as he is a Master Mason."

"I know how to build a castle," Amethyst told him eagerly. "I've helped him often at his side and have learned much about the trade."

"What is his name?" asked the archbishop.

"He is Clement Mason," said Amethyst. "He is my late mother's brother."

"Of course," said the bishop. "He is working as we speak, on a castle in the far north just on the border of Northumberland."

"That's right," said Amethyst excitedly. "He sends me missives often, telling me of his progress. He wants me to come visit him, and I am considering it."

"He sends me missives as well," said the archbishop. "The church has made a large donation for the building of the castle since it belongs to one of King Edward's best border lords, Earl Marcus Montclair."

"I have heard the earl is very wealthy and this is one of the biggest, most luxurious castles to be built yet," said Amethyst. "My uncle has been working on it for years now."

"That's right," said the archbishop. "Actually, your uncle has told me that his assistant has recently died and he has asked me to find and send him a new one at once. If you are as knowledgeable as you say, would you like to go and fill in as his assistant until I can find one that would suit him?"

"Really?" she asked. "I would love to do that."

"Then I'll make certain the proper arrangements are made. But you will have to leave at once."

"Can I go, Papa?" asked Amethyst, looking over to her father for his approval.

"I don't know, Amethyst. 'Tis a dangerous profession, and no woman has ever been accepted into the trade," answered the earl.

"They will accept her if the order comes from me," explained the archbishop. "Do not worry."

"You've let me travel with Uncle Clement once before," Amethyst reminded her father. "I promise I will be careful and mind him."

"Then, I suppose it will be fine," her father said with a smile. "I know you will be in good hands."

"Oh, thank you, Papa," she said, giving him a hug. Then she reached out and hugged the archbishop as well. "And thank you, too."

"This is just temporary," he reminded her. "Until I can find someone with the proper qualifications."

"I understand. Oh, I am so excited I can hardly wait."

"Now, I feel I must warn you," said the archbishop. "Lord Marcus is not very . . . friendly shall I say. He is known to be dangerous and hardened, as well as very temperamental. After all, he is a border lord. So don't expect him to welcome you with open arms, or even to talk to you for that matter."

"That's fine with me," said Amethyst. "I can do the talking for both of us."

"Someone who talks more than my little dove?" asked Lucas with a grin. "That's hard to believe."

"Amber is the quiet one out of the twins," said Earl Talbot. "If you don't like noise, then you were lucky to get her."

Lucas pulled Amber to him and kissed her, looking deep into her eyes. "I am the lucky one is right," he said. "Because I never thought a devil such as me would end up with such an angel. And I am happy I will be spending the rest of my life with one of the **Daughters of the Dagger – Amber.**"

FROM THE AUTHOR

I think the story of Lucas and Amber is my favorite of the *Daughters of the Dagger Series*. Through my research, I discovered that the church during the medieval times was very wealthy and also powerful. Sometimes even more powerful than the king. The priests, bishops, and nuns were not always as pious as they were expected to be. Actually, it was not uncommon back then to hear about a pregnant nun. Priests or bishops also often had mistresses and even children. The Winchester Geese were prostitutes, legalized by the Archbishop of Winchester in order to make money for the church.

I also found the medieval pilgrimages to be fascinating, as well as the amount of importance people put on relics. People believed that they could be healed by just touching a relic or that by buying one, they could pave their way to Heaven.

The Regale ruby was really given to England by France, and kept in the Canterbury Cathedral at the shrine of St. Thomas Becket. Many church relics were often stolen between rival churches – I think not unlike a college nowadays stealing the mascot of their rival school.

The next and final book in the **Daughters of the Dagger**

FROM THE AUTHOR

Series is *Amethyst – Book 4*. This journey will let you experience the building of a medieval castle.

Daughters of the Dagger Series:
  Prequel
  Ruby – Book 1
  Sapphire – Book 2
  Amber – Book 3
  Amethyst – Book 4

This is followed by my Highland **Madman MacKeefe Series**, with the first book being about the girls' brother, *Onyx – Book 1*, who they thought was dead.

Aidan – Book 2, is next, followed by *Ian – Book 3*.

Thank you,

Elizabeth Rose

ABOUT ELIZABETH

Elizabeth Rose is a multi-published, bestselling author, writing medieval, historical, contemporary, paranormal, and western romance. Her books are available as EBooks, paperbacks, and audiobooks as well.

Her favorite characters in her works include dark, dangerous and tortured heroes, and feisty, independent heroines who know how to wield a sword. She loves writing 14th century medieval novels, and is well-known for her many series.

Her twelve-book small town contemporary series, Tarnished Saints, was inspired by incidents in her own life.

After being traditionally published, she started self-publishing, creating her own covers and book trailers on a dare from her two sons.

Elizabeth loves the outdoors. In the summertime, you can find her in her secret garden with her laptop, swinging in her hammock working on her next book. Elizabeth is a born storyteller and passionate about sharing her works with her readers.

Please visit her website at **Elizabethrosenovels.com** to read excerpts from any of her novels and get sneak peeks at covers of upcoming books. You can follow her on **Twitter, Facebook, Goodreads** or **BookBub.** Be sure to sign up for her **newsletter** so you don't miss out on new releases or upcoming events.

ALSO BY ELIZABETH ROSE

Medieval

Legendary Bastards of the Crown Series
Seasons of Fortitude Series
Secrets of the Heart Series
Legacy of the Blade Series
Daughters of the Dagger Series
MadMan MacKeefe Series
Barons of the Cinque Ports Series
Second in Command Series
Holiday Knights Series
Highland Chronicles Series

Medieval/Paranormal

Elemental Magick Series
Greek Myth Fantasy Series
Tangled Tales Series

Contemporary

Tarnished Saints Series
Working Man Series

Western

Cowboys of the Old West Series

And more!

Please visit http://elizabethrosenovels.com

Elizabeth Rose